Married Past Redemption

Stanley Middleton was born in Bulwell, Nottinghamshire in 1919. He published his first novel, *A Short Answer*, in 1958 and went on to publish 45 novels in a career spanning fifty years. He was joint winner of the Booker Prize in 1974 with *Holiday*. Stanley Middleton died in July 2009.

Acclaim for Stanley Middleton

'At first glance, or even at second, Stanley Middleton's world is easily recognisable...The excellence of art, for Middleton, is an exact vision of real things as they are. And because he is himself so exact an observer, his world at third glance can seem strange and disturbing or newly and brilliantly lit with colour.'

A.S. Byatt

'We need Stanley Middleton to remind us what the novel is about...One has to look at nineteenth-century writing for comparable storytelling.'

Ronald Blythe, *Sunday Times*

'Middleton writes carefully, but his touch is light and astonishingly assured. One rarely reads dialogue as good as Middleton's; it makes his characters instantly alive.'

VS Naipaul

ALSO BY STANLEY MIDDLETON

Married Past Redemption

STANLEY MIDDLETON

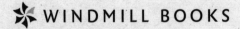

WINDMILL BOOKS

TO PAUL HELM

Published by Windmill Books 2014

2 4 6 8 10 9 7 5 3 1

First published in Great Britain in 1993 by Hutchinson

Windmill Books
The Random House Group Limited
20 Vauxhall Bridge Road, London SW1V 2SA

Addresses for companies within The Random House Group Limited can be found at:
www.randomhouse.co.uk/offices.htm

The Random House Group Limited Reg. No. 954009

www.randomhouse.co.uk

A CIP catalogue record for this book
is available from the British Library

ISBN 9780099591948

Typeset in Plantin by Pure Tech Corporation, Pondicherry, India

Printed and bound by Clays Ltd, St Ives plc

Time turns the old days to derision
Our loves into corpses or wives;
And marriage and death and division
Make barren our lives.

A. C. Swinburne, 'Dolores'

It is not good that the man should be alone; I will make him an help meet for him.

Genesis 2:18

It is so far from natural for a man and woman to live in a state of marriage that we find all the motives which they have for remaining in that connection, and the restraints which civilized society imposes to prevent separation, are hardly sufficient to keep them together.

Samuel Johnson, Letter to Sir Joshua Reynolds,
March 1772

Romances paint at full length people's wooings
But only give a bust of marriage.

Lord Byron, *Don Juan*

Think you, if Laura had been Petrarch's wife,
He would have written sonnets all his life?

Lord Byron, *Don Juan*

I

A large young man crossed the stone bridge, dated 1833, and turned right along a gravelled path. At this point the river was no more than six or seven metres wide, both banks tidied with concrete steps. August sun scorched, and the water did not appear unduly shallow; only a few hundred metres back it had been confined underground to a culvert but here it flowed at speed. Long, narrow bunches of weed stretched in the direction of the current, swaying below the surface, vaguely illustrating velocity.

The City Corporation had been dutiful so that paths were meticulously kept, and almost litter-free, while ten-foot trees, mainly lime with occasional silver birch, had been planted recently, on either flank, and flourished. Seats for the elderly were posted at intervals and on this side of the stream near where one path crossed by a metal bridge, a meccano-like structure, a neat play-park squatted surrounded by a thick, low wooden fence, displaying its slide, its miniature roundabout, swings, rocking horse and seesaw. No pensioners patronised the benches and only one child and its fluffy-haired mother trampled the bark-strewn surface of the playground.

David Randall, the young man, dabbed sweat from his forehead. Not a breeze tempered the ferocity of the sunlight. Buses and lorries braked noisily at the traffic lights on the main road. He paused to watch two blackbirds, male and female, scrabbling together in the long grass. It was late in the season for mating, he thought.

He took to one of the benches, uncomfortably, unfastened two more buttons of his open-necked shirt and flapped an edge with thumb and index finger, but without relief. The mother idly turned her son on a small, clumsy

1

carousel where the child stood in silence, too hot to shout or to show pleasure.

'Will that do?' The mother's voice in the ferment of town noises squeaked as clearly as if she stood only a step in front of David. The boy economically signalled that his ride should continue.

'Oh, you,' she said, and leisurely speeded the wheel. 'That's enough,' she called after a minute. 'Or we shall never have your dad's tea ready in time.'

Her son made no complaint, trotted off at her side, his hair fairer than his mother's. David Randall, leaning back, followed their small, bright progress.

An elderly man, in dark clothes, black coat and black cap, pushing a pram piled with packaged groceries, nodded as he passed.

'Warm,' David said ironically.

'To' 'ot by an 'alf.' The man had stopped, turned his head. 'I can't do wi' it. Don't know why people goo traipsin' off to Spain for their holidays.'

'They are prepared,' David answered. 'They can lie about in next to nothing and sip iced drinks and dip in the sea.'

'Yes, sir.' The expression acknowledged Randall's size and educated voice 'Still, you wain't catch me divin' in here.' He pumped a thumb in the direction of the river and tottered on, pram wheels creaking. 'My wife thinks I'm daft enough.'

David stood, brushed at his hair with his left hand, crossed the bridge, walked back along the main road towards the marketplace, turned right and moving vigorously up the hill, over the river again, passed the foyer of the high and narrow town hall, the dull church, and moved towards The Orchards, his grandfather's house. Still on the main road, he shoved with his shoulder at the back gate which gave suddenly. The old man hadn't fastened the bolts; somebody must be at home. David closed it behind him and walked up the ten tall steps into a garden greenly crowded with apple trees, and where blackcurrant bushes diminished an already constricted path. He stepped down into a yard vivid with geraniums, begonias and fuchsias in pots. The back door stood open.

'Anybody there?' he called, without answer. He rapped a tattoo on the knocker; his grandfather was slightly deaf. The effort brought no result. He tried again with vehemence, then stepped into the kitchen. 'Anybody at home?'

A figure occupied the middle doorway. Polly, his grandfather's second wife.

'Oh, it's you, David.'

'None other.'

'I thought your grandfather was down here somewhere. I was upstairs. I don't know where he's got to.'

Polly was stoutish, big-bosomed, still pretty, with well-shaped arms and legs. She wore a light-blue dress open widely at the neck, no stockings, white sandals, an apron. Her limbs were deeply tanned. Her hair, tinted into three tones of blondness, curled handsomely.

'Am I disturbing you?' he asked.

'No. I'm going to decorate the small bedroom. I'm moving the things out now. Then I'll clean up and fill cracks.'

'A big job?'

'No. Two or three days, if he'll let me get on with it. I thought you were on holiday?'

'I came back last night.'

'Did you have a good time?'

'Very.'

'You look brown. When do you start work?'

'Monday.'

Inside they heard a noise as of clumsiness, then a shout.

'Who is it, Poll?'

'David.'

'Who?'

'Oh, come and find out,' she muttered to herself. 'He's been asleep somewhere.'

She made way for her husband. Broad-shouldered, with a ruffle of grey hair, George Randall was dressed in stained flannels, a collarless shirt, a too tight pullover. The hands

3

on the doorpost spread wide-fingered, heavily veined. He coughed, tried harder, searched both pockets for a handkerchief.

'Oh, it's you,' he said, poking at his moustache. 'I thought you were away.'

'It doesn't look like it, does it?' his wife said.

'I didn't say he was. Only that I thought so. Mistakenly, it appears. What have you done with my stick?'

'Nothing.'

'Helpful, as usual.'

'You've dropped it somewhere, and forgotten,' Polly answered.

The grandfather stood upright, opened the handkerchief he held in his hands, and examined its variations of impurity.

'A disgrace,' he said.

'Hand it over.' Poll held out a hand on which her husband draped the grimy square. 'Find yourself another. I shall never get that clean. That's for certain. I don't know how you make 'em so filthy.'

'No.' George Randall appeared to consider the mystery.

'Well, my Brylcreem boy, take David into the parlour, and I'll bring you a drink. Lemonade, David?'

'Please.'

'And my stick.'

'What do you want that for?'

'To stir my tea.'

David followed the old man's stumbling path. Stifflegged, feet wide, the grandfather helped himself along with one hand on the wall. As soon as he entered the parlour David saw the missing walking stick on the floor by a chair. He returned it, once George Randall was sitting down, puffing.

'Don't tell her. I shall never hear the last of it.'

Grandfather Randall and his wife conducted a continuous verbal warfare, not without ill temper, though each appeared fond of the other partner.

'Tell us about your holiday then.' The old man sat stiffly. David offered a few sentences about the house by

4

the sea near Aberdaron, the beaches, the boats at Aber-
soch.

'What were the women like?' George leered.

'I had Alison there with me.'

'You had, by God, had you?'

'We swam every day, though the water was coldish.'

'What, after all this sunshine?'

This led George on to his struggle with the drought, his
sparing use of the hose compared with that of the idiot
next door who sprayed his lawn day and night.

'All he's got. Two rectangles of grass and a few neme-
sias. Bought them as bedding plants at the greengrocer's.
And this is the man who lectures me about water tables
and greenhouse effect.'

'Does he know anything about it?'

'On paper only. He was, I am ashamed to say, a teacher.'
That had been Grandfather's own profession. 'A graduate.
One of these modern subjects. Sociology. Economic history. Aetiology.' His strong voice tailed off. 'What's aetiology?'

'Isn't it the study of causes? Especially diseases. Greek
αἰτια.'

'He wouldn't teach that then.'

'Where does he work?'

'He doesn't. He's one of those who took early retirement. That's another of his fancy words. Enhancement.
About his pension. He isn't sixty yet, and there he is
trimming his lawns with a trilby hat on. And his wife's as
bad.'

'Have they a family?'

'Not they. Never got round to sex.'

These neighbours had moved within the last two years
into the bungalow built on what had been the tennis court
of the Victorian rectory. Polly had marked them down as
quiet, polite people, keeping themselves pretty much to
themselves, but George's aggressive advice to Mr Cooper
over the brick wall had led to a pedagogic return of
information, all general, all useless, culled from a quality
paper at the weekend.

Grandfather was still excoriating sun, drought, Cooper, old age in about equal measure when his wife brought in the drinks. She listened as she put down the tray, poured tea for herself and her husband, passed over David's deeply iced lemonade.

'They're a decent pair,' she said mildly. 'You wouldn't have to go far to find worse.'

George Randall blew on his tea, muttering.

'They're ignorant.' His large eyebrows met.

'Look who's talking.'

Polly sat down next to David. She looked pleased, perhaps because she had fetched out the best china in David's honour, though he wasn't using it. Her husband preferred large mugs. David raised his glass to her. At forty-eight, looking younger, she was exactly the same age as his father. She had been married to George for seven years.

'I don't suppose you've got a word in,' she said to David, 'edgeways. Tell us about your holiday.'

'He's done all that.'

'Yes, but this time there'll be somebody listening to him.'

David proffered her a few sentences of information.

'Did Alison enjoy it?' Polly asked.

'Very much. It was so quiet. And we were pretty energetic. We hardly took the car out.'

Polly smiled, said she had been to Criccieth as a child.

'It was just after the war when things were still tight. And there was barbed wire, and pillboxes everywhere.'

'Have you been to see your father this summer?' The old man asked, rudely switching topics.

'No. I think he's in France.'

'Have you made any arrangements to go down there?'

'No. Have you heard from him?'

George Randall scowled, blowing derision at the far wall.

'I see you've found your stick,' his wife mocked, 'where you dropped it.'

'Shut up, woman. How can I follow a train of thought with your everlasting interruptions? What was I saying, David?'

'That you hadn't heard from my dad.'

'No. Nor expect to.'

Polly smiled again, broadly, benignly. 'We saw him on the television last week. On Channel Four. Reviewing some book. Now what was it about? The French Revolution? The Russian Revolution?'

Her husband groaned out loud.

'It was Russia. And he looked extremely smart. A light summer jacket and a beautiful shirt and tie, with his hair smooth, and parted. But it's quite grey now.'

'Been so for some time.' George, grimly.

'And I thought he looked thin. Wasn't it you, David, who told me that the telly makes you look fatter than you are?' He shook his head in denial. 'I must have heard it from somebody. He must be like a rake.'

Her husband demanded another cup of tea. David stood to pour, but Polly waved him down.

'You won't put the poison in,' she said.

'I'll have to write to him before long.' David resumed his seat, stretching his legs. 'Alison and I are thinking of getting married.'

'When?' Polly, interest alerted, returned her husband's replenished cup.

'Oh, Christmas, end of the year. We've not fixed a date yet. But I'll ask Dad when he's free. He's the one with the strictest schedule.'

Grandfather Randall snorted contempt, slapping the arms of his chair with flat palms, a tantrum of thuds.

'Will he come?' he asked, recovering.

'Don't know,' David answered slowly. 'I honestly don't know.'

'I don't see why not.' Polly. 'After all, you're his only son.'

'In whom he is not well pleased.' Grandfather, apt with misquotation, and cross.

'How do you know?' Polly demanded. 'You haven't seen him for a couple of years. Except on the box.' She drew herself straight up straight. 'There was a lovely article about him in the *Post*, while you were in Wales. They sent a young lady to interview your grandfather. Very smart she was. Black short dress. Beautiful black tights and buckled shoes. And a great gold chain round her neck. Really big. Like the Lord Mayor's.' She narrowed her eyes at her husband. 'And you should have seen him. All over her, he was. Butter wouldn't melt in his mouth.'

'If you think I'm going to spread family disagreements all over the local paper, you're a bigger fool than . . .'

'Renowned for his tact.' She cut him off.

'Vernon has done well for himself.' George Randall spoke in a different, softer voice, at a measured pace, disinterested and judicial. 'Whatever we may say, he's found a place for himself in the world. And it's no good you two sitting there grinning like Cheshire cats, you can't deny it.'

Polly giggled out loud.

'You old hypocrite,' she said.

'I have nothing much to say in favour of Vernon's character.' He glared, daring them to laugh. 'But he has made his name known. As you have not,' to Polly, 'nor I, nor David.'

'Give the boy a chance.' Poll danced her empty teacup in the saucer.

'He was outstanding even as a child.' The tone was solemn. 'We could see that he would be a somebody.' The grandfather had reduced his voice, with wonderful skill, to a whisper, every hoarse word carrying. 'And he has not disappointed us.'

Polly poured herself another cup of tea, each bustling movement directed to thwart her husband's utterance.

'We've changed our tune,' she said.

David's father, Vernon Randall, had made a notable name for himself as a journalist and television presenter. An only son, he had been bright and attractive as a child, had excelled at school, won a history scholarship to Oxford, had been taken on by the *Yorkshire Post*, then the *Guardian*, first in Manchester and almost immediately in London where he had slaved at his career, drawn attention to himself in the proper quarters, had written highly praised radio plays, two successful satirical novels, a book of far-eastern travels often described as a modern classic, and made frequent television appearances both as a political and literary commentator, and recently as a correspondent and newsreader. As soon as he had obtained his first employment he had married a fellow history student at Oxford, Louise de Courcy Barker, and a year later David was born.

Louise had looked after her husband, apparently putting to one side any ambitions of her own. She had taken a first while he had a 'good' second, whatever that meant, but modestly admitted she'd concentrated on the history syllabus while he'd lived the full life of learning. She had admired her husband, put up with his irregular hours and frequent absences, tidied their home, kept their visitors impressed and happy, cared for the baby, acted twenty-four hours as an unofficial secretary to Vernon, made sure he was at the right place at the right time in the proper clothes with a clean shirt. To give him credit, Vernon realised how valuable Louise was, and said so often. He had kept her mind alert, he boasted, by putting pieces of literary and historical journalism in her way; these she had always done quickly and well, though sometimes he had taken them over, spruced them up, and made three or four times the fee that she would have earned for them. Money had never been a problem, even when Vernon spent madly, since Louise's grandparents had left her property in London which kept the family's finances more than steady. When David started school, Louise, always well organised, began a piece of research, and later joined, by invitation, as a junior editor the office of a magazine of popular history.

Louise relished her work, started on a book, but realised that her marriage was shaky, if not yet in ruins. On Vernon's insistence, they had moved to a larger house, part of the de Courcy estate, but he, once a puritan, self-obsessed worker, had now relaxed, begun to enjoy his fame or notoriety, made love to friends' wives if they were attractive enough, to bimbos, to colleagues, never

9

seriously enough to land him in trouble with anyone but his wife to whom he talked openly of his liaisons. She heard him in a silence which he misjudged.

They had divorced when David was nine, and Vernon won access in the courts to his son, though his travels made regular meetings difficult. Louise now worked full time, wrote a second book, this time on fourteenth-century politics, and by the time David had reached the sixth form, worked two days a week as a part-time lecturer in history at Queen Mary College. She seemed satisfied with life, and spent at least a week each summer with her son at her husband's father's home in Beechnall. David, fond of both grandparents, often remained longer, went with the old people on jaunts to the east coast or to Derbyshire. When he was just seventeen his grandmother suddenly died. Louise and David were at the funeral, while Vernon, in China, made no attempt to attend, sent flowers and a paltry note of sympathy. Grandpa George read this and swore with violent vulgarity in front of his daughter-in-law and grandson. Louise, taken aback by the outburst, cried in protest, but her son judged the sexual fury of the language was justified. Vernon, on his return to England, at once visited his father's house, where he met a churlish reception. When, a year later, George married 'Polly' Moss, née Walker, arrangements were hurriedly made so that Vernon, this time in South America, could take no part. His present, an antique writing-desk, was handsome and he made no mistake over the letter; his congratulations to the couple were expressed at length, elegantly and with real affection. George, reading between the lines, castigated his son as a hypocrite, but did nothing to prevent a short visit. Polly, always her own woman, found much to admire in her stepson, who chose to be charming; she made him welcome but never cauterised the wound of half-hatred in her husband. Vernon was a viper, self-obsessed, without loyalty, even human or humane feelings, must never be trusted. George would hear no reason.

Whenever the old man raised the matter with his grandson, David maintained that Vernon, for all his faults, had dealt justly in his financial provision for Louise and her son.

'He can afford it,' Grandfather blustered. 'All arranged by an accountant. He wouldn't notice it.'

'But it's basic. If that's wrong, so's everything.'

'There speaks the solicitor.' George Randall wagged his finger.

'Nothing the law can do would make him love or go back to Louise.'

'So it was her fault, was it?'

'I didn't say that, as well you know.'

They enjoyed these arguments nearly as much as Polly who, certain now that David could hold his own, confined her interventions to smiling nods of approval at the younger man's careful pertinencies. Not that this saved her from her husband's wrath.

'Take that damned daft expression off your face, woman,' he'd shout.

'And then be accused of glowering. No fear. There's no pleasing you.'

And the old man would grin like a shamefaced child properly caught out but knowing he'd escape punishment.

Now this afternoon as his grandson asked how he was, encouraged to grumble about arthritis and hot weather George Randall felt himself lucky, nearly said as much. The room was large, dim, with a single window, though its walls were plain white and the furniture sparse, one table with flowers, two beige armchairs and a settee, one tall flower-pot stand, a small sideboard and a cane chair with bright overplump cushions more suitable for a summer afternoon on the lawn.

'How's this new house of yours?' he asked.

'Fully furnished. Ready for inspection. Will you come round?'

'Ask Poll.' The old man in mock humility. 'Has Alison moved in with you yet?'

'No. She'll come when she's ready.'

'Before the wedding?' The grandfather grimaced over his question.

11

'I expect so. I'm not pressing her.'

'Very wise.' Polly. 'But won't you be needing a bigger place then, David?'

'Yes, I imagine so. We're talking about it already.'

They chatted and drank until George with a burst of energy invited them to inspect his horticulture and bustled outside. They emerged by the south door into the larger part of the garden which sloped gently down, terminated at a stone wall over a lane. The paths had been left unstraightened here, apple and pear trees sprawled, and below the terrace and small lawn under the house windows lay a wide bed of flowers, Polly's property, hollyhocks, dahlias, phlox, gladioli, two corners guarded by, shaded by tree peonies. Blossoms were colourful still, if paler on account of the heat.

'We need rain,' David comforted.

'He won't let me use the hosepipe.'

'Water's short,' George Randall grated. 'We'll use it for food, because that's sensible, but to keep flowers blooming is ridiculous.'

' "Man shall not live by bread alone",' David intoned.

'Don't you get encouraging her. Anyhow, who said that?'

'Jesus to the Devil.'

'Not inappropriate,' Polly, audibly, but to herself.

Grandfather Randall laughed out loud, and led them out beyond the beansticks, still delighted with his wife, until they reached the far wall and stood under the huge, flopping buddleia, heavy with scented flowers, but high, out of their reach. Butterflies and bees busied themselves, stealing the old man's nectar.

Polly pointed up, entranced. George shook his stick.

II

Polly Randall looked with undisguised pleasure at Alison. They had finished a round of inspection of indoor plants in the young woman's flat on the university campus.

'Feed them,' Polly advised, 'but don't over-water. They look marvellous. You don't need any advice from me.'

'Beginner's luck.'

Polly was immediately reminded of similar advice some months back in the huge bedsitter the girl had rented from a friend. They had talked about the Victorian spaciousness of the room and its south-facing windows, and how she should set about improving it with plants.

'How long have you been here?' Polly had asked.

'Almost a year.'

'Will you stay?'

'No, the university has offered me a flat in one of the hostels.'

'This is a beautiful house. You'll be sorry to leave.' They stared together at the lime trees in the garden.

'I know, I know.'

Alison's voice was subdued. She remembered moving into that place. She recalled her bitterness.

Heartbroken, she had walked out on her lover to take up the offer of a room with Jane Southall, a friend from an aerobics group. They had talked once about Alison's unhappiness, her struggles with herself, her dead love for Henry Corbett, the unsatisfactory nature of her life.

'I don't know where to turn.' Alison, wide-eyed. 'What to do.'

'Leave him.'

'I love him. Really.'

'You only think you do. Listen, you have a week. At the end of that Caroline's going. You can have her room. Pack your kit when he's out, and come.'

'You sound so sure.'

She had done exactly as her friend counselled. Physically it had been easy, emotionally draining. In her new bedroom, in an empty house, she had lain across her chair, sobbing. Her whole body had screamed, but in killing silence. She needed to run back to Harry, but knew she must not. She had loved him; she loved him still, she decided. He began to write her letters, to the university where she was doing post-doctoral work. Ripped in ambivalency she did not reply. Once he appeared at the flat, but she had hidden herself, asked Jane to swear she was out, had crouched to hear that sonorous voice on perfect behaviour outside in the corridor. She wanted to rush to him, but hid herself behind the settee in case the suspicious Harry had flung her door open. He did not, thanked Jane with a politeness to turn any girl's head, and walked downstairs; Alison listened to every step. She had not dared to creep to the window to find out which car he was using.

'He's gone,' Jane said, when Alison stumbled into the kitchen.

'What did he say?'

'You should answer his letters.'

'And?'

'And nothing. I didn't like him. He's what you call a young fogey, is he? Tie and waistcoat.'

Henry Corbett was beginning to do well as a barrister. He was clever enough, had confidence in himself, had good legal connections, looked handsome, more so in wig, gown and bands, but hectored, in court and out. Alison had met him soon after she had arrived in Beechnall from Oxford to do a Ph.D. He was impressive, and twelve months later, after hesitation, she had moved into his flat with him. She had been happy for nearly a year, or believed herself to be so. Henry had been attentive, and though he spent a good part of the day in chambers or court, since he had no intention of neglecting his career, she did not complain, finding his spacious rooms conducive to work, and there she concluded the writing of the thesis in good time. He had introduced her to friends, family and a wide social life amongst lawyers and in county society, had taken a distant, useful, if haughty interest in her research, and then seven months into their relationship had found her or the world unsatisfactory. He would have denied this. She discovered later, though not directly from him, that he was not making the progress at the law which he expected of himself. He did well enough; he set himself high standards of achievement; but one, at least, of his contemporaries, a man not matching him in ability, was doing better, and Henry could not bear to be outstripped. Again, if he had been questioned, he would have claimed Robert Haig-Jones's success was due to luck, and that in the end his own assiduity and talents would redress the balance. It did not feel like this to him; he dismissed these arguments as specious and took out his anger on Alison.

He accused her of being non-supportive, unsympathetic, more immersed in her books than in him. The evening meal which she always prepared he dismissed as skimpy, half-cooked, thrown together, finally uneatable; she made no great claims for herself as a chef, but felt she had improved with practice. His complaints grew wider: the tidiness of the flat, her appearance, her behaviour in company or in private, in bed or out were all condemned and at length which forced her to suspect that she was not to blame. Sometimes Henry bawled at her in front of other people, and though he would always apologise when she taxed him about this in private he would be as likely to fly into a rage on the very next day after his abject regrets. He made ponderous mock of her work on best-forgotten poets, stupid Greek or Italian texts, translations of the Bible, theatrical atrocities, ill-argued critical theses, gobbets of lunatic history. When she received her doctorate, he refused to attend the ceremony; when two months later her professor encouraged her to apply for a temporary lectureship, which she later obtained, Henry grew scathing about the waste of public money, and acidly underlined what she had herself confessed to him, wrongly, that she was second choice and had only been offered the job because somebody else had turned it down. Alison tried to be reasonable, but could not always control herself, answering him back, once to such effect that he madly drummed the table-top with his fists before collapsing into tears.

Then Alison was afraid at his weakness, her success.

Henry Corbett, thirty-four years of age, had been married, though the union had lasted only a short eighteen months. Now he began to compare Alison, unfavourably, with Francesca, his ex-wife. She had understood his needs, had assisted, had listened as he talked about his work, had frequently typed for him, had ministered, his word, to him.

'All you're interested in is some Italian poet nobody's ever heard of.'

'Correction. You've not heard of.'

'The same thing.'

'Are you sure?'

'You're a sarcastic bitch.' Henry roused himself. 'Do you understand anything about life outside those dusty, fusty books of yours?'

'I do my best.'

'You don't. Francesca used to question me about the court.'

'You've never encouraged me to do that. The opposite, in fact.'

'Francesca . . .'

'Francesca!' Alison stood, walked away from the table where they had completed the evening meal, an hour and a half later than she had expected since Henry had finished his day in the lounge bar of the Prince of Wales' Feathers with a couple of like-minded colleagues. She sighed, marched back to the table, began to stack the dishes. Henry writhed in his chair.

'Leave that alone,' he commanded, in his stentorian court voice. 'We're supposed to be having a discussion.'

16

'They won't wash themselves, you know.'

'Sit down.'

'No.'

Alison continued clearing the table, outwardly un-ruffled, though her legs shook. She carried a full tray out to the scullery.

'Are you going to listen to me?' he enquired on her return. 'Or not?' He looks gross, she thought, sitting there twisted in his chair, shirtsleeved with his waistcoat rumpled up from his trousers. He had run his hands through his hair so that it lay back in curving porcupine spikes and his fingers were greasy.

'I'm paying attention.' She began to fill the tray.

'You aren't.'

She did not reply. He rolled about, scratching his ribs with noisy fingernails. His breathing grew coarsely audible.

'I'll ask you once again,' he tried a silky politeness, but he sounded throttled, 'to hear me out.'

'I am listening.'

'Leave those things alone, will you?' More angrily.

She continued with her chore, taking care to make no noise. The room, large enough, uncluttered, seemed to contract about her. With her back to him she could not see him, but every creak of his chair cut into her. He stood up; she heard it with dread.

'Alison.' A strong voice.

She did not turn.

'Alison.'

She straightened the last piece of crockery before swivelling to face him.

'Well?'

He struck her flat-handed across the cheekbone. The blow landed heavily, in an explosion of pain, knocked her over. The sudden impact, leaden and fiery, cracking between her ears, toppled her sideways so that she found herself on the floor, crumpled on to her knees, covering her face with her fingers, broken and unscathed crockery scattered around her.

17

The room furnished her with domestic sounds, a clock ticking, the radiator's metallic mutter, the sweep of a passing car on the road outside. He did not move. She knelt clutching her cheeks, eyes tight shut to curb hysteria.

Finally, she could not remember how long it took, she put her hands down to the carpet, pushed and found that she could stand. Once on her feet, cheek smarting, head blocked and dizzy with pain, eyes still closed, she did not know where to turn. She supported herself uncertainly with her left hand on the table-top. She ventured a glance. Henry had retreated to the hearth, stood large in front of the black and polished marble surround.

Without thinking she moved towards the door.

She walked like a ghost, trying to rid herself of her body. When she put her hand down to turn the knob, he spoke. She did not expect it.

'I'm sorry,' he said.

Alison stopped, hand down, door ajar. She did not speak.

'I'm sorry, Alison.' His voice seemed to bubble. Neither moved. 'I should not have done that.'

Again a pause, an awkwardness of silence before she pulled the door open, stepped into the hall, closing the door with infinite care not to make a sound, stood irresolutely listening. She caught nothing within and tiptoed upstairs holding on to the balustrade. She locked the bedroom door, and wept. Later, undressed, but sleepless, she heard him try the door, once; he did not knock or speak.

Next morning she made her way downstairs at her usual time. Henry was already at the table. He had cleared the debris and washed and put away last night's dinner things, had laid the breakfast though neither ate a great deal on working days.

'Good morning,' he said, when she entered. He was eating cornflakes. 'Coffee's made.'

'Good morning.' She forced the greeting barely out.

'How are you?' He smiled, encouraged by her reply, spoke heartily.

18

Alison helped herself to cereal, poured coffee, not hurrying.

'I don't want to talk.'

His face fell, but he continued eating.

'We shall have to, sooner or later,' he said reasonably enough, but angering her.

She began to toy with her food, though she was not hungry, demurely lifting the spoon, force-feeding herself. He finished his meal, gulped down his coffee, packed bowl, spoon saucer and cup, not his custom, and stood.

'See you tonight. I should be home before six.'

She acknowledged this with a deeply formal bow of her head. Then minutes later she heard him leave; only then did she rise from the table to ring her friend Jane, arranging to move the following Monday.

'What will you do until then?' Jane replied.

'Keep myself to myself. I shall be all right. He's going down to London to see his father.'

'Get your things together. Don't let him see. I'll hire a van for Monday. It'll take no more than an hour.'

It had been easy.

Her cheek was unmarked though it felt bruised. Henry left for London on Friday evening and did not return until midnight on Sunday. She had prepared a meal and had retired to bed, locking the door. They had not slept together since the assault, and had talked in constricted sentences at table, when he had been as apologetic as his nature allowed. His attempts to be helpful about the house had seemed pathetic, and she had ordered him to concentrate on his own affairs. Their final breakfast had been cheerful on his part as he had learnt from his father that an aged aunt, now dying, had bequeathed him a considerable and unexpected sum in her will. When, later in the day, he read her laconic note of explanation he would be both surprised and considerably hurt by her exodus.

Jane Southall arrived, with her van, ten minutes late, at eleven forty; Alison was ready and they were out of the house inside half an hour. Alison had seen to it that there was food in the refrigerator, had propped her note conspicuously on the dining-room table and had pushed her keys through the front-door letter box.

Unhappy in the new flat over the first five days, she was much on her own because Jane was at work, she began to prepare her lectures for the next term. The OUP now seriously considered publication of her rewriting of her doctoral thesis, and she had arranged a fortnight's holiday in Italy at the beginning of September. After a week, she began to prize herself and her luck. She was glad to have rid herself of Henry Corbett, and though shaken by his one unexpected Saturday intrusion, the sound of his voice both disturbed and frightened her, she read his letters with critical amusement. Her flight had damaged his pride, but he lacked the skill or the emotional freedom to write his complaints naturally. She might have been a client who had acted imprudently and needed to be set right. He professed love in the same clichés he would have used in an explanation to a layman of a legal judgment. She felt sorry for him, but glad she had escaped. He did not appear again in person, she did not run into him socially, and after a month, there had been an extra burst during his holiday in Morocco, the letters petered out.

Perhaps six months after this at a party and two days later coincidentally at a concert she had met David Randall. Now she was engaged to be married.

'Do you like this new flat?' Polly asked. Alison had moved to the university campus.

'Yes. I was grateful to Jane. It was a godsend at the time.' Alison had spoken earlier to Polly about Henry Corbett.

'Ah, ah. But now? After you're married.'

'I suppose I shall move in with David. He's talking about a bigger house. Now that prices are low. Of course, my job at the university runs out at the end of this year.'

'And what happens then?'

'That's the snag. I'll have to look round, and there aren't too many openings these days.'

'They won't keep you on here?'

20

'Jack Ryder would if he could, but I don't think it very likely.'

'David will have to make himself responsible, then. He should begin to do nicely now. You don't meet many poverty-stricken solicitors, and he's in with a very good firm. Lamberts are solidly established, I can tell you. He'll do well, won't he?'

'I'm sure of it.'

They walked out into the yard and the long stretches of garden. Her flat was on the top floor. The houses backing on to hers were distant and grand, three huge storeys, detached, with wide gardens and trees, sycamore and lime, out-soaring the roofs, built for the well-to-do, later incorporated into the university grounds.

'I like David,' Polly said. 'He seems very steady. For a Randall.' She looked at a rose bush withering in a corner between brick walls. 'We'll give that a bucket or two to be going on with. When I first met him, that's eight years ago now, he was just about to start at the university here, and he and his mother came up from London in the summer holiday. She didn't stay long. David always had a fortnight, sometimes longer, with his grandfather, in the long holiday, ever since he was quite small. They enjoyed each other.'

'Did David's father ever come?'

'Not to the best of my knowledge.' Polly had found a large, heavyweight watering can and was soaking the ground. 'Look at that, running off.' She paused to admire her cunning irrigation. 'Though Vernon had access to the boy, he wasn't always able to take advantage of it. I mean, he went abroad or was out filming or whatever they do. And Louise, David's mum, did her best to poison the child's mind against her husband. Not that I blame her. I went through a sticky divorce and I did my bit maligning Father, I can tell you. I couldn't help myself.' Polly marched her can sturdily back to the outside tap.

'It was quite a long time before I found out who David's father was,' Alison said. 'He never boasted, as I think I would have done.'

21

'He gets on quite well with Vernon.'

'But your husband doesn't? At least to hear him talk.'

'Oh, George's bark is worse than his bite. He likes to see himself as an old-fashioned, moral, crusty schoolmaster, and he keeps shouting out that you could go round the schools and find at least one thousand five hundred men who'd read the news and interview politicians as well as Vernon does.'

'But is it true?'

'That's what I try to tell him. The potential may be there, but Vernon has fought his way up to where he is. He had the temperament, the ambition, the drive, while the other one thousand four hundred and ninety-nine stick back at home lecturing their sixth-formers.'

'And what does he say to that?' Alison asked. Polly rarely visited her, and both were enjoying the conversation.

' "Thank God", that's what he says. What they're doing is more valuable. They teach, over a long period, whereas Vernon gets an admission of something or other out of a politician, or makes some poor minister look a fool, and wins praise for enlightening the public. But George says it's mere entertainment, surface-skimming. The television, he reckons, can do nothing but trivialise.'

'So you don't think he admires his son much?'

Polly examined the soil round the bush.

'We'll give this another,' she said. 'Half-measures are never any good.' Back along the path. 'If you ask me,' she called back over her shoulder, 'he does think quite handsomely of his son, but he remembers him as a boy. Vernon was on the arts side; he was good at maths, I believe, but didn't follow his father. On the other hand George belonged to that generation who esteemed poets and writers. And so. So. Perhaps he saw Vernon as a Shakespeare or a Keats. I don't know. Certainly Vernon must have been outstandingly attractive as a child, not only physically, but mentally and in his ways.'

'You think George is disappointed, then?'

'Once you reach his age, and he'll be seventy-three next birthday, you're pretty well bound to find life a let-down.

He's not so lively; he has his aches and pains; he's slower picking new ideas up. And yet in his mind he's just as active, retains all the old yearnings and ambitions, though he knows now he'll never accomplish any of them. And I think he misses his captive audience; he taught on to sixty-five, and that's unusual these days.'

'He still has you, Polly, to keep him young.'

'Um.' She replaced the watering can, only to swear in a whisper and refill it. 'He married me in his last term as a teacher. Hundreds of his pupils turned up. Well, perhaps not hundreds.'

Once more she brought the can into play.

'How long has he lived in that house?'

'He bought it almost as soon as he came out of the Air Force. That would be, oh, 1945, or '46. Vernon had been born during the war.'

'And his first wife?'

'Edna. She was three years older than he was. She taught English, like you. At some private school. He met her when he was in the RAF during the war. I think her parents lived in Cornwall, but she was teaching in Lincolnshire when they met. She lent him her bike. It was very trusting of her. And when he brought it back, he invited her to a dance or a party.'

'Did you know her?'

'No. I saw her. I must have done, at school functions. He taught both Fiona and Godfrey at the grammar school. They used to call him "Killer" Randall.'

This family chit-chat comforted Alison. She listened to the emphatic voice, watched with admiration the conversation combined without difficulty with horticultural byplay. She became one of the family, steady, sure now that she had done right to accept David's proposal of marriage. Her relationship with Henry Corbett had seemed, at the end, a period of imprisonment, physically comfortable until that final blow, in no way impeding her academic progress but preventing her, notwithstanding social outings, a hunt ball or two, barristers' get-togethers, formal with judges and deputy-lieutenants in attendance or in saloon bars, three uncertain visits to the Corbett parents' home in London, which neither of the young people had enjoyed, from realising herself. It was, and this perhaps in hindsight, as if Henry had taken her over, made her his chattel, and she could not exactly understand, then or now, why she had acquiesced in the absorption. She had considered herself a woman who knew her mind, who could trade condition for condition in her dealings. She had done her Ph.D. at Beechnall and not at Oxford because her tutor there had signally failed to show any enthusiasm for her subject while Rupert Melluish, the man she was now replacing for three years, saw exactly what she was about and demonstrated his interest in her proposal.

'My youngest, Godfrey, was the same age as David. They were both just off to university when George and I married. I've enjoyed being George's wife.'

'Does he never annoy you?'

'Oh, often. We both have our little ways.' Polly looked round. 'I'll come round one afternoon and smarten this up for you.' She hesitated. 'That's if you don't mind.' They both laughed. Polly laid a not over-clean hand on Alison's arm. 'I was terrified when David told us his girl was a doctor of philosophy. George said, "She'll need to be", but I think he was pleased.'

III

The date of the wedding was shortly fixed: the Saturday before Christmas.

Polly had laid down that George must buy himself a new suit. He groused with vigour, but prepared to obey, once consulting Alison as to what she considered proper.

The wedding would take place in the parish church nearest Alison's flat. The university had no chapel; some secularist Victorian philanthropist had insisted on this condition before he disbursed his savings, and so although there was now a thriving department of theology one found no corner for Anglican or other worship. Alison expressed regret. 'Does it matter?' David asked, slightly puzzled. 'You can have the university chaplain.'

They looked over St Mary's, a beautiful thirteenth-century church, hidden in trees not fifty yards from a main road. The vicar, a young man, with large red ears, expressed delight, said that he did not use the 1662 Prayer Book, but he would certainly do so on this occasion, and reminded Alison with a smirk that she would be required to promise to obey her husband.

'I don't mind that,' she answered. 'I expect he'll be sensible.'

'But if he isn't?' The vicar leaned forward, biting on his thumb, comically.

'Then I shall consult God again.'

The clergyman coughed into a clean handkerchief, and concluded arrangements.

'I don't expect you to obey me,' David told her with a cheerful insouciance, on the way out.

'Neither do I expect you to make exorbitant demands on me.'

'And if I do?'

'I shan't obey you.'

'Then let's cut it. Jug-ears there wouldn't mind, and I wouldn't, and nobody will be surprised.'

'No. We'll leave it in. It puts you on your mettle.'

That puzzled David more than he would admit, but he answered humbly, 'Yes, I think I see what you mean.' She knew he spent some of his time at Lamberts on divorce arrangements.

Vernon both rang and wrote to say that he and his wife, Karen, would come. 'Louise will be there, I take it?' he asked, and at David's answer his father sniffed heavily. 'It's a long time ago,' he chided himself, and said no more. He asked what wedding present they would like; they left it to him. A week later he telephoned to say he had bought for them a massive early Victorian sideboard, 'the most beautiful piece of furniture I have seen this year'. David thought there was no room for such in his maisonette, but Vernon argued that there was plenty in George's place, and it could be stored there until David bought a house big enough to go round it.

'Typical, typical,' George ground out.

'But will it be beautiful?' Polly.

'If you like that sort of thing. But Vernon sees it as a bargain or an investment and so you must have it whether it fits in with your plans or with any other furniture you possess.'

'We could sell it.' Alison, who excitedly wished to keep it.

'You wouldn't sell a wedding present?' Polly asked, scandalised.

'Tell you what,' George interrupted. 'I shall enjoy putting a high gloss on it when I've got rid of the woodworm and sealed the cracks.'

'Wouldn't Vernon have noticed them?' Polly.

'He would. And have pointed them out. And have had the price reduced. And would know I'd do something about faults if it was parked here. There are no flies on our Vernon.'

'Don't let David hear you talk like that.'

'He's a solicitor. He's doing nothing else all day but learning about people's sharp practice. It won't surprise him.'

'It's his father, George.'

Grandfather Randall slapped his thigh and rocked in his chair, chuffed with himself.

The wedding, Alison insisted, would be quiet and the invitations limited to relatives and close friends. Even so the list was twice as long as she had guessed. The pair spent much time arguing over those entitled to attend. Both were surprised how easily arrangements were made for such an important event. Alison was persuaded to wear white. Her mother and father, divorced and both remarried, had accepted her invitation.

'It's not a good omen,' Alison had said out of the blue. 'Our parents' lack of matrimonial success.'

'People live so long these days. People aren't used to marathon running.'

'Is that good?' she asked.

'It keeps my pay packet full. That, and conveyancing.'

Alison would be married, it was decided, from George Randall's house and the reception after the ceremony held there.

'But look at the work it makes for you,' Alison objected on Polly's suggestion.

'It will save you no end of money,' Polly argued. 'A caterer will provide the meal, and we've plenty of room either on the lawn for a marquee or inside if you think it'll be cold in December.'

'Give her her head,' George counselled. 'She's a bossy-boots, and'll enjoy nothing better than ordering the banquet, and pushing us all about.'

'Not to speak of cleaning up the confetti.' David.

After further consultation they asked George Randall to give the bride away. Alison's father had declined, saying he preferred to skulk out of sight, in anonymity.

'Is he like that?' David asked her.

'He's up and down. And perhaps we've hit him in a period of self-reappraisal. I don't know. I suppose we

27

ought to visit him, but he lives so far away. And we ought to offer at least to visit my mother. We could manage that one Sunday.'

'As you wish.'

'I know you think it doesn't matter, that we shall all meet soon enough, but I should like to show you off. I'm proud of you.' She patted his broad back.

One Saturday afternoon in October, as they were walking towards the town centre in sunshine, enjoying the displays, dodging the pedestrian loiterers in streets festival-bright, Alison at a shop window was suddenly greeted from behind her back. The voice frightened her and she turned.

Henry Corbett, in mufti, an open-necked shirt, casual denim jacket and jeans, smiled at her. His teeth gleamed large and regular against a sunburnt face; his hair neatly pomaded. She had not met him once in the fourteen or fifteen months since she had dodged out of his flat. He seemed genuinely pleased to see her; the voice was warm, but she shivered.

'How are you, then? Long time no see.' The vulgarism jarred.

David Randall turned, angrily she thought, from the shop window. His movement was slow, deliberately delayed, insulting. She exaggerated.

'David, this is Henry Corbett.'

Corbett put out a hand; the two men shook. David stood bigger than Henry, an inch or so taller, but more strongly built. He knew the history; twice or three times she had described their time together, her disappointment, his assault, her flight. The men, her men, faced each other, but now without aggression. She had considered Henry as big, but he seemed slim, almost effeminately so. His voice, commenting on the fine weather, had not changed, but she could not help her naive pleasure at judging him diminished by David's solid size.

David said, politely, without emphasis, that he had seen the other in court, and mentioned the case.

'You work for?' Henry enquired.

'Lamberts.'

'Ah, yes. They occasionally employ me.' He smiled modestly, as if the firm called him in to unblock the sinks or replace washers on taps. 'And I meet one of the partners socially. We play bridge.'

Henry surprised Alison. He had never mentioned card games during her interregnum. Now he stroked his chin socially. Conversation withered. They parted, amicably enough.

'He seemed pleased with himself,' David offered after a few yards.

'He always is, in company. Is he any good? In court? What's his reputation?' She piled the short questions nervously.

'Oh, he'll make a living. He's not afraid to put a bit of work in on a brief.'

'Is he good at cross-examination or addressing the jury?'

'I think so. A bit high and mighty. Oxbridge manner. But that's not altogether a disadvantage.'

'He'll never be the top of the tree?'

'He wouldn't be on this circuit if that's what he wanted. But no, he'll do all right. He's quite intelligent. He'll take silk in the end and find a minor place on the judiciary.' David laughed at his own formality of expression. 'He's said to be a bit overbearing, but he knows what he's about. Plays bridge, it appears, with the right people.'

David's judgement, delivered without emphasis, carried easily to her as they dodged between people on the pavement. He spoke with a confidence she admired, even wondered at.

Not many weeks before, she had picked him up from his office. As his car had been in for repair, and as she had finished the marking and administration of exams, she offered to drive him to his house that Friday.

'There's no need. I can easily catch a bus.'

'I should like to see you at work.'

She arrived at ten minutes to five; he said he'd make sure his desk was clear by then.

'And suppose something urgent comes in late?'

29

'It's unlikely.' David spoke without flurry. 'But if it does I shall be in first thing Saturday morning to deal with it. Easy.'

Lamberts' offices were within five minutes of the city centre. A plain early nineteenth-century house with a portico, a low wall and iron railings, its orange brick and pale stonework had been recently cleaned. A receptionist sat at the end of the rectangular corridor or hall; only the space round her desk was carpeted, a square island of olive green on the grey marbled floor. It was tasteful, Alison decided, and pleasantly cool this hot afternoon, puritanical, more like a private library or museum. She walked the length of the hall to the desk, where the young woman in charge looked up from her typewriter. On either side of the hall were heavy ornate wooden doors, polished to a dark gleam, with brass knobs and finger-guards. Alison's heels had clacked disconcertingly. She gave her name announcing that Mr Randall expected her.

'Miss Hunter to see you,' the girl reported to the telephone, head pleasantly cocked. Alison could make nothing of the crackling reply. The receptionist pointed with a long palely varnished fingernail. 'The first door. He'll see you now.'

Alison retraced her clicking steps, knocked on the top right panel, opened and marched straight in. The weighty door moved without a murmur. When she closed it the mechanism, hinges and lock, worked soundlessly.

David sat at his desk. The room was much larger than she had expected, lit by three long windows, lace-curtained, each with shutters. The walls were oatmeal and the paintwork brilliantly white on windows, shutters, tall skirting-boards, radiators and the large surround of the fireplace at David's back. The fire basket had been blocked off with a sheet of painted wood in front of which stood, she could see once she had crossed the carpet, a triple screen, rather small for the purpose, embroidered with flowers. She liked it at once and said so.

'I think one of the nineteenth-century Miss Lamberts did it,' he said, rising from his desk. He rounded it, kissed

30

her and led her to a chair. There was a formality about him to match the room. He reseated himself. 'Give me a minute. I'm just clearing up.' The wall to her right was furnished from floor to ceiling with shelves, neatly packed with law books, many in sets. In front of this stood a table with a word processor. David had, however, an old-fashioned fountain pen in hand with which he signed two documents before consigning them to long envelopes and replacing the top of his pen with a flourish.

'There,' he said. He straightened papers, stood, approached, kissed her cheek.

'Have you read all these?' Alison pointed to the shelves.

'No fear. They go with the room. We'll just walk across the hall to say hello to Albert Frankland, the principal. I warned him you were coming.' David had now sealed the envelopes, which he carried across the room. He held the door for Alison, but once out in the corridor, he dashed to the desk, said cheerfully to the receptionist,

'In the post, please. At your leisure. No hurry about either.'

'On my way home,' the girl said. She looked at the addresses. 'They'll be there first thing Monday if not tomorrow.'

David knocked at the door on the opposite side of the corridor from his and was invited to enter. He ushered Alison in before him.

'May I introduce Alison Hunter, my fiancée.'

This room stretched larger than David's, with more legal tomes, though these had a slight untidiness about their arrangement, as if after use volumes were carelessly replaced. On the walls hung three portraits in oils of bewigged gentlemen, all youngish, all in eighteenth-century military costume. Albert Frankland's ample desk was covered with papers, arranged in shallow piles, while his blotting pad, green, wide and leather-bound was littered higgledy-piggledy with hand-written notes.

This room boasted a settee, two wide armchairs and a polished gate-leg table, but no computer or word processor, not even a manual typewriter. An electric bell

31

between the sheets on the desk-top, and a door in an alcove to his right behind Mr Frankland suggested that secretarial duties were carried out elsewhere. A white telephone made the sole concession to modernism.

Frankland rose.

He was a small man, with a fine head. His face was unlined but healthily scarlet; his iron-grey hair was thinnish on top but curled handsomely above his ears and the nape of his neck. He held out a hand.

'I'm glad to meet you, Dr Hunter,' he said. 'David has often spoken about you.'

His suit was impressive, a three-piece dark grey over a cream shirt and a plain, maroon tie. His shirt cuffs, showing an inch or two when he shook hands, were beautifully starched. His grip was both firm and warm. He signalled the young couple to sit, but did not return to his chair, parking himself lightly, unofficially on the front of the desk, hands clasping the edge. He looked comfortable there, but Alison wondered if this informality might not disturb his papers.

Frankland welcomed her, speaking temperately, in a bass voice. He invited them, at his wife's instigation, he said, to dinner at his house, and this they arranged with an opening of three diaries and a handbag. He offered a word or two about the building, and spoke uneasily of the office block going up behind high board walls on the other side of the road.

'I don't know whether I approve. The architects have tried to be sensible. I don't have much taste, and I've been bought off, I fear, with a bribe. We are responsible for the legal work. But even so . . .' He lifted well-manicured hands.

He posed the question whether these buildings would be admired in a century or two. 'They are spacious, and, well, geometrically balanced, and have a puritanical plainness about their appearance. And we never know what people will approve of a hundred years ahead.'

Alison explained why she considered these lacked lasting aesthetic qualities. Frankland listened, eyes mischievously alight, to her lecture.

'You're probably right.' And he sighed. 'I wish I had your confidence in these matters.'

Alison looked closely at him, feeling her certainty drain away, but vigorously continued her argument.

David listened without interruption to their exchanges, an expression of quiet content on his face. So might a schoolmaster appear when two of his bright pupils crossed swords at the debating society. In the end he asked to be excused while he fetched his 'luggage'.

Alison enquired about the portraits.

'They're two brothers and a nephew; all belong to the Coupe family. They served in India at the end of the eighteenth century. And a Miss Coupe, great-granddaughter of Joseph,' he pointed at one wooden-faced young man, 'married a Lambert in the 1850s. That's how these came into the family.'

'Are there no Lamberts in the firm now?'

'Bill Freckleton, another of our young men, he's not in this afternoon, had a mother who was a Lambert, a direct descendant.'

Frankland passed information without fuss. He seemed to anticipate the next question and answered with lucidity. He was now talking about David.

'We're very pleased with that young man. My old friend, Alfred Woodhouse, in the law department, recommended him. He did well at university and even better in the Law Society examinations. Of course, it's an advantage to pass academic examinations, but it's not everything. A lot of our work is dull, needs conscientious slog, and that sometimes riles clever young men. But David's always cool, calm and collected. He did his time here, as I suppose you know, and . . .' Frankland, she guessed, had been about to regale her with some anecdote about David's care or conscientious application but, for whatever reason, had thought better of it. 'He's very large. He looks like a rugby player. That inspires confidence. You'd be surprised how many of our clients need, above all else, a big comforting presence. I see you smile, Dr Hunter . . .'

'Alison.'

33

'Alison, but you're an academic. You'd want a sound legal opinion from a lawyer, advice based on knowledge and experience, but . . . You're still smiling.'

'You're a romantic. I'd just want somebody who'd make a proper investigation and then supervise the buying and selling of my house.'

'You are right. But even with conveyancing we have. . .'
Again he checked himself from supplying an illustration.

'Is he good in court?'

'Oh, yes. All our young men have to do a certain amount of court work. We don't like it. It's often time-consuming in an uneconomical way. One sometimes has to hang about waiting for some long-drawn-out case to be concluded before one's own comes up. But we have our duty. And yes. David's good. He argues well, knows the law, or makes sure that he has read it up, and puts his points without flurry. Magistrates like that. They are amateurs. They don't want histrionics; that seems too patronising. They want to be convinced by reason and knowledge. I'm talking in generalities. Magistrates are like everybody else; they all differ. But. And when David's in a higher court, he makes sure that his barrister is properly briefed. Yes, for such a young man he is doing extremely well.'

At that moment the paragon returned, carrying a brief-case, a light mackintosh hanging over his arm.

'Are you expecting rain?' Alison asked.

'It might before Monday. I could put it in my briefcase if its appearance offends you, but we've only fifty yards down the street before I throw it in the back of my car in the park.'

'Good,' she said, coolly, and all three laughed.

'I see you're kept in order,' Frankland muttered.

'Of course.'

They made their farewells. The girl in the hall had gone and her desk-top shone polished and empty. Even the telephone had been packed away.

'How long will he work?' Alison asked.

'No idea. Until he's satisfied.'

'He had an enormous number of bits of paper.'

34

'And he'd be able to list them all. From memory. They say he's the best pure lawyer in practice in Beechnall. Whatever that means. And he'll sort that lot out before he goes home. And I don't think it matters much to him whether he'll make money from it or not. It's interest that counts.'

'That only means,' she answered, 'that he has plenty to live on.'

'I suppose so.'

They moved down the street at a spanking pace, hand in hand. When they turned into the alleyway which led to the car park, David spoke again.

'Did you like him?'

'Yes. He's rather as I imagined him. But he went out of his way to be pleasant. And invited us to dinner.'

'That surprised me.'

'Why?'

David, unlocking the doors of his car, reserved his answer until they were both seated with belts buckled.

'He told me a week or two ago that he and his wife were splitting up. We had both worked on an hour or so over the odds, and once he had locked the place, he thanked me, and we walked along here together. Just as we were about to make for our cars, he put his hand on my sleeve and said, 'I don't know if anybody has said anything to you, but Eleanor and I are separating.'

'Is that a legal word?'

' "Separation"? Yes. Can be, but not in this case. He didn't look it, but perhaps he was a bit embarrassed at having to tell me.'

'Did he give you any explanation?'

'He just muttered something to the effect that they hadn't hit it off for some years. He thought I ought to know so that it wouldn't come as a surprise. He wouldn't, he said, want me to be caught out by it. He's a careful man, and never likes to appear unprepared.'

'That's what he said about you. A comforting presence.'

'He'd mean it as a compliment then. And now he invites us to dinner. Perhaps he'll give us a drink at home, and then whip us out to a restaurant.'

'Perhaps they haven't split up yet,' Alison suggested. 'He mentioned his wife. He'd consulted her.'

'Nobody has said a word since. In the office or out. He asked me not to speak about it. To anybody. So perhaps he's imposed the ban on us all.'

'How old is he?'

'Fifty-five, fifty-six. You'd think at that age, with the family out of the way and no shortage of cash, they'd be able to put up with each other. She must be used to his working long hours.'

'What's she like? Have you met her?'

'Oh, yes. At their house, and at office functions. She's just what you'd expect he'd choose. White hair. Not quite twinset with pearls, but that way inclined. Conservative Party Conference type. I thought she was lively. In her mind. She played the piano to us, once. Some Brahms.'

'Did she play well?'

He nodded, gnawing his lip.

'Oh, yes.'

IV

Alison Hunter parked her car outside her fiancé's maison-ette. They'd drive up to Albert Frankland's house in David's Volvo. He had decided.

She hummed her pleasure, a tune from the Mozart Sinfonia Concertante for violin and viola.

That morning as she had been working in her room at the university, writing a new lecture on Wiat, her professor had knocked at the door. Jack Ryder was a smart man, baldish and, though incisive, mild of manner. He knew a great deal so that he felt no need to shout opponents down; he demonstrated their ignorance quietly, almost charmingly. His period was mainly contemporary; he had written three excellent books, one of which had made the reputation of the poet Thomas Dewer. He contributed long, magisterial articles to the *TLS*, the *London Review*, the *New York Review of Books* and the learned journals, and people crossed him at their peril. He was forty-five, looked younger in spite of disappearing thatch, and no one understood why he did not occupy an Oxbridge chair. He had recently published, almost offhand, a magnificent study of Alexander Pope before which reviewers, even academic rivals, had kowtowed. He was now writing a survey of poetry in English in the 1980s. He had smiled at Alison one morning as he described his labours. 'Nobody will thank me for it. Who'll buy it?' His Pope had just sold out a third enormous American edition. 'Everybody I miss out will hate me. But that's what I must do: look for quality. I don't want to produce mere lists. And those I deal with won't be altogether pleased. They'll see my praise as lukewarm.'

'Why do you bother, then?'

'I know, Alison, that I seem very old to you.' He wore, she remembered, that morning a particularly up-market

37

denim suit and his complexion was youthfully immaculate. 'But I am in some ways still the daft, idealistic student I was twenty-five years ago. If criticism is to be written at all, and I sometimes doubt its usefulness, it has to be done with a proper ferocity. And that means the majority will be rejected, and those that remain for consideration will be scrutinised without fear or favour. I'm writing for that lad of twenty hurrying up Mill Street or Sidgwick Avenue in the east wind to read Yeats or Hardy for the first time. I owe it to him. And he'd reject scholarly blether.'

She had laughed. His voice had been so unemphatic, his choice of vocabulary so near journalese that she thought Ryder might be testing her out, inviting her to an examination of the lexis of his cherished beliefs. One never quite knew where one stood with him. Should she take him on, his voice would nowise harden, but his answer would be incisive; he'd ask her to rephrase for him, and then, in a quiet, quiet sentence, mock her stumbling, demolish her objections.

'You're an evangelist,' she said.

'Right. And I'll make sure the news I bring is good.'

She approved of Jack Ryder. He was as crafty as his enemies claimed, but he had learned a great deal and had a mind to make up about that knowledge.

This morning he had called on her to report that he had just received a letter from Rupert Melluish, the man she deputised for, now in Boston.

'I doubt if we shall ever get him back.' Ryder looked thoughtful. 'That's what I want to talk to you about. At the very least, you know how cautious he is, he'll have an extra year, but I don't think he'll come back at all. That means you'll have this year and next with us.'

'Thank you.'

'I'd sooner have you than Rupie. You're a human being. He's a dry-as-dust. And he was disappointed not to get the chair here. Oh, I'd have him made up to reader, then to a personal professorship, all in good time, but he wouldn't, couldn't love me; nor could Carolyn. So I think

38

he'll stay out there. He likes the money. And he gets on with his work. And his children are off his hands now.' Melluish was older than his professor and had, as a research student, supervised Ryder in his first year at Cambridge. 'You think I don't approve of Rupert, but then I don't know. He's a worker; he has standards; he will take his share of departmental chores . . .'

'But. . . ?' she tempted him.

'He's dead. If I wanted a course of six lectures on, oh, let's say, Spenser so that even the ignorant would know the right dates, critical highlights, the best quotations, I'd nominate Rupert. But none of these students would ever turn to Spenser again once they'd left the university. Oh, the clever ones would make use of him in their finals, and that's better than nothing, but once every fifty years we might have a poet sitting in the classes, and then what?'

'He'd make his own way, whatever lectures we gave.'

'You're right; possibly; probably. But try not to think it. Work as if it wasn't true.' Ryder looked out from her window, over a square with trees and paths, a stone fountain, turned off, in the centre. 'If he goes, I'll do my best to keep you.'

'Thank you.'

'And to that end I want you to spread your wings, move out of your period, and lecture on Yeats as a special subject to the second year. Beginning next term.'

That surprised her; Ryder's first book, highly regarded and still in print, had been on Yeats. The professor now threw Yeats at the smeary glass:

> 'That grammar school of courtesies
> Where wit and beauty learnt their trade
> Upon Urbino's windy hill.'

He swung round, hands in pockets, advanced slouching. 'I thought: Alison would know about that. She's read Castiglione. And then: I'd like to know what Alison Hunter makes of Yeats. She's done Plato. She has the Latin and Greek and Italian.'

'But no Irish.'

'As much as Yeats. Will you do that for me?'

'Yes, Jack.' He had surprised her.

'Good girl. I'll come and listen to you.' That was doubtful.

Ryder saluted, half militarily, and left the room.

Alison knew delight as she reported this to David. He, newly shaved, spruced up but not gaudy, straightened the jacket of a grey suit she had not seen before. He was pleased and said they should start looking for houses. They were still exchanging ideas about size and style when he parked outside Albert Frankland's home, a huge semi-detached villa, with a great horse-chestnut tree in the front garden, branches high over the wrought-iron railings and the pavement.

Frankland answered the door. He wore a linen jacket and an inappropriate, tartan bow-tie. He ushered them immediately upstairs to an enormous, heavily furnished but attractive drawing room, its velvet curtains already drawn. The host seated them in comfortable armchairs at a distance of five metres from each other at either side of a marble fireplace, and civilly provided drinks.

'We made this into another sitting room,' Frankland explained, 'after we had finally got rid of the family. We're high here, and so have a superb view over the town. An urban landscape with a large sky becomes fascinating, a constantly changing spectacle of light for idle old men like me. I can sit here with an unopened book in my lap staring out for hours.'

The door opened; his wife entered.

Eleanor Frankland had been a beautiful woman, but now the fine face was deeply lined. She made no attempt to cover her withering neck. Her figure was slim still, and the flame-red and orange dress suited as it contrasted with her pallor. The helmet of hair was snow-white. She stood shyly by the door, still holding the handle.

'Oh,' Frankland said. 'Eleanor. You know David Randall. Come and meet his fiancée, Dr Alison Hunter.' He seemed keen on her doctorate.

40

Mrs Frankland advanced, shook hands with both, murmured greeting. Her attention was, they thought, directed elsewhere. She accepted a glass of sherry, but drank none of it.

'These young people must be hungry.' Frankland spoke heartily. 'By this time.'

'Dinner won't be long now.' Eleanor's voice was suddenly stronger. 'I've left my daughter slaving over the stove. She's visiting us, and was foolish enough to say that she liked nothing better than cooking.'

'It's true,' Frankland countered.

'I didn't say it wasn't.' Eleanor stood again. She had barely sat, though she did nothing in a hurry. 'I've taken her at her word, I tell you. You'll meet her. She'll dine with us.'

They talked about the weather. Mrs Frankland confessed that she sometimes watched cricket on the television. 'I don't understand it, though I used to follow Albert when he played.'

'Was he good?' David asked.

'No,' Frankland replied.

'I can't remember.'

They answered together. Frankland asked if there were to be any interesting plays or concerts once the university term began.

'I guess so. Dates are fixed already, but parts can't be auditioned for until the students have arrived. They're going to perform Purcell's *Fairy Queen* in the spring. I guess that it will be good. The professor's a live wire.'

'Will you be in it?' Frankland.

'I might sing in the chorus. And they keep asking me about the staging, though I'm no expert. It's outside my period. But a man in the education department is very good. Up to all the tricks and special effects they need, and I help him out.'

They talked easily until Eleanor suddenly ordered:

'Albert, go and see to the wine, will you?'

He left the room at once.

In the hiatus Eleanor asked David if the name Randall was common locally.

'I don't think so. Half a column in the 'phone book. With a few e-double ls, and some le-s.'

'Wasn't there a poem about a man called Randall?'

David looked at Alison.

'Yes,' she answered. 'Hopkins. "Felix Randal". But he was single l. "Felix Randal the farrier, o is he dead then? My duty all ended." '

'It's a sad poem,' Eleanor muttered. She had seated herself. Now she diffidently asked Alison about Gerard Manley Hopkins, and was rewarded with a short lecture, and in answer to a second question with a few sentences on the Jesuit order.

'You're not a Roman Catholic, are you?' Mrs Frankland murmured.

'No.'

Mrs Frankland nodded as if the reply merited consideration.

'I have no religious convictions,' she said in the end, frowning, touching her hair as if she had spoken out of place. She stood again. 'Daddy and Jennifer are taking long enough. Perhaps it would be advisable if I checked up on them. I'm sure you can occupy yourselves profitably on your own for a few minutes. I like to know what's going on. Even if I can do nothing about it. Which is often the case.'

She left the room, her sherry untouched.

Alison and David lifted eyebrows, together, and shook their heads in comical interrogation, signifying the unusual nature of Mrs Frankland's behaviour.

'Not much small talk,' Alison whispered.

'Not used to visitors, perhaps. But that can't be right.'

'Not used to young people. Who's the daughter?'

'I've no idea. I don't know anything about the family.' David rubbed his chin. 'He sometimes mentions Julian. He's a consultant physician.'

They sat in companionable silence, sipping their drinks, waiting for the door to open again. The room was not too hot, well worth looking over, and their chairs large and very comfortable.

'I could drop off here,' Alison said.

'Have you been working hard?'

'Not really. Clearing up bits and pieces so that I shall be ready for the beginning of term.'

'Are all your places taken?'

'Yes. We shall be oversubscribed. They all did well at A level this year. All scored the required grades.'

'So you'll have to take them?'

'Yes. Somehow or other.'

'Why have they done so well? Are the standards slipping?'

'They say not. Perhaps we get clever people who put us down as first choice, really want to come.'

'Is that likely?'

Alison smiled modestly, spread her arms. Outside, elsewhere in the house, silence was absolute. The two concentrated spuriously on their drinks, feet nervously together. When they heard footsteps outside, David raised a monitory finger. Frankland opened the door, swiftly, with a swoop.

'We are ready for you now.' His expression was pleasant. 'It's downstairs again, I'm afraid. Leave your glasses here.'

They followed him out.

The dining room, its walls panelled in dark oak, struck them as dimly lit, compared with the hall, though the large table held six burning red candles. Frankland, head of the board, put Alison to his right and David diagonally opposite her. Places were set at the far end and across from David, though the size of the table, polished and without a covering cloth, made for wide spaces between the diners. The cutlery gleamed heavy, big, old-fashioned, valuable.

'They'll be in,' Frankland said.

They, wife and daughter, arrived carrying large bowls of soup on two trays. Introductions were made to the daughter, Jennifer Fisher, a dark-eyed sallow young woman with large hands.

'My favourite.' Frankland, appreciatively, spoon at the ready. 'Marrowbone.'

43

'We have tried to accommodate you,' the daughter said, in a far-back voice. 'Anything to oblige.'

Mother and father began to speak together, perhaps to erase the sourness of Jennifer's announcement. Frankland afforded precedence to his wife who described her butcher, a young man who understood more of his business than pork chops and sausages. If one believed her, he had been consulted, had approved and provided the meat. 'It is very hard to know what is best on these hot days. I find my appetite is blunted.'

All finished their soup without difficulty.

Alison said of her generous helping that it alone was substantial, delicious, and nourishing enough to have kept her working all through a long afternoon of tutorials and study.

Mother and daughter rose together, militarily precise, to clear the plates, and after a short pause to bring in an enormous joint of cold beef which Frankland stood, with a clashing of knife and fork, to carve. They helped themselves to salad, rice, home-grown carrots, tomatoes, some Indian and Greek vegetable concoctions, three sorts of potatoes, dishes of pickle. The table's broad area now glowed colourfully crowded.

This time the daughter joined her mother in a set piece on the advantage of beef over fowl on a day of this sort. They made an attempt to include their guests, but the most monosyllabic answers satisfied their attempt at politeness before they rattled on between mouthfuls about meals they had eaten and where. They punctuated the discourse with descriptions of what each dish contained, and recommended this, that or the other delicacy in an offhand virtuosic way.

When Frankland commented on the beef, which melted in the mouth, he was dismissed by his daughter.

'Albert's taste is bland. And conservative.'

This led to a digression from Eleanor on fashions in eating, and later a competition between Alison and Jennifer to describe the exotica they had eaten in a Thai restaurant both knew in Oxford. David, amazed at his

44

fiancée's memory not only of tastes but of names, learnt afterwards that Alison had patronised the place only twice in her life.

'How do you remember, then?' he had asked.

'I just concentrated on the one or two things I knew about. I've a good memory for words.'

'And what about Jennifer-girl?'

'Oh, she's interested in cooking. And she'll have a book at home on Thai cookery so she has plenty to work on. Probably her bits and pieces had no connection with the Sala Thai. You mustn't forget we were both using a very basic, elementary knowledge, and there were no experts there to show us up.'

'You fooled me.'

'Yes. But you know nothing about it. And you wanted to be pleased. Moreover you don't give your opinion on a subject until you've made sure that you know what you're talking about. I could just about hold my own with the Fisher.'

'Did you want to?'

'Want to what?'

'Hold your own?'

'I'm competitive. And that's one of the ways it shows up. I've no more interest, really, in Thai cuisine than you have.'

Mrs Frankland now included David in the conversation and he had replied with a cheerful, judicious, confessed ignorance, describing his grandmother's suet puddings, apple and blackberry, spotted dick, jam roly-poly with white sauce. He spoke attractively, and Alison noticed how eagerly the other women plied him with questions. Frankland at the end of the table concentrated his efforts on filling their glasses with claret, or offering further slices from the joint, politely encouraging gluttony.

The pudding which Jennifer brought in was a syllabub.

'It lacks substance,' she warned David.

'Isn't that the idea?'

After cheese they took coffee in another downstairs room, smaller, with three book-lined walls. Here they sat cosily. David refused brandy. Jennifer, next to him, now questioned him about the difficulties of conveyancing a piece of land she was buying. David carefully took her through the transaction, with brief explanations for his opinions, pointing out what she, or her solicitor, should enquire into or know. The ten leisurely minutes were observed, not interrupted by the other three, and had about them something of the formal, artificial nature of an oral examination, as if Albert Frankland had set the situation up to test the knowledge and approach of his employee.

Jennifer, her chair drawn close to David's, leaned too near, laying her hand on his forearm, for an examiner. She seemed unaware of the other three people in the room, but answered and asked with a sober clarity. Alison guessed that the women had been drinking steadily all evening, but now, only with this slight overexaggeration of gesture was she betrayed.

Once Jennifer had been satisfactorily instructed, the conversation became more general. Eleanor quizzed Alison about her reaction to the city, while Frankland wanted to know about the education of her students. Talk flew in animation as they produced evidence about the fall, or otherwise, of standards. Frankland gave a drily humorous, rather censorious account of the law students of his day.

'Did nobody work hard?' Alison asked.

'Of course. There were as many assiduous people there as in other departments. And we had a higher proportion of overseas students than most. But on the whole, my contemporaries came from the middle class, knew their way around, knew which corners could be cut and how.'

'And weren't the examiners aware of their tricks?'

'Of course. And I guess they approved. They probably felt that those who in the end actually went out into the world to practise law as barristers or solicitors, as opposed to academic lawyers, were none the worse for worldly knowledge and so they turned a blind eye to the helpful crib books. They did not want practitioners stuffed to the crown with knowledge of judgments and precedents; they thought that men of the world, who had, mind you, the know-how to lay their hands quickly on the right books and who were careful and self-esteeming, were what clients needed.'

'And what do you think?' Alison pressed him.

'There's some sense in the view. And if you were taken on in a good office, or good chambers, you'd learn soon enough where to look or whom to ask. Much of our work is, after all, routine, or dull.'

Alison did not allow him to rest with this thesis, and chivvied him to his pleasure.

Frankland never held any length of conversation with his wife. The couple were polite to each other, but if one engaged elsewhere in banter or argument the spouse did not interfere. Jennifer called her parents by their fore-names, but made no attempt to inveigle them into speech together. The atmosphere held no menace; exchanges were interesting, sometimes sharp, often enlightening; politeness ruled.

At eleven thirty Alison, looking at David, said they must leave. They parted warm-heartedly, with hand-shaking, and a drift out on to the front drive. Albert Frankland came down to the pavement to wave them off.

'Do you want to spend the night at my place?' David asked, driving away.

'No. I'm too drunk.'

He made sounds of lewd encouragement, but drove her straight home. He left her flat at two in the morning, sated.

Next day when he thanked Frankland for his hospitality, the older man stroked his face.

'We were certainly pleased to see you. I, especially. Alison is a charming girl, clever and quite breathtakingly beautiful.' The expression surprised. 'You're a lucky man. The sad thing is that we shall not be entertaining people like that any more. My wife is, has . . .'

'I'm sorry.'

'Only my daughter's appearance made last night's occasion possible. My wife flatly refused to raise a finger.' He waited for comment.

47

'I'm sorry. I didn't realise that . . .'

'She would in no way incommode you. When I told her I had invited you, she said I must then make my own arrangements to entertain you. I called on Jen. Fortunately she was willing and able to come. I imagine my wife thought I would have to cancel the invitation, and that she'd score over me in that way. It's sad. But she did not want to involve you. Once you'd crossed her threshold, she would act with what she considered propriety, help Jennifer to serve, talk to you. She wanted to make me feel insignificant, by having to cancel the invitation I had made to you. I certainly felt most uncomfortable.'

'I, we didn't notice anything.'

'You're kind to say so. But . . .' David wondered what had happened when Frankland had returned to the house from bidding his guests farewell. Would his wife have disappeared? Or stayed to quarrel? And on whose side did Jennifer come down? Would Frankland have to provide his own evening meal today? 'As I say, it is sad. But I am pleased that you and Alison were not unduly troubled by our domestic disagreements.'

He said no more, standing behind his desk, shirt collar perfect, face unclouded, hair shining. With a beautifully manicured hand he rang the bell to call in his secretary.

V

Alison and Polly Randall sat together.

They drank tea with lemon in Polly's sitting room, while the older woman advised about arrangements for the wedding. Grandfather Randall had called in at The Oxford, as he did usually on Wednesday, to play dominoes with two friends and argue the world to rights. He walked, even in winter, the half-mile because he claimed that the landlord had made an effort to cater for him and his like. 'We need to be near the bar, to have comfortable seats, respectable décor and furniture, warmth or coolness according to the season, and quick service. What we do not want is music, muzak, pop records, one-armed bandits, Space Invaders and other flashing foolishnesses that brewers deem necessary accompaniments to beer-drinking.' He shaped his sentences for Alison's pleasure.

This evening, hearing that Alison had arranged to visit, he threatened to stay at home, and in fact delayed his departure by half an hour to pass the time of day with his granddaughter-in-law-to-be.

'He's very fond of you,' Polly said, after George had taken up his stick and stumped out. 'He's pleased that David has chosen "such a marvellous girl". His own words. "Chosen?" I said. "Alison's chosen him." '

'But he thinks highly of David, doesn't he?'

'Yes, he does. David's quiet, and sensible, and isn't frightened of him. I suppose it comes of sitting advising people all day. "He's got an old head on young shoulders," George says, and when I ask him if that's good, he compares David very favourably with his father.'

'I see.'

'David's a human being. Vernon's a phenomenon.'

Polly had shown herself utterly efficient, had contacted caterers, and printers for wedding invitations and orders of service, florists, the firm to provide the Rolls-Royces and chauffeurs. She had valuable local contacts and loved organising.

'Have we forgotten anything?' Alison would ask timidly.

'Not if the pair of you have consulted the ecclesiastical authorities.'

Polly laughed, knowing full well the young couple would make no mistake there.

'Consult. Latin. Consulo, ere, consului, consultum, takes the dative case.'

'Oh, to be clever. I gave Latin up after one year.'

'There's nothing clever about it. It's a snippet of knowledge I've not been able to jettison.'

'Are you glad you learnt Latin?'

'I think so. Yes. On the whole. It's a good foundation for my sort of job.'

'I've not missed it.'

Alison enjoyed desultory conversation with Polly. For an hour or two it removed her from her careful writing and reading, her work with students, her communication with colleagues, her letters and faxes abroad, even, if truth be told, from her lovemaking. Here she stood on earth, solidly, not swaying on the fragile scaffolds of scholarship, nor scudding diagonally upward through the clouds of ecstasy to the brilliance of a lover's consummation. In this house she spoke to a woman who had looked about her and understood what she had seen. Alison had never talked like this to her mother; memory interfered too radically. The breach had too much of a finality for easy repair. Alison had despised her mother in adolescence for her whining, her attempts to blacken her ex-husband's character in the girl's eyes, her constant appeal for help and comfort which her daughter could not easily give. Alison had little leisure at the time, immersed in her studies, enjoying an unexpected new mastery at school. For the first time in her life in command of herself, she had no intention of surrendering to her mother's petitions, but could not help feeling guilt.

Now she talked with pleasure to an older woman who wanted no more than warm friendship, who gave more than she took, who seemed sane, mature, with common sense to spare.

Alison spoke about the visit to the Franklands' house, and the situation between husband and wife there.

'Would you have known there was something wrong if David hadn't mentioned it beforehand?'

'I don't think so.'

'Then she did very well. When Tom and I were breaking up, he couldn't do a thing right for me. You know, I considered myself a balanced sort of woman, but I was in such a state that I hated him for breathing. It took me all my time to stop myself screaming at him just for being there.'

'And this was just at the end?'

'The last two years. Growing worse by the day. I married too young, I was twenty. Fiona was born when I was twenty-two, and Godfrey the next year. I loved Tom when I married him. I can remember it now. Tall, dark and handsome.' She wagged her head in mockery of herself. 'Very considerate; he was an engineer, and chose to work away from time to time. He had two long spells in the Gulf. But this wasn't unusual. I knew all about this. We managed. He threw his glad eye round. I caught him once. But I could put up with that. Well, just about. It gave me something of a hold over him. But by the time we'd been married twenty years, we'd had enough of each other.' Polly tapped the arm of the chair on which she sat brightly upright, unhurt apparently by her confession. 'We'd had the best of each other sexually, though that could still be good; the children were making progress at school. Tom's firm was doing well, but that meant he had to put in a great deal of time there. We didn't find much pleasure either staying at home or going out. When I think about it now, I guess most marriages come to this sort of state, but people, if there are advantages, adapt to the circumstances and make themselves a bearable sort of life.'

'But you didn't?'

'No. Neither of us. We were too youthfully minded, immature if you like, with too much energy to spare. He was a good-looking man, late forties, doing well, fussed over by the women at work. And he didn't want to come home to carpet slippers and stodgy meals and discussion of the children's UCCA forms for intellectual stimulation. If he'd been a bit older, or less lively, that's what he would have enjoyed, but he didn't. He gadded about.'

'And you?'

'Yes. That's the question. I put my surplus energy into hating him. First of all, I suppose, I thought it was unfair, but instead of taking up good works, or playing squash or golf until I'd no strength left for brooding, I sat at home and nursed my neurosis. It was the time of life, beginning of the menopause, I guess, though I'd have denied it if anyone had asked me. I felt sorry for myself. I stayed in my beautiful house and refused to help myself. And, as I tell you, in the last couple of years he hadn't put a foot right. I couldn't bear the expression on his face; if he told me something interesting he'd done, I was jealous that he'd had the opportunity. I loathed him.'

'You seem to be blaming yourself,' Alison said.

'Well, I know more about my side of the coin. When I think about it now I'm surprised that I managed to work myself into such a state. I'm basically sensible. If Tom had made some effort to appear sympathetic, we might have patched things up. But he was too busy, too preoccupied, too pleased with his new status to bother until I was beyond redemption. And this different, mad Polly, must have surprised him.'

'Had you no friends?'

'I was cunning. I could hide my hysteria from them. They didn't know. Well, sometimes.'

'And the children?'

'They were working hard at school. And caught up with their own teenage problems. They knew something was wrong with me. They couldn't help seeing. My behaviour with them was bizarre in the extreme, sometimes.'

'Doctors?'

'Oh, dishing out tranquillisers. And I looked on them as Tom's friends and allies. Bloody men. As I suppose they were. And when I demanded divorce, Tom was only too glad to comply. He'd had quite enough of my lunatic goings-on at home and embarrassing behaviour outside. He made a generous settlement, I'll give him that. I'm not so sure he couldn't have wooed me back to sanity, if he'd made the effort, but he didn't.'

'And how did you first meet Tom?'

'At a party. Friends of my parents. I can remember to this day my excitement when I realised that this gorgeous young man, he didn't seem too young, was interested in me. We'd been to a disco or two, and the theatre, once in London even, and to restaurants. And then he proposed marriage.'

'Where?'

'In his car. It seemed impossible to be so lucky. But I can only recall it with words. None of the physical feeling. I have to say something to myself like "I danced on rainbows". That's the best I can manage. I had got exactly what I wanted. We bought a house. Tom worked for Plowright-Marshall then. It was before he began travelling regularly abroad.'

'Were your parents happy about it?'

'Surely. Tom was very presentable and had great prospects. To prove how well he was doing, we moved house three times in six years, up-market. I was pregnant inside the first year and delighted. We had a boy and a girl by the time we had been married three years. We had the money so that I could stay at home and look after them.'

'Then what went wrong?' Alison loved the simple question.

'I did. That's the top and bottom. It took some time. We changed. So does everybody else. Tom spent a great deal of time abroad, and then in his office. He had an affair or two, but nothing lengthy or serious. This is as common as breathing. But I couldn't put up with it. It made me hate, and fight, and scream.'

'But why?'

'Frustration, I guess. What else? I'd no career, nothing to turn my hand to. I could see the children leaving home in a year or two, and there was I on a straight run for the crematorium, with nothing much to occupy me. Blame hormonal change, if you like. It played its part. But I had two years of such violence of feeling that when I screamed for divorce Tom was only too willing.'

'And did you really want it?'

'Really?' There was a sarcastic edge to Polly's echo of the adverb.

'Well, you married George almost immediately.'

'I see. Fiona had just started university and Godfrey was in the upper sixth. I'd met George, he was their housemaster. He was a widower, Edna had died the year before, and he was about to retire. You know what he's like, bluff John Bull; he proposed.'

'And you accepted straight away?'

'You think I should have been more circumspect in view of my disasters? It never crossed my mind. I'd been lucky for the second time.' Polly laughed. 'And are we happy ever after? Well . . . We get along. I'm happier than I deserve to be, considering my tantrums the first time round. But I shouldn't be troubling you with this rigmarole. It's enough to put anybody off. I'm not against marriage. You must realise that. Enjoy your engagement. The weeks when I knew for certain that I'd hooked Tom were the happiest in my life.'

'More so than the birth of the children?'

'Yes. I may be unusual, but yes. More so. Make the most of it.'

'I'm older than you were, Polly. I'm twenty-six.'

'And more sensible, I'm sure.'

'What about the second time round? Were you, er, elated then?'

'Quite different, quite different. I was coming round, making head or tail of myself, and I realised that Tom was out of the way, Fiona gone and Godfrey almost off. And old 'Killer' Randall was making a fuss of me. I could see he was embarrassed by it because he obviously expected me to turn him down. There was a twenty-four-year difference between us for a start. And George had nothing like the income Tom had, though there'd always been some money about with the Randalls. But he proposed.'

'Were you surprised?'

'Not really. He always made his intentions clear. And he has a great deal about him. A bit aggressive. But you'll have noticed. He can stand up for himself. He stumbles out with it. He was in the RAF in the war. He was aircrew, a pilot.'

'I didn't know. Does he talk about it?'

'Not much. He will occasionally come out with something, but no more enthusiastically, oh, that's the wrong word, forcibly, emotionally involved than about anything else. But of the people he trained with, I think one in twenty survived. It's appalling to think about. All those clever young men. All killed. He was extremely lucky. And these were all people he knew well, his friends, what he calls his "dirty drinking pals". It must have made a great difference to him.'

'Don't you wish you'd have known him when he was young?'

'Yes. No. It's impossible so I don't think about it. He was married to Edna two years before I was born. I'm the same age, within a month or two, as David's father. So. I've seen photographs of him. In his uniform.' Polly shook her head as if she found difficulty in coming to terms with what had happened. 'We've been married seven years now.' She stroked her face. 'It's worked out well. Don't ever expect everything to be perfect. I think I did. I was so green. I remember my first big row with Tom. We hadn't been married more than three or four months. And he was late home from work.' Polly pulled a wry mouth. 'I wasn't much of a cook in those days. Did it all from a manual. I've still got it. I still use it, though it's dropping to pieces. So I liked to know exactly when he was coming home, and then I'd just about get all the things finished and right together. Well, this day I had one hell of a struggle. Everything went awry. But I didn't give up, and by half five when I expected him it was all coming to completion.'

Alison smiled now. Polly seemed relaxed.

'And?'

'He didn't turn up. Six o'clock came. Half past. No Thomas. Seven. He came in large as life at ten past seven. I'd been doing my best to keep the meal hot and eatable; it was pork chops and apple sauce, about all I could manage in those days, but by the time he came, well, burnt offering just about describes it. And there he was, all smiles. He'd had an important meeting with one of the Jardines. It had started at four thirty and dragged on. Frederick Jardine was a very important client. The family lived, live still, at Hoveringham Hall. And the pair had gone out for a friendly drink afterwards. I could smell alcohol.

' "I'm sorry, darling," he said. "I should have 'phoned. But I wasn't sure. I might just have been home at half past five. But there were loose ends. He's sharp is Fred Jardine, and thorough. Anyway we cleared it all up in the end. And a good long contract for the firm." '

'He put his arms round me. That should have softened me. It didn't. I could smell the whisky on his breath. I wriggled away from him by thumping his chest, and I shouted out, "You're drunk." I can still remember the expression on his face. "Oh, come on, Poll," he said, so high and mighty. I'd strained the peas into a colander, a great big silver thing, and I snatched it up and threw it at him. It went nowhere near him. I don't know to this day whether I intended to hit him, but peas sputtered all over the room.'

'And Tom?'

'He just walked out. Ten minutes later he came down again, helped me clear up, I was sitting snivelling on a stool, apologised again, said how thoughtless he had been.'

'And you made it up?'

'Yes. There and then. And he didn't hold it against me. I think he understood. Of course it made no difference. Next time his work demanded he was late, then late he was. He'd try to ring me up. And I suppose I got used to

56

it. But then, later, a lot later, I couldn't stand it any more, threw restraint aside, bawled and screamed.'

'It doesn't sound like you, Polly.'

'No? That just shows how little you know me. Or how little I know myself.'

Polly walked about the room, tranquilly enough, but unusually so that Alison wondered if she needed the exercise to calm herself.

'I shouldn't be telling you all this.' The voice was normal. 'It's enough to put you off matrimony.' She chuckled. 'Or put you off me.'

'And where does Tom live now?'

'Out at Keyworth.'

'Is he . . . married?'

'Yes. His secretary. One of them. Anne. I know her. She was a nice girl.'

'Do you ever meet?'

'With Tom? Only once or twice, outside court, in the eight years.'

'Has he a new family?'

'No. He hasn't. That's odd, because Anne Sowbridge is a sensible woman. Not just a pretty face. She would make a good mother. Fiona and Godfrey like her. They took to her when they went over to see their father.' Polly spread her arms wide. 'So we're all happy. What's the next thing? I don't know. Godfrey's engaged now. His wedding, perhaps. Fiona, she's not married. She's your age. But she's too busy. She's in dress design. London. I often wonder if my performance hasn't had a bad effect on her.'

'Is she sensible?'

'I guess so. And she knows such a lot more than I did. I went into marriage ignorant, and I remained so for long enough.'

'Why was that?'

'These matters are discussed. On telly, by agony aunts in the local papers. In my day all we had were old wives' tales.'

'But,' Alison objected, 'they were the swinging sixties. In fact you were married the year before sexual intercourse began.'

57

The look of Polly's face, crumpled puzzlement, delighted Alison.

'It's a quotation from a poem,' she said, 'by Philip Larkin.'

'It sounds like "Eskimo Nell",' Polly grimaced.

Alison left before George Randall returned from his dominoes. As the two walked out together to the car, parked in the lane at the end of the garden, Alison felt again the rush of pleasure in the other woman's company.

'When I talk to you here I feel as if I've joined a real family,' she confided.

'We're bits and pieces.'

'But you fit.'

'Sometimes.' Polly took her arm. 'We've had our moments. And our moments. And our off days. When George told me that David was going out with a lecturer at the university, I thought, "She'll be talking about *Paradise Lost* all the time." '

'I know what you mean.'

They kissed warmly, squeezing each other, both optimistic.

'Do you have to get George's supper ready?'

'No. He won't want anything more. He won't have drunk much, either, but it will be enough to get him and his prostate gland up four or five times in the night. But he's quiet with it. I'll give him that.'

Polly watched Alison drive away under the boughs of oak and lime trees which once bounded the rectory gardens.

VI

David walked into the corridor at Lamberts at ten minutes to nine.

Outside October sun brightened the walls of splendid houses, flashed from brass plates, but did little to take the edge off the morning's cold. David, early, had beaten the secretary to it so that the guardian desk had stood empty. The cleaners had left behind them a pleasant smell of disinfectant and furniture polish. Albert Frankland opened the door of his office with a small blaze of light.

'Ah, David. Would you come in for a moment?'

He had, David concluded, been waiting for him.

Frankland closed the door, commented on the weather. His room dazzled with the morning.

'Sit down. Or not, as you please. I shan't keep you long. I want to thank you for the invitation to your wedding. Very tasteful.' Frankland raised his eyebrows. 'You should see some of the monstrosities that are sent these days.' He frowned, suddenly, forming a sharp dark cleft between the silver eyebrows. Social conversation was over. 'In my case, there is a slight, that is the wrong word, complication.' He spoke jerkily and walked two yards or three either way. Now he laid a hand on his desk. 'Eleanor has gone. Has left me. That will perhaps not surprise you. I shall send on your invitation to see what she says. I do not know where she is staying, nor have I attempted to find out, but I can always reach her, I understand, through Jennifer, my daughter. You have met her.' Again the tapping of fingers on the polished surface. 'I don't think Eleanor is with her.'

David watched his principal. Frankland said nothing for a few moments to allow the younger man to outline, for himself, like a good lawyer, the problems that were inherent in the situation. Then he could compare and contrast the difficulties he envisaged with those described by the client. David, on the arm of a chair, kept silent, head cocked in interest, waiting for Frankland's exposition. Even in his embarrassment his boss did not fail to instruct, thus indirectly, his subordinate.

'You see the snags. I most certainly want to attend, and have already marked the day and time in my diaries. Now it is possible that Eleanor may also wish to be present. One of the few, the very few things, she said to me after you wrote thanking her for the evening at our house was what an attractive couple you and Alison made. But my presence may inhibit her attendance. You see that. It will be a matter of negotiation. So, I cannot give you an immediate acceptance.'

'That's all right.'

'You will explain my dilemma to Alison, if you please.'

'She'll understand.'

'I'm sure. Though,' the voice dropped in pitch and volume, 'it's more than I do. This has shown me how little we lawyers know what is going on in our clients' minds, the stresses, the contradictory promptings, even the violence, when we are dealing with cases like this.'

'Perhaps it's as well,' David murmured.

'We explain the law, you mean, and that is where our responsibility ends. You're probably right.' He drew himself up straight. 'She told me, one evening, that she was going to leave the next day, and that from that time I would be on my own. I argued against this as reasonably as I could. But nothing. I was, in fact, beginning to hope that the breach was being, at least in part, healed. We had lived on, uncomfortably, I grant you, for a month or more, and I played my cards as quietly as I could. Then, it is a fortnight ago, she made her announcement. Nothing had gone badly wrong in the week before. But I realise it now, she had been making her preparations. She packed a fair amount of clothes, enough for a month's holiday, say. But the house is full of her belongings. I suppose she and Jennifer, I believe they're in this together, can call in at any time during the day and help themselves to whatever is required.'

'You're not thinking of changing the locks, then?'

'I see no need for that.'

They could hear in the office next door Frankland's secretary setting about her day's work. Footsteps of the girls had clapped along the corridor; greetings had been vaguely heard as other colleagues arrived, collected mail or left instructions.

'You'll say nothing,' Frankland had instructed, 'except to Alison.' He pressed the bell.

The side door flew open immediately as if Mrs Wakefield, his secretary, had been waiting at the keyhole. She would have heard nothing; they had kept their voices lawyerly low.

'Good morning, Mr Frankland, Mr Randall.'

They greeted the smiling young matron. The day's work had begun.

'Thank you, David.'

Frankland's face, clear of worry, assumed untroubled alertness as he sat and signalled his secretary into the client's seat as the young man left.

David admired the old man and his coolness. Presumably his pride had taken a dent, and the appearance of acting circumspectly played a large part in the priorities of older members of the Law Society. Did Frankland take his evening meal at a club, and do his own laundry? And Jennifer, the daughter, appeared to side with her mother. And Mrs Frankland? The rift must have been deep for her to leave the comfort of her home. As he settled to his day's work David forgot the Franklands except that a faint mortification at first spoiled the morning's brightness.

Two days later, Alison, walking into the centre of Beechnall from the university, thought the matter over. David had talked to her on the telephone, and had seemed ambivalent about Frankland's predicament. He had suggested, with provisos galore, that perhaps Albert was himself relieved by Eleanor's departure and for that reason could keep such a phlegmatic appearance. David reported with great accuracy; it was almost as if he had taken a shorthand note. She was impressed; David must have been interested to pay such close attention.

She walked easily now among the mansions of Victorian lace manufacturers in streets still leafy in sunshine. The term had begun, lurched out of inertia. She had worked morning, afternoon and evening in the weeks before October the first, and now with the administrative chores covered, and the students' first assignments under way, she had freed herself for three hours to walk to town on a nonexistent errand. She would look frivolously into shop windows and at the faces and clothes of pedestrians; she'd keep out of libraries and bookshops and offices, and edge thoughts of wedding arrangements to the margins of her mind.

The variation of the buildings intrigued her. All were large, even the smaller houses, but some were straight-fronted parallel to the roads while others had an almost gothic darkness and size behind high walls. True, gardens had been divided, and town houses, maisonettes, executive four-bedroom fancies had been rushed up while many of the great mansions had been divided into flats with rows of names like tab-stops on a Wurlitzer in each Romanesque or Regency doorway. Once, there had been money about, and individualism. Every man of means, or his wife, had chosen to live in affluence and within a few minutes' carriage drive of work but in huge rooms different from those of the neighbours, with severe fantasies of plaster work adorning the high ceilings and daring the merchant next door to match the capriciousness of the employed artisan's imagination.

And outside, on the streets, forest trees, limes, beeches, planes, horse chestnut grew with here and there a silver birch, flourishing so that the sky seemed crammed with foliage, sometimes bridging and darkening the whole width of a road. 'High overarch'd embower', she quoted Milton, with unforced pleasure. These outward and visible signs of an earlier prosperity lifted the heart of casual pedestrians a hundred and twenty years later.

'Oh, good afternoon.'

A diffident voice greeted Alison from behind.

Eleanor Frankland smiled uncertainly. Alison turned. In a light coat, hatless, hair in a band, Eleanor held in front of her a multicoloured plastic shopping-bag. The two women asked after health, commented on the clement St Martin's summer, on the beauty of the trees. Alison, out of kindness, explained why she found so much enjoyment from the houses. Eleanor listened obediently and the pair lifted their eyes to playful, small clouds in pale-blue sky above the foliage.

'The leaves are just beginning to turn.' Eleanor pointed pointlessly. 'I like this season.'

Alison said why she walked this part of the world. Almost eagerly Eleanor answered her.

'I live here now. Not far from here.'

Alison waited politely.

'I've left my husband. I've taken a flat.'

Alison offered a sympathetic face, murmurs of compassion.

'It's not far from here. Less than five minutes away. Would you come and see it?'

'Now?'

'I know it's a nuisance, but . . .'

'Yes, please. I'd like that.'

'Thank you.'

Mrs Frankland's voice had the accent of her class, but she spoke vaguely as if her breath was running out.

They set off together, not very fast, pausing now and then to allow Eleanor to make comments on the few front gardens not hidden behind high brick walls. They went downhill, physically and socially, to the bottom edge of the magnates' estate where the streets protected the higher reaches from the main road below with its roaring traffic, glass-fronted factories, warehouses and workmen's cottages. On this drive the houses were substantial by modern standards, semi-detached or in terraces of three, originally for high-class clerks or cashiers, with short, largely neglected front gardens, low walls, but quite handsome entrances. The two women left the pavement level by two steps and a Gothic arch into a corridor and thence straight upstairs. On the first floor Eleanor unlocked her flat. The metal frame on the door lacked a naming card.

Alison felt colder inside the house than out, and chillier still in the room. Though they could see sunshine on distant roofs the large window here seemed shadowed, perhaps by the turn of the street or by the outjutting of the house next door, so that the first effect on her was of half-darkness. Once her eyes were accustomed to the light, or lack of it, she could make out the long rectangular shape with a table over by the windows, two armchairs and a settee, with sideboard behind, ranged in front of an uninteresting fireplace and hearth. The end of the room nearest the door stood bare with two large suitcases unsuitably placed as if to combat vacuity. The walls, without pictures, were papered in a lifeless striped pattern, the tint that of mild scorching. The carpet buckled almost colourless, its design worn away, its tasselled edge uneven, and at one spot near the settee worn to a ragged hole. The place looked clean enough, but shabby; furnished rooms worn to nonentity by a rapidly changing series of careless tenants.

Eleanor switched on a light without much effect.

'It's comfortable,' she said unconvincingly.

Alison was invited to sit while Eleanor moved through a second door into a kitchenette to fill a kettle and turn it on. The visitor stared at the frayed carpet by her feet, at the ill-painted surround of the fireplace with small discoloured tiles, two of which were badly cracked. The coal scuttle in the hearth, with a battered one-bar electric fire, was ugly and empty apart from a scatter of slack in its bottom; the wooden fender, chipped and stained, matched the concrete beneath it in dullness. Nothing was square; constant misuse had distorted right angles and straight lines.

Though the chair was comfortable enough, Alison sat uneasily, squinting out of the window at the three tall storeys of the houses opposite, and listening to the preparation of tea. When Eleanor finally returned, carrying a wooden tray with an oversized brown teapot and cheap cups which must have been part of the furnishings of the flat, the guest brightened her expression.

'I've hardly got used to where things are kept,' Eleanor began.

'How long have you been here?'

'A fortnight. It seems both longer and shorter.'

Alison sipped her scalding tea and put down cup and saucer on the carpet by her feet.

'Are you here all on your own?' she asked.

'Oh, yes. Jennifer found me the place. Some acquaintance of hers who owns rented property.'

Alison refused a proffered biscuit, and Eleanor, after some useless alterations on the surface of the tray, sat down sighing.

'It's convenient,' Eleanor said. 'Large enough. There's a big bedroom which I will show you, with a huge bed.' She laughed nervously. 'Of course, I'm not settled.'

'You'll stay here?'

'I shouldn't think so. But it will do for the transitional period.'

'Are you lonely?'

Eleanor considered the question.

'Yes, I suppose I am. But then again that's what I wanted.' She shifted heavily on her hams; her chair springs squeaked. 'I needed time to myself. With no social duties or pleasures. I'm not very used to being on my own. Albert works long hours, but during the day I'd visit friends or have them in to see me. But I wanted blank time.'

Alison stooped to her cup so that she need not speak. She determined she would not take sides. Blank time.

'They, my friends, don't know where I am. Al doesn't. Only Jennifer and now you. I'd be most grateful if you'd not give my address to anyone, not even to your fiancé. It would put him in an invidious position if his employer began to question him.'

'I needn't mention that I've seen you.'

'There's no need for that. But no clues to where I've landed.' She smirked, rather unpleasantly, at her expression. 'Jennifer won't let on to her father. She is my accommodation address. She helped me to settle here; found the place, helped move my bits and pieces, calls in, brings mail. Do you know I haven't written one single letter since I came here?'

'You like being on your own?'

'I didn't say that. I don't think, to be frank, that I do. But it's what I needed. How old do you think I am?' Alison made no attempt to answer. 'I'm fifty-three. Is that more than twice your age? I guess you find it odd that I've scuttled out like this. After all, I've been married thirty-odd years: I ought to have grown used to it. That's Jennifer's line with me.'

'And you with yourself?'

'I don't know. I really was driven to distraction this last year or two. I guess it was partially, even largely my own fault.'

'That's what Polly Randall, David's grandfather's wife, says about her divorce. Though she blames it on the menopause.'

Eleanor paid no attention.

'I don't make out that Albert was cruel. Thoughtless, yes. Or not quite that. If it came to a choice between his work and my pleasure, work won. And that may seem sensible to you. But there was no need for that on his part. He's so well established that he can make his own timetable of appointments, and professional committees and so on are fixed months ahead. We lost interest in each other. Thirty years is a long time. Or at least that's how it seemed to me. And so I've decided to test the water.'

'Any results yet?'

'Too soon. A fortnight's not long.'

'You might go back, then?' Alison, eagerly.

'Not yet. I'm the one in the partnership who experiments. Al's not dull. By no means. But he'd be content with the same rota of meals, provided they were nutritious and well cooked, the same furniture, the same style of suits and ties and holidays. His work's sufficiently interesting. Outside that everything else, me included, is secondary.'

'I always had the impression that legal work was rather boring.'

'Maybe it is. But in this last four years Albert has reorganised Lamberts. He's got rid of the old men, promoted one or two of the middle range and appointed some young men. Your David, for instance. It hasn't been easy. He's very good, for instance, with finance, and so the arrangement of terms of severance, if that's what it's called, has interested him. And some of the old stagers didn't want to leave, and had to be encouraged by favourable settlements to pack their bags. And he's organised all that.'

'I see.'

'And then he has to look to the image of the firm. Lamberts is old-established. Didn't do divorce until, oh, about twenty years ago. Except in the case of their notable families. But Albert encouraged the then principal, he's dead now, to take on Edward Blagg, an up-and-coming young man, and he's built up a tremendous reputation for the firm. The same with the commercial side. He introduced Terence Thompson and they've made a very good thing of it. Both Blagg and Thompson are partners now.'

'They're the middle-aged men?'

'Yes.' Eleanor gabbled her answers, as if to prevent interruption. 'It's all a matter of judgement. What's worth following up in strength.'

Eleanor cited examples. One of the more senior 'young men' had acquired a tremendous reputation in cases of racial discrimination. Knowledgeably Eleanor cited the times, the payments, the advantages or disadvantages over other kinds of practice. Her account was comprehensive; she held her listener by the speed and nature of the exposition. As she talked she poured out second cups of tea, without pausing. Alison gathered that two weeks of loneliness were being amply made up here. Eleanor gabbled like an expert, in expectation of effort and attention from her listener, thoroughly immersed in her explanations, certain of her power to interest.

In the end Alison interrupted.

'Two things strike me,' she said, as at the end of a student's essay.

Eleanor goggled.

'Oh, dear.' She was reduced now to a middle-aged housewife who dressed well and could produce delicacies, bramble jelly and bread-and-butter pudding. 'Go on, then. Tell me.' Her voice hung nervously low.

'First, that you must have talked about these matters a great deal with your husband.'

'Yes. We did.'

'And secondly. You greatly admired him and what he was doing.'

'I don't deny it.'

Now the eyes narrowed, the expression became crafty, cunningly cautious.

'And if that's so, I'm surprised you left him.'

Both women had now overstepped the mark.

'I left him for personal reasons, not because he was a poor solicitor.' The tone was dismissive.

'Ah, yes.' Alison spoke with soft reasonableness. 'But I've found that when one is overwhelmed by dislike, never mind hatred for a person, one can't usually say much in his favour.' As soon as she spoke she knew she was wrong. At the time she fled from Henry Corbett, she could have written a perspicacious list of the man's strengths. Eleanor watched.

'You mean, I take it, that if I can talk like this about Al, I can't really be too dissatisfied with him. I'd never thought about it in that way. I suppose there's something in your argument. Or perhaps at my age one isn't so shaken with anger as when one is young, the necessary energy's lacking. I just don't know.'

Alison admired the woman's open-mindedness. Eleanor continued to talk.

'I'm glad I left. I was reaching a stage of unreason, where I might have done something silly. I don't mean murder or suicide but I might have smashed some valuable china or attacked a good picture.'

Eleanor described how she had decided on leaving, and had consulted her daughter, who had been helpful in a cold-blooded way. 'She'd no sympathy. She felt sorry for Daddy, I think.' Then followed an account of her financial situation. Money of her own meant that she could live in moderate comfort, and if it came to divorce she'd be entitled to a fairish amount from her husband. She knew the law, it appeared.

As the voice rolled on, syllable after precise syllable, shaped sentence after sentence, it was not so much the sense of the discourse as the necessity for delivering it which struck Alison. Eleanor had to talk. Her listener confined herself to encouraging monosyllables or brief questions. Eleanor talked about the source of her family's money, and this led to her childhood, her siblings, her school. She marvellously sketched her piano teacher, a shabby organist with whom as a thirteen-year-old she had been in love. Holidays abroad, a grandmother's house in Scotland, an unexpected trip to Canada in the holiday before university. She mentioned her husband only parenthetically; nothing of their first meeting, or wedding, or early married life or the birth of the children. Only the clinically clean years of her early youth, remembered in loving detail, and offered as a reward for the patience of the listener.

'Look at the time,' Alison said in the end. 'It's nearly four fifteen.' She had been there almost an hour and a half. 'I must go.'

'I've wasted your afternoon.'

'Not at all. I've enjoyed every minute.'

Eleanor started back, perhaps on the look-out for irony, began to thank Alison volubly. They promised to meet again. Alison giving her telephone numbers received Jennifer's in return. The two women put arms round each other, hugged, both surprised at themselves.

'You don't know what a relief it's been to have somebody to talk to.'

'Ring round your friends.'

'I daren't do that. Not yet. I don't want to force things.' Slyness lit her face. 'I'm lurking. And that means silence.

That's why it's been such a bonus meeting you. I feel flushed out.' She laughed at her expression; Alison could not disentangle the ambiguity of the metaphor, but felt pleasure either way.

Eleanor escorted her guest from the room, down the narrow staircase, on to the uneven quarry tiles of the hall, where they embraced again.

The street outside seemed no more busy, though the pounding of traffic along the unseen main road sounded more insistent, with a harsher clarity.

Alison looked back to Eleanor Frankland's window with its drab curtains. They showed blank, black, polished by dust. Eleanor did not look out. A schoolgirl posted a letter as a cat scuttled across the road. A West Indian emerged from a front door to mount into his van and drive off. The sky shone; loose paper littered the gutter.

She lifted her head, thinking of bus stops.

VII

Alison and David ate Saturday's breakfast together.

She had spent the night at his flat, had been there when Polly had rung in the early evening to say that Vernon and his wife were expected and that David and Alison were invited to lunch.

'Have you only just found out?' David asked.

'Karen rang this morning. I 'phoned your home and Alison's but you weren't in. I didn't want to interrupt you at work.'

'Why not? Thanks very much. At what time shall we appear?'

'Just after twelve. We'll lunch at one. That will give them a good long morning in bed.'

'Is he all right?'

'Tired. Overworked. They haven't arrived yet. They said late afternoon, but you know what these people are. Karen's driving him.'

They discussed David's father and the change of plans lunch at Polly's involved.

'They don't give much notice,' Alison said.

'Typical of Vernon. He might know that Grandfather will want time to prepare himself. He's not fond of official visitors. And he doesn't always hit it off with Vernon.'

For the third or fourth time Alison questioned David about his father. They liked nothing better than the dissection of somebody's character.

'You'll get on well with him,' David promised. 'He'll put himself out to attract you. He always looks worn out, but I'm never sure whether that's real or not. We don't meet all that often, and we don't write or 'phone much. I was nine when he and my mother were divorced. But he's clever, astute, that is, and well read.'

71

'Does he enjoy being famous?'

'I expect so. It has its drawbacks, I don't doubt. But it's what he's always aimed for. When Grandpa nags him, he invariably replies that he's nowhere near as well known as some pop stars or footballers or comedians. But, wait till you meet him. Then you can make your own mind up.'

'I'd better drive back home to find something fit to wear.'

'Um.' David pulled a long, comical face. 'You do.'

'You've no idea,' she said.

He left it there, mildly.

They enjoyed these sessions on people. Eleanor Frankland had been discussed at length. Alison canvassed the view that it was the volubility, the gush of words rather than their sense or clear utterance which had been important. Eleanor, lonely after her decision, had found a friendly ear and had taken advantage. Immediately after her visit Alison had dispatched a card to Mrs Frankland suggesting that they meet again and proposing times and venues. That was more than a week ago, and it had gone unanswered. David thought Eleanor had moved on, to a seaside hotel or the house of a relative or friend, while the card gathered dust on the doormat or tiles.

'I'm considering ringing Jennifer.'

'Good idea.'

'But I don't want to be thought to be poking my nose in.' She looked serious. 'Has Albert said anything?'

'Not a word. He's an odd man.'

'Does he talk to you very much?'

'I'll say.'

Lambert and Partners had been marginally caught up in a notorious, continuing series of accusations and arrests over child abuse, in which the firm represented three sets of parents. Why Frankland had accepted the case was a mystery to all his young men; he could easily have suggested other solicitors who would be more used to work, and publicity, of this sort. But he did not; he thoroughly cross-examined the six people concerned, together and separately, before deciding to move to their defence. He had called in David for the final meeting, one evening, at the home of one of the accused pairs.

Next morning he had sent for the young man.

'I don't know what opinion you formed last night of those people,' he began, solemnly, 'or if it would be wise at this stage to come to any conclusion after so short an acquaintance.' The meeting had lasted two hours. 'I have decided in my mind that no blame attaches to them. Except in so far as they have acted foolishly or have been wrongly advised. They are connected by marriage and proximity with some who, I think, will be found guilty. But these are innocent. You may not like them. I do not. They have no criminal records, but they are . . . oh, not our sort. Perhaps that is all the more reason for us to make the effort on their behalf.'

David, puzzled, wondered why Frankland had put himself out. He, however, acted expeditiously, and without undue trouble had the children of these families back from care and into their parents' homes. That was right, and he was pleased with himself, even though Frankland then grumbled that he could not approve of the way these children were brought up. 'They will not be abused. Of that I am sure.'

'Why were they included with the others in the first place?'

'They were there. Contiguity. And in two cases they were related, but it was their awkwardness. Obstinacy. Refusal to co-operate with enquiries. You saw them. You had your chance to judge. They did not like us, for instance. They considered that we had no idea how police or social security offices and social workers treated them. You saw one of their homes.'

'Why did you take the case?'

'Why do you ask that?'

'It's not your usual line of country.' David found it best to answer his employer plainly.

'The Chief Constable, this is to go no further, asked me to get them out of the way. They were a complication, he said, that he could do without. They'll manage to secure convictions in the majority of the cases, he believes.'

'Why did he not just let this lot go, then?'

'It's sad. There are several interested parties representing what they would call the public interest. And one of these, I shall name no names, was determined that all the children concerned should be kept under close observation and out of their parents' reach until such time that prosecutions were fully prepared. Atkinson thought that this was to nobody's advantage, would court adverse media attention, and asked me to interview these people, and then to begin to intervene on their behalf. We have a reputation. Both for long public service, and for success. As you saw, once you began, opposition melted. Atkinson said it would. The families were reunited.'

Frankland spoke almost with warmth, but he interpreted the question on David's forehead.

'You're wondering who is paying for this. Clearly the Rhodeses and the Flemings are in no position to do so. The answer is: I am. We have acted for the public weal and done Len Atkinson a good turn. We need to make money to keep up appearances,' he waved his hand round the puritan elegance of his room, 'that I admit, but as long as we earn our livelihood, then we can score our mark elsewhere. And, you know, they may not be unconnected.'

Frankland now embarked, this was during the lunch break, on an anecdote about the length of time he had expended on a small case, worth only a few pounds to the firm, sorting out legal complications nobody else had noticed. The two or three days of search and hard thinking had not only been interesting to him as a lawyer, taking him into byways he had not encountered before, but had earned him a considerable reputation in the profession. 'These things get about, you know.' Moreover, the expertise he had acquired had been useful in no less than four very profitable affairs within the next two years.

'But the Lord is mindful of his own,' David said, lowering his eyes.

The principal did not comment on this mild mockery. He enjoyed instructing his young men, though he realised they made fun of him in private, so that when David admitted to Alison that Frankland often talked to him, he spoke the truth. To or at him. Neither, however, mentioned Mrs Frankland.

This Saturday morning the engaged couple sat in the car outside David's house ready for the drive to his grandfather's. They'd arrive at twelve fifteen, he predicted, and that was soon enough. He parked in the lane behind George Randall's and they made their way up fourteen high steps and into the length of the garden.

'You can't see the house from here,' Alison said in the orchard. Leaves were turning, but not falling. 'Not at all.'

'No. You will in winter. That's why they keep the gate locked. Polly will have opened up for us. It shows they're awake and about. Let's listen.'

Beyond the house they heard the faint buzz of traffic. The church clock struck the quarter-hour plangently.

'You look good enough to eat,' David said, kissing Alison lightly on the cheek.

'And you're very smart.' She straightened his collar as if he were a schoolboy.

They walked hand in hand towards the house.

'Forward to meet the rich and famous,' David chaffed her.

'How old is this place?' Alison asked, pausing at a second gate, squinting ahead.

'I think my grandmother once told me that one bit of it is late seventeenth-, early eighteenth-century, but the main part is Victorian. There's been so much rebuilding it's hard to say. It's really oddly put together. I think that the main road was cut out from underneath it, and that the lane there, lower on the slope, was the original city highway.' They looked along the windows; no one stared back. 'That explains the stone wall,' he pointed, 'down to the street.'

'So this would be the front of the house?'

'Yes. Still is, I imagine.'

They walked round to the side of the building, knocked at the back door.

Polly greeted them, led them through the kitchen, which smelt appetisingly delicious, to hang their outdoor clothes on the pegs in a small, unstraight corridor in the dark middle of the house.

'They're in the parlour,' Polly said. 'Real company this morning.'

'Do you need any help?' Alison. 'Out here?'

'No, thanks. It's all under control. Go in and support your grandfather.'

'Does he need it?' the girl pressed.

'Both of them,' Polly pointed towards the parlour, 'are a bit frightened of David these days. He's grown up so big and sensible, and quiet.'

'She hadn't noticed,' David answered. Alison punched him on the arm.

Polly ushered them forward. Father and Grandfather both stood.

'Come in, come on in,' George said. 'And let me introduce you to Alison.' He nuzzled her rather clumsily before he led her to Karen, Vernon's wife, who stood up easily from her armchair to kiss Alison on both cheeks. 'And this is Vernon, David's father.'

Alison turned as Vernon advanced; the pair shook hands and kissed. Karen was hugging David in the background.

Vernon Randall seemed thinner than his television image, older, shabbier, but instantly recognisable. Head on one side, he nodded, thoughtfully smiling.

'You are as beautiful as George said you were.'

The famous voice shaped the sentence as he held Alison's hand, at a yard's distance.

'Of course she is. What did you expect?'

Alison moved aside and David was briefly clasped to his father before they shook hands with equal curtness.

'He's getting bigger,' George said. Now they were all talking together, Grandfather loudest, Polly a close, laughing second. In a minute or two she had settled the newcomers into their chairs and had instructed her husband to provide them with sherry. Duty done, she made for her kitchen.

'How long are you staying?' David asked his father from the far side of the room, near to Karen.

76

'That's it,' George said loudly, with meaning. 'You ask him.'

'We shan't leave until tomorrow.' Vernon, as one purveying reason in a chaotic world.

'We're trying to get him to put his feet up for a day or two,' George almost shouted. 'He's been overdoing it again, hasn't he, Karen? He's ill.'

'He has been working hard,' she answered.

'I'm used to it.' Vernon smiled confidentially to Alison who sat by him on a settee. 'It's what I want. I don't complain.'

'He's had a turn,' George insisted. 'Heart trouble; heart attack.'

'Is it serious?' David asked his father.

'Not really. It was unpleasant while it lasted.'

'Were you frightened?' George blasted out. 'Was he, Karen?'

'I wasn't pleased, that I can tell you.' Vernon's voice, though not loud, had authority, put his father into place.

'We want him to have a few days here with us, so that he'll have a real rest.'

'Who'd choose a holiday in Beechnall?' Vernon smiled at Alison.

'We're very tourist-conscious these days,' David answered.

'When I sat for a schol. to Oxford one of the dons asked me what he should go to see if he had just twenty-four hours in Beechnall.'

They discussed what they would suggest, and Vernon talked to Alison about Oxford. He did this well, never excluding the rest, considering their interest. David noticed that Alison spoke more frequently than Vernon. By the time lunch was announced, the conversation had grown animated.

'What was all the laughing about?' Polly asked as she served.

'Gramps on inside information,' David answered.

'You talk in riddles.'

'You can't expect us to go all over it again just for you,' Grandfather grumbled.

'Why not?' Alison beating Karen to it.

'Because I've either heard it already, or it's not worth repeating.' Polly sounded as delighted as the rest.

David noticed how small a helping his father accepted, how slowly he ate, that he drank water, not wine. Vernon complimented Polly on the excellence of her cooking.

'Are you doing justice to it, though?' George bullied.

'Little and often. Like firing the Flying Scotsman.' He explained the reference for Karen and Alison, and this led Vernon's wife to a long-drawn-out, cunningly phrased question on the attraction of steam trains. George answered loudly, naming nostalgia. Vernon spoke, at length, while he talked he did not have to eat, about the difficulties of driving an inefficient piece of machinery like a steam engine. Some years ago, it appeared, he had made a film for television about the Age of Steam, and had questioned footplate men about their work.

'They all claimed, and these were still working, remember, on diesel or electric locomotives, that they preferred the old days.' He did not hurry. His son admired his mastery of the pause. No one, not even George, interrupted. 'This surprised me. In the modern cab you're sheltered from the weather, and every operation is less demanding physically; they all swore they put on weight immediately they had transferred from steam. And it was so much more difficult with steam to rectify mistakes. If you're delayed at a signal, you could not make up time as you can with a modern machine. And if you got the firing wrong, that was the driver's responsibility not the fireman's, you could actually bring your train, and the system, to a paralysing stop.'

'Why did they like it better, then?' Polly. Vernon smiled at the question he had angled for.

'Fascination of what's difficult.' Now he raised his face to Alison. 'They were like craftsmen working in an intractable medium.'

'But,' said Karen, 'if you were carving in, let's say, a very hard wood, you wouldn't want, well, things like knots to add to your troubles.'

'I am not so sure.' The sentence seemed ordinary enough, but it rang, imposed itself on them. 'There are some who positively welcome difficulties of this sort, who not only overcome them, but use them to enhance their artistry. The defect, the knot, is taken into the design, is made part of it, an important element. After all, achieving a work of art often consists in putting technical difficulties in the way of your chosen expression and then mastering them with more powerful results. Artists don't want a straight run in good conditions. A bumpy, curving track with blustery winds, gusts of rain. Forgive the metaphor and the exaggeration.'

'Is it railway or athletics?' David asked. His father wagged a finger at him.

After lunch, when Polly had stacked the washing-up machine, the party moved out into the garden, where it shone warm. Karen, however, insisted that Vernon put on a light anorak and that he button it up. David, coming out last with Polly, listened to his step-grandmother's complaints about George, who with stiffening limbs had been ordered on a desperate visit to the surgery to use a stick constantly, but refused, though he had recently bought one for himself.

'He's awkward,' Polly said. 'But I'll talk him into it. And this heart attack of Vernon's has upset him.'

'When did this happen?'

'The week before last.'

'And when did you hear about it first?'

'Yesterday. After they arrived. Karen told us straight away.'

'Did they take him into hospital?'

'Well. They sent for their own doctor, and he had him in a private clinic for tests. Some cardiac bigwig gave him a thorough going-over.'

'And handed him a clean bill of health?'

'He has angina. But you ask Karen. I don't think you'll get much information out of Vernon. I think the consultant said that if he took it more easily, he'd be all right.'

Out in the garden they found Vernon on a seat with Alison, both with serious, contented faces. Karen walked the winding paths on her own.

'Where's George?' Polly asked her.

'He went off along there.' Karen pointed. 'He did give me some explanation, but I couldn't tell what he was saying.'

'Typical. You have a walk round with David. I'll go and see what he's up to. He's no notion of his responsibilities as a host. I shall never train him.'

Polly followed her husband. David and Karen faced about, passing Vernon and Alison who waved lazily in their direction, not interrupting conversation.

'She's lovely,' Karen said. 'You're lucky.'

'I am.' David, formally.

'And Polly says she's clever too. Knows six languages. Is that so?'

'Latin and Greek and French, Italian and German. And she's great on Italian art. We shall visit Italy at least once every year.'

'Do you mind?'

'No. Why should I? She's a fascinating teacher, other things aside.' He laughed.

'It doesn't daunt you? All her learning?'

'No. I don't think so. Should it?'

'Well.' Karen fluttered her hands. 'You Randalls are a pretty self-confident lot. You think you have plenty going for you. Though you're the quietest, Vernon says. By far.'

They reached the end of the garden, and on Karen's suggestion went steeply down to look at the lane. Opposite the gate a high Victorian brick wall stretched and branches from the trees behind this roofed the cobbles. In the distance they could see and hear the traffic on the main road two hundred yards away.

'It's dark down here,' she said.

'Is that your car?' he asked. A highly polished Daimler-Jaguar stood in front of his.

David began to offer information about the lane, once the high road from the city, about the stone bridge over the river below them in the valley, the marketplace, old vehicles and animals, the railway, the dyers and bleachers.

'It seems so rustic,' she said, re-entering the lowest gate back into the garden.

As they were about half way up the long flight of steps Karen, who was leading, turned and announced,

'I'm worried about Vernon.'

'This heart spasm, or whatever? What happened?'

'I was out. He had chest pains, and rang Jonathan Douglas, our doctor, who lives only a few doors away. Luckily he was in, and came round. He sent him to see Sir Francis Dugdale, the heart specialist, and it appears that your father has angina.'

'Was this the first sign?'

'I'd heard nothing before, but apparently there's been pain. And these must have been pretty frightening, because Vernon had been to see Jon about it already.'

'And said nothing to you?'

'And said nothing to me.'

Karen had now turned away from him and faced the right-hand orange-brick wall enclosing the steps. She could not see over the top ahead of her, though shrubs grew in apparent wildness on either side of the cutting. He stood below, the substantial wooden door closed behind him.

'He'd never complained?'

'I knew he was off colour, but then he often is. He works too hard. He reminds me all the time of a demented student just before finals. And because he goes to interesting meetings and dinners and conferences it tends to hide how furiously he flogs himself. He'd an incipient ulcer, I knew; he was anaemic from time to time. He'd flop out at home, exhausted, and after an hour or two pick himself up and set to again. But I'd no idea there was anything wrong with his heart.'

Karen looked at the pointing of the bricks on either side of her, testing the roughness of the mortar with a finger-end.

'Jon Douglas had him into this clinic in no time, before I knew anything about it. I was away that day in

81

Hampshire, moving from place to place, so they couldn't 'phone me. I found a message asking me to ring Jon. He was very comforting, said it wasn't serious, but didn't want to take any chances.'

'And nothing appeared in the papers?'

'Not a word. He'd had his tests, and was back at home before the press got wind of anything. It might have been flu for all the time he had off work.'

'And what did the experts say?'

'Angina. No damage to the heart itself.' She now rested a hand on the wall, leaning obliquely in this part-darkened place. Wind stirred the thin branches, the foliage above. 'Tablets. Watch it. Try to take it easy. Have a holiday.'

'Is that possible?'

'Yes. He's coming to the end of a fairly intensive stretch, so he's due for time off. The trouble is that he'll have a fortnight in some warm place, not too far distant, and be back and up to his eyes in it again. He's an employee of the Beeb now, and they've done him well since he transferred, but his contract only has a year to run, and then he's seriously considering going freelance.'

'Is that tricky?'

'No. He says no. New channels and so forth. But one can never be sure. A shift of fashion and you're dropped. Oh, he's plenty of contacts. We shan't starve. For the present. Anyhow, I could keep us jogging on.' She straightened, looking down serious-faced at David below. 'There is one worse thing.'

'What's that?'

'The man himself.' She breathed in noisily through her nostrils. 'Oh, let's get out of this dark place. I don't know why we're standing here, do you?'

'So people can't hear what we say.'

'You're a level-headed young devil.'

Karen ran up the rest of the steps and on to the bottom end of the garden path. The wild leaves and stems black against the sky from below now translated themselves in the sunshine to spreading orange berberis and cotoneaster salicifolia both rich with berries.

'Promise of a bad winter.' David said, fingering the bunches.

Karen would be thirty-five at most, he decided, slim, fair-haired, rather severely dressed, in blouse, skirt and jacket, as if for the office.

'About Vernon.' She looked about her; they could see no one. The world was out of earshot. 'He's disturbed. I put it in that silly way, because neither of us knows how we stand. It's altered him. Before, he was like all creative people, down one minute, up the next, manic depressive, but now it's as if he's frightened he's going to die. He's not old, by the standards of today. He's forty-eight, and yet it's as if mortality . . .' She broke off. 'He seems to be asking himself, and not just occasionally, but all the time, what is the use of planning and working and looking ahead if at any minute it's all going to be snatched away from him.'

'Is that likely? Medically, I mean.'

'I went to see Jon Douglas, and he says no. It isn't. If Vernon acts sensibly he could live to old age.'

'Yes, but what's "acting sensibly"?'

'That's it. He must take some physical exercise and not just lounge about. He'll probably do that, talk himself into good habits, but it's this other thing. Vernon works so hard and does so well because he finds it fascinates him, and he is praised and flattered. Yes, I know he's made some enemies, and there are plenty of people who are envious of him. But he's doing something that's well paid, I put that first these days, and highly regarded, and difficult, you heard what he said, that's an advantage, but, above all, fascinating, worth doing in itself. But . . .'

She stressed the one word foolishly hard, hamming it as she stuck the clenched right fist into the palm of her left hand.

David waited.

Karen paused to run a sentence or two over in her mind, making sure she had her meaning right.

'If he once convinces himself that he's marked down, then die he will. He won't be able to work and the stress of that will finish him. Now he knows he is not in imminent danger of death. Both Dugdale and Jon Douglas made this utterly clear, and, to give Vernon credit, I think he believes them. Now.' She was good at these reverberating monosyllables. 'What I fear is that he'll have one or two setbacks, and that will be the end.'

'Can't he take a rest?'

'For a week or two. But these old saws about being famous for being famous are true. You have to keep appearing on the TV. Once you're off, you're forgotten. And it's no use writing a book, however good that is, however long it lasts and books are pretty ephemeral these days, because the audience for it would be mere thousands as opposed to the millions you're accustomed to.'

'So what will happen?'

'What do you mean?'

'Will he chase himself to death?'

'That's my fear. I'm trying to make the most of this next week or two to steady him down. That's why we're here. When I see him on a seat in the garden chatting to your Alison, I think that that's just what he needs. But as Alison's an intelligent woman she'll say something interesting and it'll give him a lead and he'll be away again.'

'But surely he has research assistants?'

'Yes. But he's not just a front man. He comes up with his own ideas. What I'd really like would be for some programme of his to catch on so that it would have a regular weekly slot. Then topics would present themselves. He'd need to work, but that wouldn't kill him, and he'd be freed of these basic insecurities.'

'What if these programmes began to fall in the ratings? And it was suggested that they're taken off? Wouldn't that . . . flatten him?'

'I suppose so. I hadn't really thought of it, because I've so much confidence in him as a presenter, as a television personality. He *is* good at it, David. He's so contemporary, and thrusting. And he looks right; when he's dealt with a politician or a poet,' she laughed, slightly sourly, dismissing the pretensions of a literary figure, 'I can't help feeling he's asked the right, awkward questions.'

'The trouble I find,' David said, 'is that these people'll do anything but answer what's been asked.'

'Again, that's where he's so good. He points out, without rudeness, that they are evading the question, and leaves it to the viewers to draw their own conclusions.'

'That won't make him popular with the politicians.'

'No. Except, he says, most will do anything for publicity, even make fools of themselves. They think, probably rightly, that people forget what they've said, just remember they've been there, been on the screen. As to Vernon, I really believe he has this notion that TV can be a serious medium, not a set of constantly recurring meaningless faces.' Karen laid a hand on his arm. 'You think I overpraise him, claim too much for him, don't you? I love to blow his trumpet for him.'

'To his face?'

'Oh, yes. And when he's not there to hear me.'

'That's good. I approve. Why are you telling me all this, Karen?'

'You're just like him.' She flicked her skirt with finger-ends snappishly critical. 'Because I'm frightened, frightened, frightened.'

'That he'll fail?'

'That he'll feel so ill he can't think any more. That will be his darkness. He's so lively. He understands, and I mean emotionally, as well as mentally, the complexity of the world. He'll stand here and see these leaves and holes and shadows and stones, and it, it inspires him. He says it sings a doxology.'

'He isn't religious, is he?'

'Not in any orthodox sense. That's why I've brought him here. In the hope he'll rest, or renew himself seeing the places he knew as a child.' She touched her hair. 'I don't know whether it will work. He won't see eye to eye with his father, for a start.'

'Was he happy here as a boy? Does he ever talk about it?'

'Anecdotes. Amusing snippets. Eccentricities. He was born while his father was in the RAF. On flying duty. Of course Vernon doesn't remember anything about it. But think what it must have been like for his mother bringing up the baby on her own and dreading the news every night her husband was out on bombing missions.'

'You think this had some effect?'

'I've no evidence. But, yes.'

'Grandma Randall was a strong woman.'

They left it at that, walking off north-eastwards, almost parallel to, but hidden from the front of the house. Karen talked of her career; she was working for the BBC TV Drama Department. They were not, she admitted, doing quite so well financially now after the years of argument. Yes, they'd had to sack some people. Yes, this was her first holiday of more than four days this year. She wasn't complaining. 'I've really enjoyed making my ends meet. And my job gets daily more intricate and interesting. I work long hours. I don't need too much sleep. I usually manage to be home at night when Vernon staggers in and needs pampering.' They'd been married nine years. It seemed longer, she said.

David remembered the occasion. He had not been invited to the wedding, or if he had his mother had refused the offer on behalf of her sixteen-year-old son. He recalled the photographs in the Sunday newspapers next day, it was the beginning of the era of his father's fame, his father and a young blonde girl with flowers. He remembered his grandfather's comments. The old man and his wife had made a day-trip to London by train for the event, but had not stayed overnight. Granny had been seriously ill, and though slightly better at this period, had died inside twelve months; George still held his post of senior mathematics master at school. Louise, David's mother, had complained to her father-in-law, but he had shrugged broad shoulders and said, 'It's probably the best thing he could do. He needs somebody to look after him. I'm sorry for you, Louise, but you weren't right for him any more than he was right for you. And at least he's got married.'

David could not forget his mother's sullen, set face nor his grandfather's red-cheeked bluntness. They must have heard rumours of Vernon's promiscuity. Neither had liked the stories, but both had kept their mouths shut at least in the boy's presence. Now, at least, Grandpa George spoke his mind, roughly as always.

In this October garden David tried to refigure his own state of mind. At the time he rarely saw his father in the flesh, but frequently on television. Louise seemed fascinated to stare at the face of her ex-husband in the antiseptic light of the screen; she showed no revulsion but would comment sensibly, intelligently on his performance. And the pathetic sentences she dropped out: 'He should never wear that sort of shirt' or 'Your father was always very concerned about his hair.' His classmates at school were delighted to know the son of a somebody 'on the box'. On the rare occasions the two met, neither had difficulty. Vernon did his best, and David, studiously polite, according to his mother's training, did not court trouble.

'Do you like this house?' Karen demanded.

'Yes. I spent quite a lot of my summer holidays here when I was young. I enjoyed them.'

'Would you like to live here?'

'The house is awkward. It's been built in bits. And it's not altogether beautiful. Moreover, the garden and orchard are very large. I'd have to learn to look after them. But the place is roomy and near shops and, now Grandpa's had double glazing put in on the road side, not too noisy.'

'Vernon was about five when they bought it.'

Now they had come round a half-circle and approached the terrace and lawn. Alison and Vernon were still on the seat; Vernon waved his arms in the air, pleased as punch. Alison was laughing. They greeted the other couple with enthusiasm.

'Tell you what,' Vernon said. 'Let's walk down the hill to the marketplace.'

'Do we need to buy something, then?' Karen asked facetiously.

'No. For the walk. For the devilment. Saturday afternoon.'

'We'd better tell Polly,' Alison warned. 'Perhaps they'd like to come with us.'

'I doubt it. Not Dad.'

'Go and see, David,' Alison ordered.

The four walked down the hill, Alison and Vernon in front. They pushed through the aisles between the canvas-topped stalls. The fruiterers' displays had lost their morning neatness; the dresses, underclothes, T-shirts, jeans, tracksuits seemed rumpled, turned over by many fingers; the one book-stall had no order, the scruffy paperbacks staggering. One could buy pictures, ill-coloured prints in tawdry gold frames, rolls and squares of oilcloth, pieces of carpet, children's shoes, unsparkling jewellery. Shoppers crowded the narrow aisles still, but listlessly, as if they realised the best had gone to the morning buyers, or without fervour, eyes forlornly searching for bargains among the many times discounted merchandise. The ground was littered with paper, newssheets, hamburger wrappings, sweet-packets, aleatory rippings; cardboard boxes were piled higgledy-piggledy ready for unsold objects. The patter of vendors had become hoarse and sporadic so that an outburst of cheap-jack eloquence seemed out of place.

Vernon, in a brown trilby he had picked up on his way out, walked hands in mac pockets, unrecognised.

'Does Polly shop here?' Karen asked.

'Shouldn't think so.' David. 'She'll have her own places.'

They watched Vernon and Alison in front.

'This is just what he needs.' Karen spoke categorically. 'Laying the law down to an attractive woman. That is, if she'll allow it. Will she?'

'Yes. She's very modest for one who knows so much.' They could see Vernon waving a hand about, pointing at some architectural feature. 'I wonder what they're talking about?'

'He'll be describing what he did as a boy, which shop he patronised, which trees he climbed, who lived where, who did what, what George wanted.'

'And that does him good?'

'On the few occasions I've been back with him, he forgets his present life. Perhaps he thinks I find it strange. I do. That this set of roads and houses and schools and churches and pubs, all this dullness, produced my husband.'

'That remarkable man.'

'You can laugh.' She did so too. 'But it's about right.'

They, emerging from the stalls, drew closer now to Alison and Vernon on a wide pavement so that they suddenly heard the girl's voice, strong and pleasantly confident.

' ". . . fleet the time carelessly as they did in the golden world".'

'Who said that?' David called. Alison looked back in surprise.

'*As You Like It*. Charles the wrestler.'

'Wrestling, now,' Vernon took over. 'Wrestling.'

He in spate moved ahead with Alison; deliberately the other two hung back.

VIII

On Sunday morning Polly invited David and Alison round for supper.

'Eight o'clock,' she ordered. 'Vernon will be delighted.'

When the pair drew up in the lane they discovered their hostess swanning out of Vernon's limousine in front of them. It was already dark and the two old-fashioned street lamps, one tilted, barely fulfilled a useful function.

'We've been pubbing,' Vernon told Alison.

'Where's Gramps?' David asked.

'Oh, he wouldn't go. We went out to lunch, Vernon took us, and your Grandpa says once a day on the razzle is enough. He doesn't like cold beer, except in the summer.'

They bundled themselves up the steps, Polly last to double-lock the outside gate.

'Can you see your way?' she shouted from below.

'I know it like the back of my hand,' her stepson returned.

As David reached the top step and waited for Polly he heard a crash ahead, a shout of 'Jesus', a stifled exclamation from Karen. A yard or two on Vernon had picked himself up from the path, and was brushing at his knees.

'Flagstones,' he said.

'Let me go first,' Polly said, waving her torch.

Indoors, in the light, they found a smudge on Vernon's right cheekbone, both his hands earthy and a small cut and patch of soil in the knee of his elegant trousers. Vernon swore.

'You'll be able to have that invisibly mended,' Polly sympathised. 'In fact, I could do it myself if you'd let me.'

'Don't worry.' Vernon swilled his hands under the kitchen tap, towelled them.

'Your face,' Karen said.

'What's wrong with it?' He bent to a mirror, dampened his fingers again, wiped it hurriedly clean.

'Are you sure you're all right?' Polly asked, almost in a whisper.

'Thank you.' Vernon hauled up his trouser-leg. No mark. 'I'll change these.' He left the room huffily.

'What happened?' Polly asked.

'He just tripped.' Karen's face was hard with distress. 'But he hates making a fool of himself. He loathes it.' She breathed deeply through her mouth, impolitely. 'He's quite likely now to rush back home.'

'Tonight?'

'Possible. Or first thing in the morning. And we were doing so well.'

They rid themselves of outdoor clothes and trooped into the lounge where George in an armchair read the evening paper.

'All together, eh? I hope you've not been sitting in pubs on the Sabbath Day with these heathens?' To Alison, spluttering.

'Oh, no.'

'Then have a drink with me. Where's milord?'

'He's gone upstairs to change his trousers,' Polly answered.

'*Quelle politesse.*'

Grandfather Randall rather slowly enquired about their wants and supplied drinks; Alison first, next Karen, then Polly. He puffed and coughed so that the whole process was slow, ponderous, embarrassing. He was about to hand David a glass and a can of locally brewed ale when Vernon returned. George returned both to the table-top to look his son over.

'Fit for the Palace,' he said, laughing himself redder of face, but soundlessly.

'I fell.' Haughtily challenging them to say more. No one spoke. Grandpa turned, stumbled about but passed David his drink in safety.

'Vernon?'

'Whisky, please.'

'Large or small? With water? Without? Soda?'

'Small and neat. "Infinitely small and dry." ' He smirked at Alison. The crisis was over.

When all were supplied George Randall supported himself on the drinks cabinet. He sang to himself, not loudly, but aping a big bass voice.

' "For behold, darkness shall cover the earth, and gross darkness the people." '

Still singing, he picked up the glass water-jug and walked out of the room paying not a blind bit of attention to the rest.

'Handel, the universal genius,' Vernon told Alison. 'They used to take my father to a performance of *Messiah* once a year when he was a child, and he's never forgotten it.'

From outside they could hear the voice: ' "And the gentiles shall come to Thy light, and kings to the brightness of Thy rising." '

'Max Somebody-or-other sang that. My father used to show me when I was a boy.' Vernon stood and mimed a stiffness of pose, a proud wagging of the head and a wooden movement of the arms in front of the torso. The soundless mouth squarely bit off the notes. 'A handsome, starchy man he was.' Vernon wagged a didactic finger at them, himself again. 'It shows the lasting value of ephemeral performances. While ever my father is alive, and I, and remember I never heard the man, old Max How's-your-father will still be giving his performances. It makes you think. There's somebody in your lectures,' he concentrated almost entirely on Alison, 'taking it all in, and sixty-odd years later will be copying you. With relish.'

'But compare the size of your audience with mine,' she answered.

'Yes, but they pay no attention to me. I and my like are on all day and night. Dad went to *Messiah* once a year. You preach,' he lifted his eyebrows at the verb, 'about Skelton or Howard or Wiat once annually. They'll remember you. I'm like the wallpaper. There. Fading. Unnoticed.'

George returned to the ensuing silence. He held his full jug in front of him and now merely hummed the angular line of 'The people that walked in darkness', keeping head and carrying-hand still.

'What are you lot staring at?' he asked.

'Max Somebody, the bass.'

Vernon rose again and mimed the movements, the pouter-pigeon chest, the proud shake of the head, the thrust-back elbows. His father returned the jug to the table and joined him, so that smirking, but solemnly acting, they performed with slight differences of interpretation, together.

'What was his name?' Vernon asked, impetus running out.

'Bradley,' his father replied without hesitation.

'What happened to him?'

'Don't know. He'll be dead by now.' His face soured. 'Like the rest of us.' He drew himself straight. 'I'll go to our house. Fancy you remembering that.'

He held out his hand, which his son heartily shook.

'There's hope for me,' Vernon mocked. 'In spite of appearances to the contrary.'

'Did you ever hear him?'

'No. Only your imitation.'

'Fine voice and presence. Was he a fireman? In the fire brigade?'

The old man looked round them as if for an answer. Perhaps Edna would have known. He seemed to shrink.

'They've pulled the place down now,' George whispered, almost to himself. 'The chapel.'

'Would you go even if it still stood?' Vernon light-heartedly.

'You know bloody well I wouldn't.' George breathed heavily, sighing, wiping trouble from his forehead with finger-ends. 'Not even to hear *Messiah*. Gramophone records have spoiled us.'

'And CDs are even better,' Polly said.

Grandfather grunted. This was a sore point between man and wife.

Over a cold but lavish supper David enquired how long his father was staying.

'Depends how long Polly can put up with us. I'll tell you what I really would like, and that's to go up to the university for a day and hear Alison lecture. Is that possible?'

'Yes,' she answered at once. 'It will be unusual. The general public never come into lectures here. It's not like Oxford.'

She considered the matter shortly and named a day. Tuesday.

Outside the room on a corridor David met his grandfather. 'He's in love with your Alison already,' George grunted.

'Vernon?'

'Who else?'

'So are you,' Polly answered. 'And don't you deny it.'

At the end of the meal, just after ten o'clock, George suggested bed. 'Vernon's resting. Karen needs the sleep. I'm dog-tired.'

'What about Polly?' David asked.

'She'll be glad to get us out from under her feet.'

'You make me sound as ungracious as you.'

'And these young people have to go to work tomorrow. Give me a torch and the keys, Poll, and I'll let them out at the back.'

'I'll do it.' Vernon, on his feet immediately.

'You'll get lost.'

But Vernon walked them through the garden, down the precipitous steps and out into the lane. Alison said she'd ring him from the university the next day to make arrangements for his visit. Vernon shook hands with David, kissed Alison, waved them graciously away.

'Grandpa says that Vernon's in love with you,' David said, once they were on the main road.

'Are you jealous?'

'I'd be surprised if he wasn't.'

'He's impressive, isn't he? He doesn't throw his weight about, but you can't help seeing how easily he makes a point when he wants to. It's as if the whole of his personality is concentrated on what he's saying. Eyes, body-language and that beautiful voice.'

'You talk about mutual admiration societies,' David twitted her.

'He is a somebody,' she said, stabbing him with a finger. 'You're like everybody else, fascinated by television personalities.'

'You do like him?' she asked; timidly, he thought.

'I was brought up by my mother to believe that he was the cause of every evil in the world.'

'And you believed her?'

'I was at an impressionable age.' David bounced his hands on the steering wheel as he drove, exorcising unreason, putting away childish things by the infantile act. 'She thought she had set him away on his career, supported him, made it easy for him, and then once he began to be really successful he walked out.'

'Is that anywhere near the truth?'

'That's the short form. My mother thought she was more gifted than he was; she did better at Oxford than he did. But luck ran his way. She was tied up in the house with me, and had one miscarriage, if not two. She spilled her disappointments all over him, but he was determined to make his way. In the end he walked out on us.'

'With another woman?'

'I think there were others, but that wasn't the cause. He didn't want to slave hard all day and come home to constant complaints and bickering, if not worse. Vernon knows his way round, especially where it concerns himself. He made excellent financial provision for us.'

'And you used to go and see him.'

'He had access to me, yes. But he worked irregular hours and at that time was abroad quite often. And Louise, my mother, was as awkward as she could be. So I didn't visit him too often. But he sent presents, remembered my birthday and so forth.'

'You don't altogether blame him?'

'No. He was ambitious. And my mother embittered.'

95

'Shall I meet her before the wedding?' Alison asked.

'A bit unlikely. We'll go down if you like. She'll make us welcome.' He spoke without enthusiasm. 'She seems to have come to terms with her life.'

'She never married again?'

'No.' He looked as if he'd offer some further explanation, but clamped his lips and accelerated.

On Tuesday morning, the appointed day, Vernon arrived at the university on time, nine thirty. He found the place gloomy under the north-east wind. Alison led him indoors, introduced him to the head of department, Jack Ryder, and the two men accompanied her into the ten o'clock lecture. It was the first time she had known the professor to attend. The students looked slightly affronted at the advent of the older men. One or two whispered with manic vigour as if they recognised Vernon.

Alison had warned Vernon that he would be bored, that it would be telling him nothing new, that it was for first-year students who a few months back had been at school and had to be weaned carefully from the form-master's fad-bottle.

In fact, the lecture not only enlightened, but excelled.

Alison did not wear a gown, he was surprised to note, but an expensive dress in autumnal colours and patterns of lines. Her hair was taken up into a knot at the crown of her head, exposing forehead and neck. She looked both beautiful and vulnerable. But there was no mistaking her mastery of the subject: Sir Philip Sidney's *Apologie for Poetrie*. 'These children will have to read this book in detail, and will all write extended essays on it, and be asked to paraphrase passages or comment on them in the first-year examinations. And, remember, some of them have never read any Shakespeare or Chaucer, nothing earlier than Wordsworth. I know, I know.' She laughed at him. 'But there it is. I've got to make sure that they understand when and why the book was written; I'll sort out some of the arguments and comment on their strengths and weaknesses. But we mustn't forget that they won't have a clue why Sidney feels it so important to refer to these old Greeks. My God, they're ignorant.'

Vernon sat immersed.

Alison warned her students they'd be puzzled by the first page, but claimed that this was Sidney letting his readers lightly into the subject with this talk of the riding master. Her exposition was clear, and she knew when she was likely to bore or lose her listeners, and threw in an aside. She told them exactly how to read, pencil in hand, and even stipulated the length of the summary. 'Put a half-page section into one sentence,' she argued. 'It's possible.' She traced Sidney's arguments, but warned them not to come back to her with her own words. 'Look at this as an exercise in the use of the language. God knows we don't do enough of that in this place.' One student looked over her shoulder in protest to the professor.

The students stood back at the end of the lecture to let the two men walk to the door. One young dandy, his hair flopping into blue-black spikes, cheekily said to Vernon, 'You're not thinking of televising Dr Hunter, are you?'

'I've done worse,' Vernon answered gruffly.

Outside, as they walked three abreast in the corridor, Alison, in the middle, apologised for the elementary nature of her instruction.

'Just my level,' Vernon answered. 'As far as I remember the lectures I attended, the dons merely mumbled through their own preoccupations whether they had relevance to the students, the syllabus, schools or anything else. I knew nothing about Sidney. But you made me believe in, admire, this all-round gifted man. I was convinced for a few moments that literature and thinking about literature were important. There aren't too many who can do that for me these days. And I'll tell you this, I might even get hold of a copy and read it.'

As they moved along Alison noticed that people stared at Vernon, thought that they knew his face, placed him sometimes and then dismissed their conclusion as unlikely.

He did not appear to pay any regard to this attention.

When she left them for a few moments in the common room Professor Ryder looked apprehensive when Vernon enquired if Alison's lecture was typical.

'That's difficult to answer. The OUP are publishing her first book. She's a real scholar.'

'And the rest of the department aren't.'

'I am not saying that. They're good on the whole. I inherited some rubbish from my predecessor. But by and large they know a great deal, try hard enough and produce some first-rate work. We came out highly among English departments in this last curious assessment . . .'

'But Alison?' Vernon expected her back any moment.

'She's a real teacher as well. Her lectures are entertaining. She's not afraid to simplify. But I tell you, woe betide any smart-arse who tries to question her. She set about one such this spring in the correspondence columns of the *TLS*. Her letters were quite unlike her. She's rather quiet; she's so beautiful, I think, that she has no need to talk her way into favour. But those letters. They were cold and furious. I wouldn't have liked to have been on the receiving end.'

'Were they justified?'

Ryder wagged a minatory finger.

'You mean that we academics fly into tizzies and tirades over trivial matters. Yes, Alison was properly correcting some unsupported assertions.'

'Will she stay on here?'

'If I have anything to do with it she will. At present she's a temporary replacement for Rupert Melluish, but he won't come back here from America.'

'Was he any good?'

'Another real scholar. He supervised Alison's Ph.D. Has written five outstanding books. He's helped the department towards its reputation. The authorities should have given him a personal professorship before now, but they didn't, so his wife insisted he try America. And he's found a home there. He won't come back.'

'He's a loss?'

'As a scholar. But he was nowhere near Ally's class either as a teacher or a human being.'

'You could do with them both?'

'This isn't a perfect world.'

98

Alison returned, smiling, with another woman, whom she introduced as Susan Bailey.

'You don't half look serious,' she ribbed Vernon, using a kind of cockney accent he'd never heard from her before.

'We were discussing you.'

'Do continue, then.'

'No fear.'

Susan Bailey, a thin, unkempt, rather harassed-looking middle-aged woman, sombrely sipped her coffee.

'What's wrong, Sue?' Alison asked.

'Oh, nothing. I'm caught up in a problem I can't quite see my way round. I ought to be able to do it. I've racked my brains and tried every trick and wrinkle in the trade, but I can't see my way into it, never mind through it. That's why I've come out here. I did a nine o'clock lecture, and then got down to this bloody thing, but . . .'

'Is it something important?' Alison.

'Is it hell! But I ought to be able to sort it out.'

'Will you be able to? In the end?'

'I expect so. I've done all the hard bits. I don't like to be beaten. Especially when I know it's there for the taking if I weren't so bloody obtuse. But talk about something else.'

'Will that edge you into it?' Ryder, foxily.

'It will not.' Susan Bailey opened her dark eyes wide on to Vernon. 'I'm sorry, I didn't catch your name.' Vernon offered it. 'I've seen you reading the news, haven't I? You're not the man Alison's about to marry, are you?'

'No, that's my son.'

'I'm sorry. I don't live in this world.'

Susan's face was blotchy, with heavy pouches under the eyes and a forehead wrinkled and slightly scaly. She wore no rings on her brown hands.

'I didn't realise,' Susan continued, 'that Ally here was marrying into the aristocracy of the media.'

Vernon, very gently, explained his place and importance on the small screen. He spoke with decent humility, classing himself as a lively pygmy, even inside the ephemerality

99

of television reputations. Alison watched Professors Bailey and Ryder who, listening intently, were won over by Vernon's civilised and restrained judgement of his position. He described two recent programmes, one on divorce, one on AIDS, and how they, he and his producer and team, had set about them. Bailey and Ryder were quick with questions, interrupted often, were courteously answered, even corrected. Before he'd been talking five minutes he'd collected a small audience who, diffidently at first, began to take part. Vernon held his seminar consummately together. Alison, delighted, watched her colleagues, who usually went about their coffee break singly or in knots of two and three, minding their scraps of business, their privacy, what one had called in her hearing his privity, cohere to become eager students. It was, she thought, a little miracle. Vernon handled them with admirable care. He sorted their questions out for them, surmounted objections, made every interruption the source of enlightenment, and every speaker the object of his goodwill. True, the subject fascinated, but here was a master at work.

After twenty minutes, the group broke. Lectures had to be delivered; professors had some administrative meeting to attend. Compliments flew, un-British handshakes from those departing. Alison led Vernon up to her room.

'I've never known that before,' she said.

'Everybody's interested in the telly, even dons.'

'Their questions were much the same as those of anybody else?'

'Yes. Given the different level of sophistication. Some of them were quick on the uptake. Your friend, Miss, Mrs Bailey doesn't say much.'

'How old do you think she is?' Alison asked.

'Fifty?'

'Thirty-eight. And she's been a professor here for five years. She's a mathematician. They say she's very good.'

'Is she married?'

'Yes. Her husband's a don at Cambridge. They have a house there. They meet when they can.'

'But it doesn't seem important?'

'I've never asked her. She will mention him from time to time. But, important. I just don't know. She's a weird lady. Not simple. She's sharp as a needle when she wants to know something. And in her interests.'

'Feminist?'

'Mildly. Rather "green". They tend to tie up. At least here. She's very bright, very distinguished in her subject. I once saw her when she was working and her face had quite changed. She looked absolutely arrogant as she concentrated, as she scribbled away at her equations or whatever they were.'

'She's highly regarded?'

'An FRS.'

Vernon and Alison took a turn in the university park before lunch. Though the sun was bright, the raw air clawed the sinuses.

'Are you enjoying yourself in Beechnall?' Alison asked.

'Yes. So far. Karen suggested we came. I have to rest, or go steady. I didn't want to travel abroad. Not for a week. Nor did I want to stay at home. There'd be too many 'phone calls. So Karen dragged me up here. She'd consulted Polly, of course. "You ought to meet David's fiancée," she told me. So up we come. I didn't expect more than one night. I don't get on with my father.'

'Why's that?'

'Basically I think he resents what I've done. My salary he describes as obscene. And he thinks that there are people as well qualified, as gifted as I am, slogging away as teachers or lecturers at a fraction of what I earn.'

'That's not the way he talks about you.'

'Possibly not. He'll have notions of loyalty. Perhaps he'll speak more frankly once you're married to David.'

'Does he think he ought to have done just as well?'

'I doubt it. He won't see himself as a television person, front man or anything else.' Vernon rubbed his chin, looking down at the copse below. A squirrel darted. 'When he was in his twenties he was sent on these bombing missions over Germany. Most of his friends were killed. It must have affected him.'

101

'Does he ever talk about it?'

'Never. He answered my questions when I was young. But in a very ordinary way. As if he'd been, let's say, an engine driver, something a boy admired. He answered technical queries. And he spoke about his comrades, saying how good at their jobs some of them were. And he'd mention that this one or that one was killed. And was only twenty. But always without emphasis. Never angrily. It was the same with his own near misses. And once he said, in a grudging way, "It was the high point of my life." I once gave him *Catch-22* to read. I don't know how far he got with it, but he handed it back and said, "It's no use expecting me to read this," and that was that.'

'I see.'

'So I make every allowance I can for him, but it's not long before we're getting on one another's nerves.'

'This time it's better?'

'We've not been here long. Karen and Poll have gone into town shopping today. He'll be left on his own with something to complain about. That'll suit him. I asked him if he'd like to come up here with me, but he said that you'd be trying to work, and not wanting a couple of old men gawping at you. He's very fond of you, you know.'

'I'm glad.'

'He approves of David. He's a big, solid, clever boy who is careful. Not like him, short-tempered, or surly. Nor a fly-by-night like me. And he's sure David acted with marvellous sense when he fell in love with you. That's great. A real bonus.' Again Vernon stopped, again he held his chin and examined the sunshine among tree boles. 'Last night he said this to me, he was asking me about my heart attack, "Every time I'm ill now I wonder to myself if this is the beginning of the last time. It's never been so before." That quite scared me. I thought he'd live to be a thousand.'

They returned to lunch in the staff club where Jack Ryder joined them again. During the meal Vernon listened to gossip, said little, appearing pleased. Equally admirably, he encouraged talk, laughed with such *élan* that the other joined in. He exuded success. People passing their table smiled, pleased with celebrity. The vice chancellor, to whom he was introduced, invited them to his office at three fifteen for a cup of tea. On the way out of the dining room they met Professor Bailey coming in.

'Have you solved it yet?' Vernon asked.

Her eyes slowly focused on him; she had no idea what he wanted of her. 'Your problem. The one you told us about. That you couldn't see your way through.'

She shook her head.

'No. It's not very easy to concentrate here.'

When the mathematician had gone, Ryder said,

'She does her real work in the mornings at home. It's unusual to see her here. She had to give a lecture, I imagine. Or had a meeting.'

Since both Ryder and Alison had two o'clock tutorials, Vernon was accommodated in an armchair in a comfortable staff room with, at his request, a copy of Sidney's *Apologie*. He found that as dull as he expected, and was slightly annoyed, not only by the Elizabethan spelling but the printing of 'v's and 'u's. This seemed mere scholarly pretension, either to con the students into a sense of shared mystery or to make the text less accessible to any plebeian who tried to read it. He found no difficulty in understanding what Sidney said, but had little sympathy with the approach. The claims for poetry were both pompous and naive. Now he began to question himself how he would convince, for example, a Channel 4 audience that Heaney or Hughes or MacCaig or Hill had anything of lasting importance to say in their art. Would an up-to-date Plato exclude such poets from his ideal modern Britain? Or would our poet, our maker, be a creator of television scripts? Could a contemporary philosopher be found who'd even judge such matters worth his consideration? He laid the book aside to stare out of the window.

Park and trees lacked light, but in the far distance he could make out grey, flattish complexes, factories of four or five storeys he guessed, covering acres but to him grey smudges rising from muddy ground. He wondered what these places made: chemical, pharmaceutical, electrical, electronic goods? On their wealth this university depended. Poetry would not assist them, but, the possibility vaguely existed, one of Professor Susan Bailey's conclusions, solved conundrums, might just point the way to some process, some means to money.

He returned to his chair in the warmth, picked up his book, and almost immediately nodded off. He woke after ten minutes, sat still in the strange place. He was used to catnaps in aeroplanes, departure lounges, waiting rooms, out-of-the-way hotels; he boasted that it was one of his strengths that he could drop off for a few minutes in an inhospitable place and wake refreshed. As he rested, arms along his chair, he breathed easily, sensing a restoration in himself. It was more. He glanced about the room; seven easy chairs, three low, black-glass-topped tables, a dark-brown, unpatterned carpet, walls and ceiling uniform magnolia, the four windows brilliant white. No pictures adorned the walls: the surfaces of the tables, unbroken, without even an ashtray, shone as if polished the moment before. He could hear sounds from outside: footsteps or a snatch of faint conversation, and the hum of traffic from a greater distance. He moved only his hands on the mock leather of the chair arms, quite still, quietly comforted, different, a new man.

Inside himself, without force, ostentation, he felt renewed, freshened. It was as though he had been healed. He had been lifted, undeservedly blessed. Even in the joy of the experience the old journalist cast round, without spoiling the wholeness, the completeness of his attention, for a comparison. A picture of a garden presented itself in sunshine under a new fall of snow. He had been remade. He felt no exhilaration, no whirr of wings into the upper air, merely a sense that all in himself was well, and that in the simple act of recuperation his view of the world had been changed. He knew quite clearly that this could not be objectively, scientifically so, but the knowledge did nothing to shake the perfection of his content. He lived in a marvellous universe, complex or maybe icily empty, but this speck of dust had been filled with a glory, a silent, unmoving, momentary certainty of, no, not beauty, of its own rightness inside the system.

Vernon savoured the new man. He needed to do nothing, merely to sit as a part of the fitness of things. These were factory-made tables and chairs, not works of art, but they supported him, encouraged him to believe in a miracle. 'Time be stopped, and eternity be begun,' he told himself in a Wold Grunter voice, and as he spoke he realised, but not sadly, that the experience was now over, that the supreme calm, the brightness, sun on snow had ebbed away; he was vulnerable again, a man. Smiling, he stood up, slightly dizzy, wistful but not unhappy. He could not be robbed of these unruffled seconds. They came from inside him; he neither praised nor blamed supernatural intervention, attributing the experience to his own body.

A splash of sunshine suddenly illuminated the paint of one architrave of the windows. The weather had been dull, cool all day, but at once the beading congealed into marvellous detail in the purity of the light. His heart danced. He held his breath, for here again was the moment renewing itself, returned to him in the beauty of woodwork and paint cut clean by the sun. He waited, hands slightly forward of his trunk, asking.

Almost at once he realised that this was no repetition; sun through clear glass on worked wood and new paint delighted still, but not transcendentally. He looked, was glad, was slightly disappointed when the sun faded and he was left studying a grey neutrality where before pure white, perfection of light and shadow, of masterfully achieved shape had existed. Rapid steps took him to the window; he massaged the paint with fingertips. Outside the sky stretched dead, with one, insignificant, jagged tear of white and blue. The sun had not, not shaken him from there. He craned for a second, sought an important opening but failed to find it.

He walked back to his seat, breathed deeply, picked up his briefcase, went out to the lavatory where he cleaned his teeth. He invariably carried brush and dentifrice; a few strokes and the tang of peppermint, he claimed, sharpened his wits. He emptied his bladder, swilled hands, combed hair and approved of his appearance in a mirror. Out in the corridor he wished a pleasant good-afternoon to a girl in jeans who approached. She clutched her folder, smiled brilliantly and clattered away downstairs as he returned to his armchair.

This room lacked distinction.

Warm, neat, useful, ordinary but yet . . . inside the place he had glimpsed the numinous, had been himself extraordinary for a short time. He walked to the window; the cloud broke; small patches of blue sang strong. A dart of sunshine caught him as he stood. When it flicked out, he returned to his chair, consulted his watch, but did not pick up the *Apologie*.

Within five minutes Alison called in.

'Nobody's disturbed you?' she enquired. 'Not likely, this time in the afternoon. Have you been bored?'

'Not at all.'

'You look really pleased with yourself. You do.' He did not answer her. 'Let's go and pick Jack up. We've got ten minutes before the VC wants us.'

He did not talk, but nodded, smiled as she offered explanations.

'Pleased with himself' flatly but accurately described what had happened to him. Without self-deception, show-ing off, he had been allowed to evaluate his place in the world and find it good, utterly satisfying. This had noth-ing to do with his achievements, his status, his popularity; that and the curiosity or awe with which these academics regarded him were only minimally part of it. He had been exalted, without earthquake, fire, hurricane, into a state of blessedness. He pulled a wry face at the phrase in his head.

'Does the vice chancellor usually dispense tea in the afternoons?' he asked. One had to walk on earth.

'I've no idea. He must have meetings galore.'

'Have you been to his office before?'

'Once. On a small deputation. About money. As you'd expect. Funding a course.'

'Sympathetic?'

'He listened, yes. He made a note. Nothing's happened yet. But we'll be one of scores of similar petitioners.'

'Did he seem worried?'

'I can't say he did. No. He asked the right questions, made sure we had done our homework. He consulted Jack about it. Later.'

'Ryder knew you were going?'

'Yes. Advised us to ask for the interview. And to put our case on paper.'

'And?'

'There it stands.' Alison laughed. 'Our scheme wouldn't be Jack's number-one priority. So.' They had finished the conversation outside her room. She seemed perky. 'Loo across there.' She pointed. 'I'll be ready when you are.'

From the window at the end of the corridor afternoon sun flushed and reddened the world. Vernon whistled.

IX

That night in bed Vernon gruffly described the experience in the common room to Karen, his wife.

Both were laconic. He wanted her to understand the power of the event, but would not overstate. She, puzzled, for he had never mentioned an equivalent happening, took it as a sign that he was physically cured. He had, ever since she had known him, been prey to violent swings of mood, euphoria to depression, and she had many times noted the use he made of his temperament in his work. But now, behind his reticence, the deliberate curbing of language, he seemed to be making a larger claim.

Karen clung to him, stroking his thin shoulder-blades, pulling him close. Later they made love, but cautiously, not straining his heart. When they had finished, they lay naked, flank to flank.

'Did you tell Alison about what had happened?'

'No. You first.'

'Will you tell her?'

'It's possible. I wanted to let you know so that I could think about it. It was, I need some old-fashioned word, a boon. That's it.' Vernon giggled, embracing his wife again.

'It was, I take it, extraordinary?'

'Oh, yes. Unique as far as I was concerned.'

'But you described it flatly. To me. Is that because the words don't exist for it?'

'It's the power of it. You'd have to cite huge numbers, infinities for its strength. And yet it was calm, easy, quiet, dignified, no rush.'

'Did you think you saw things differently? Was your body changed?'

'No. Chairs looked like factory-made chairs as far as I can remember. I didn't escape either from the room or from my body. Everything became perfect. That can't be right, can it?' He held her nakedness against his. 'Things were as they were, me included. And yet they seemed part of a privilege granted to me.'

'Can you feel it now?'

'In the same way one feels a cramp in the calf when the violent pain's done. There's a shadow of discomfort. I have a reflection of this perfection. Don't worry. I shall grow out of it, I don't doubt.'

'So you will tell Alison? Or David?'

'If it comes up.'

'What about your father and Polly?'

'You can tell them.'

'You're sure you wouldn't mind?'

'You can please your dead aunt.'

She loved this rough, grandfatherly brevity.

That morning at coffee, when Vernon had gone out for a walk, she tried, not without embarrassment, to describe to George and Polly what had happened. Polly listened, but on the move, refilling cups, offering the biscuit box, while George sat, uncomfortably, as if his joints ached, pulling his mouth about. The cross-examination, when it duly arrived, came from Polly. Was this usual? Typical of Vernon? Had it left any mark on his behaviour? Was it religious? Was Vernon?

Karen answered as carefully as she could, admitting she was as puzzled as they were.

'You'll have to ask him,' Karen said.

'I wouldn't dare.' Polly laughed. 'And what does the master of the house think?'

'That you could put yourself out to get me another cup of coffee.'

'That's no answer.'

But she responded to his bidding. George rolled about in his chair, not speaking of his son, breathing heavily, troubled.

Before lunch Vernon, meeting his wife on an upstairs landing, grasped her by the shoulders.

'You've told them, then. About this university thing.'

109

'I did. You said you didn't mind.'

'Polly mentioned it. What did George say?'

'Nothing. He writhed about on his cushion. Perhaps he was thinking.'

'Polly seemed quite pleased. In an amused way.' Vernon let his wife loose, turned, clamped his hands on the stair rail and looked down. 'They don't believe it happened. That's not quite true.' He talked as if he was gently persuading someone below on the ground floor. 'They think I felt pleased, because I liked the look of Alison, or physically better, and that I've exaggerated beyond all measure.'

'Why should they think that?'

'That's the rational explanation. And I guess my father's view that my training as a journalist and my work on television encourage such heated conclusions as I reached.' Vernon raised his face. 'I am, Karen, a professional sceptic.'

'They see it as a religious thing?' Karen asked.

'No. Lack of judgement on my part. Media hype. Screaming for attention. An attempt to make myself more interesting than I am.'

'Have they said that?'

'Not yet. But it's on the way. That's how I might view it.'

'And how would you answer yourself?'

'I couldn't. It's the intensity of the emotion that makes this different from, let's say, pleasure. And yet there were no pyrotechnics, no blinding mysteries.' Vernon turned, grinning. 'Pure white light, without rainbows. A certainty that for a few seconds everything was balanced, that there was no dross, that I had been allowed to glimpse or grasp real happiness.'

' "All manner of thing shall be well"?'

'I don't know about "shall be". For the present. That's all.'

'The timeless moment?'

'Except I didn't think about it in that way. And it didn't leave me changed. Perhaps that invalidates it, but I'm still the man I was before it happened, except that I have been handed this, this, oh, present.' He coughed over his word.

110

'That could change you.' She advanced the statement carefully.

'What could?'

'A pressie you liked.'

Downstairs the matter received no mention over lunch. In the afternoon Polly took Karen into town shopping while Vernon drove over, by appointment, to Mansfield to visit an old college friend.

'Don't forget I'm not made of money,' George Randall warned the women at the back door.

'He's generous,' Polly said at the bus stop. 'He'll be pleased if I overspend.'

Karen enjoyed the shops, bought herself two dresses, delighted with provincial prices. She enjoyed Polly's company, confessing that she thought they'd stay for one night only. The break had improved Vernon in all ways.

'You know, he expected to quarrel with his father.'

'What about?'

'Any pretext. He thinks George disapproves of him. Every time he faces some new challenge, and is praised for it, he's pacifying his father.'

'You'd think anyone as successful as he is', Polly answered, 'wouldn't need that.' She laughed. 'He's only to compare his salary with George's pension.'

'God. He wouldn't do it. He thinks his programmes are nothing like as valuable as his father's maths lessons. And George worked on his own. Besides, there was give and take.'

'But Vernon teaches, literally, millions. Compared with George's thirty at a time at most.'

'Nobody learns anything from him, he thinks. They blink at the screen.'

'That's not true. Look at the money these television appeals raise. They persuade people to dip into their pockets.'

'I won't argue. But you won't convince him.' Karen touched Polly's arm. 'He says that George has aged this time. Is that right?'

'I don't notice it so much. He's seventy-two, and he's less nimble, and has some pain. He's still lively. We've been married seven years now, and it's been good.' They caught sight of their standing elegance in a shop window. 'I wasn't sure. We were creatures of habit. I was sore, and George bereaved. But we've changed enough to be happy.'

Karen looked about her, wondering how often such serious confessions were made in street exchanges. At the end of the expedition she pointed out David's office.

'It's a beautiful building,' Karen said.

'And large. There are at least ten or a dozen solicitors in the practice. If not more. And David, one of the new boys, has one of the best rooms on the ground floor.'

'How did he manage that?'

'By chance, he says. Somebody left. Nobody else wanted to pull his roots up. But that's typical of him.'

'You're pleased with him, aren't you?'

'I've always liked David. He's big and dependable. He has his grandfather's strengths and his father's energy, but all within reason.'

'And Alison?'

'She's a different kettle of fish. Quick and clever.'

'Vernon says she gave a superb lecture,' Karen said. 'I wonder if he might employ her in television.'

'Yes. She's unusual. She doesn't try to impress you. She's very modest, and a tremendous worker, David says. It frightens him.'

'He's not an idler, is he?'

'By no means. But she goes on and on without getting tired or losing concentration.'

'Will marriage suit her?'

'I expect so.'

'And children?'

'A family's never been discussed in my hearing.'

Though both women complained when they returned of damage to their feet, laughingly as they kicked off their shoes, they were enlivened by the afternoon. As they prepared the evening meal Karen talked of her family, originally refugees from the Nazis in the 1930s. Her father, a consultant in paediatrics, had been born in Germany, but only just.

'Were they Jewish?' Polly asked.

'Only partly. But my grandfather, a lawyer, just brought himself over and set up a furniture manufactory. He's still alive. Over ninety. He has made a great deal of money, and says he has forgotten his youthful ideals. He's just a bit like George.'

'Who is?' Randall coming in on them.

'My grandfather Lodtz. My father's father.'

'He's ninety,' Polly said.

'And still at work?' George rapped his stick on the kitchen floor and shuffled out.

When Vernon returned he seemed not only tired, but disconsolate.

They ate the evening meal in a subdued silence, neither of the men responding to conversational baits of the women. At the end Vernon mumbled that he'd go to bed.

'Are you all right?' Polly asked.

'Yes. Very tired. Alfred Bridge did nothing but complain.'

George Randall inveigled his son into staying downstairs for a glass of whisky. 'It shifts the cholesterol,' he claimed. The father then began to tell them, rather charmingly, what everyone should know about mathematics. He blamed his fellow pedagogues. 'The trouble with mathematics is that it's very easy to lose your pupils, and you have to be on the watch for that all the time. And that slightly inhibits instruction.'

He spoke without gruffness, or rancour, dealing with a world that could be set right with common sense and a moderate change of method. Vernon listened with only half attention, but smiled, seemed soothed. He went upstairs at nine o'clock, and claimed next morning to be restored.

Polly walked them in the afternoon round the local park, leaving George at home. Under enormous lime trees they strolled leisurely enough along the paths as Vernon pointed out where he had played football, been chased by the park keeper, done his early courting or chiking.

'What's that?' Karen demanded.

113

'Playing Peeping Tom on the lovers.' Vernon coughed. 'Preparation for a journalist's life.'

'Did George know what you were up to?' Polly.

'I expect so. Human nature doesn't change.'

They did not walk far or fast, careful not to tire Vernon who that evening was to dine at David's. In dampish sunshine they looked about, enjoying the ordinariness, saying nothing in particular, being good.

As Karen drove her husband to his son's house she asked about the afternoon.

'I thoroughly enjoyed it. I love that place. There's nothing outstanding about it, but I know it so well, and it hasn't changed much. And I've changed a great deal.'

'For the better?'

'No. When I was young, anything seemed possible. Not that I saw myself as Tolstoy or Dostoevsky, but I was in touch with them in a way that isn't possible with me now. I know my limitations as I didn't as a boy. I was nobody then, so I could be everybody and everything. "O hurry to the ragged wood".'

'Who's that?'

'Yeats.'

'It's doing you good up here. I was dreading it. I thought we'd be here for a few hours and then back home.'

'You're teaching me sense, Karen.'

In David's house, Alison and her fiancé were waiting. The four settled almost immediately to their simple evening meal, eating slowly, talking at a great rate, sparingly drinking white wine.

'Did you know', David asked his father, 'that you were on the telly yesterday?'

'No.'

'They repeated your interview with Thomas Turner.' Vernon pulled faces. 'Lateish last night. They had to postpone something.'

'Did you see it?' Karen asked Alison.

'Yes. This time and before.'

'Was it good?'

'I thought it was excellent the first time, and even better the second.' Alison laid down knife and fork, kept them waiting. Vernon scratched his upper lip, and she directly addressed him. 'You asked the questions I wanted asked.' She poked a finger at David. 'No, that's wrong. And arrogant on my part. Especially about music.'

Thomas Turner was the composer.

'You seemed to make me understand something of what he was doing when he settled down to think or write music. And you did it without poking ideas into his head. Too many interviewers flash their own notions, instead of allowing the artist to say his piece.'

'You have to sometimes. Some painters or musicians are not good with words.'

'But he is?' David.

'Yes. He's a cultured man. Has read a good deal. Is interested in language, in philosophy.' Vernon frowned, swayed in his chair like his father. 'And yet when he's composing he drops all that, concentrates on notes and rhythms, seems a different being.'

'But when he's setting a libretto? Or a poem?'

'There it is. But the cultured Harvard professor disappears. There's this shaman, snatching music out of the air, forcing it, if needs be, making it. And he seemed willing enough to talk about that. Once the process was over, he resumed the learning, the charm, the cultivation. I wasn't sure when I'd finished the interview, and it wasn't difficult for me, whether we'd got over what he was trying to say.'

'What d'you mean?' Karen asked. The bright-voiced interest caused David to look up. That's how a woman should treat her husband.

'I thought it might come over as too bland, too beautifully expressed. There was something strange about this man crouched at his desk composing. Something not quite civilised, primitive, weird. Oh, I know he's learned, with his music, so they say. A great contrapuntalist, a master of form. But, but, but. And I thought we might have lost the oddness of it all.'

'You didn't.' Karen again. 'Did he?'

'No,' Alison answered. 'At the end of the programme I felt that some part of his strange world had been opened up to me. I didn't exactly understand what was going on, any more than I liked the bits of his music you played. Though I've bought a CD of his string quartets now. But I was made to see him as a man out of my star, both in kind and quality.'

'He was very nervous.'

'Really? That didn't come across.'

'He thought I might question him about parts of his private life he didn't want brought up. He told me that he felt guilty.'

'Does that affect his music?'

'Must do, must do. But he was brought up to music, like Bach or Mozart. And they were both composing on their deathbeds. Turner would do the same. Whatever happened to him would be changed into music, but it's the nature of the change that's so marvellous. Most of us are guilty, or lovesick, or shocked or embarrassed from time to time, as well as uplifted, but we can't use these emotions as he can. He's found the means to transmute them. Most of us don't.'

'His music convinces you?' Alison asked.

'Oddly enough, no. I don't know enough about it. I'm old-fashioned. The three Bs. But I couldn't help feeling that something important was going on here. The fact that I was too ignorant to understand it doesn't mean much.'

'Did you see the programme, David?' Karen asked. 'Twice?'

'Oh, yes.'

'And what did you think?'

'Dad didn't get in the man's way. The cameraman or whatever you call him was good, too. He wasn't jerky, dodging about. He let one look at Turner's expression, or mouth or forehead, or at Vernon's profile so that I could study faces as I do in real life.'

'Is that important?' Karen asked. 'In your legal work?'

'I always do it. It's interesting. I'm not saying, of course, that I can tell when people are lying from their expression. But it adds something to the words they're offering.'

'Something misleading sometimes?' Vernon asked.

'I suppose so. But I'm in no hurry. Telly interviews always seem to be cut off just at the interesting moment. I can check and recheck what's said. And most of my clients try to make their own side right.'

'The best television interviewers,' Vernon now spoke slowly, 'show a sense of wonder. They may know a great deal about the person they're quizzing and his, or her, subject. And so they should. But this background information should never knock out of their minds the fact that they are talking to a somebody, to someone with unusual qualities, and this sense that here they are dealing with something out of the ordinary should be conveyed to the viewer. That's vital. And it doesn't matter whether one's talking to a philosopher or a comedian.'

'And how does one prepare?' Alison asked.

'This one doesn't. Or can't. I find out as much as I can, and I've had first-rate research teams . . .'

'Not that you don't terrorise them,' Karen interrupted. Vernon showed his teeth.

'. . . but I'm amazed from time to time. I'm easily impressed, perhaps. And I try to get over all this background information because otherwise the viewer will be puzzled, or feel cheated or not properly done by, and then my amazement, my sense of the character's difference from the rest of us will be wasted.'

'Do you sometimes interview people who do not rouse this wonder in you?' Alison, straight-faced.

'Of course. But even then . . . I'm interviewing some politician, who's not quite being straight with me, or hasn't properly thought it out for himself, or is, as is usual, just making sure that he, or his party, appears in a good light, and I suddenly think, How has this man, this human being, manoeuvred himself into this position? And then I see the boy winning scholarships, president of the union, seeing his opportunity in politics, keeping his eye cocked

117

for opportunities, being called for interview at No. 10 and all the rest of it, and the banalities don't seem quite so dull.'

'But what if they are dull?' David asked.

'I see what you mean. You're implying that I try to make something out of nothing just because human beings are always complex, always have a complicated history behind them. I don't think it matters. Dull blether will always come over as dull, for all I can do. True, I have to try to expose the fallacies in his arguments, or bluntly ask the questions he's doing his best to avoid, but at least I've caught my own interest.'

'Isn't catching him out in a lie or an evasion more important?' David again.

'I don't think so. It's too easy to trip even the most persuasive speakers up if you're well prepared, but if I treat my junior minister in the same way as I would have treated Einstein or T. S. Eliot, then . . .'

'That's not possible,' Alison said. 'You couldn't help being impressed by what Einstein or Eliot had done. They'd altered the world for you.'

'And so might this twit when he puts your income tax up.' David, judicially.

They enjoyed themselves round the table, in no hurry to move from one delicious course to the next. Alison finally went out for the pudding.

'Spotted dick,' Vernon almost shouted. 'With white sauce?'

'Of course. What else?' David answered.

'My favourite. I haven't had it since I was a boy. This is the stuff to clog your arteries. Atheroma, here I come.'

'Eat it slowly, and make it last,' Karen warned.

'My mother used to make this on Sunday.' Vernon.

'Did your father like it?' Alison asked.

'Loved it. "Ah, stodge," he'd say, and tuck in. And my mother would say, "George, whenever will you grow up?" '

After the meal they sat in the small, cleanly room, with its three framed photographs of trees, its narrow bookcases, its puritanical carpets and comfortable furniture.

'Will you live here after you're married?' Vernon enquired.

'We're looking for a house.' Alison.

'Alison has too many books for this place. And we'll both need studies.'

'So you're looking for some Victorian, gothic mansion, are you?'

'Not really. My mother and my stepfather have an enormous place, an old rectory, and the cost is prodigious. Madeleine, my mother, has started taking students in and young business-people. It's company, she says, and helps to defray expenses. But they were talking about a bungalow in the grounds when Fred retires.'

'When's that?'

'He's only fifty-four now.'

'He'll never retire. He's too interested in his work. He's an architect. Works abroad a great deal.' David spoke without emphasis.

'What's his name?'

'Frederick Payne.'

'I know of him. I believe I met him once. Has he reorganised his rectory?'

'Oh, yes. He's done it really well.'

'He's very modern, though, isn't he? That new college at Oxford? And that mega-church in California?'

'He goes his own way, but he's scholarly, appreciates the past. Won't fill his rectory with steel tubes and furious lifts and mad lighting.'

'Are they coming up to the wedding?'

'If they're back from America. They have some almighty conference. Fred's speaking to change the architectural world, and daren't throw up the chance. Or at least, that's Madeleine's story. She's not given to exaggeration.'

'And your father?' Karen asked. 'Is he coming?'

'Yes. He and Peg. They'll come. He's a schoolmaster, like David's father. And a poet. He's publishing his first novel this year at the age of fifty-two.'

'He's not Julian Hunter, is he?' Vernon asked.

'Yes, he is. He'd be pleased you knew his name. He thinks nobody's ever heard of him.'

'*A Morning on Tenterhooks*,' Vernon murmured. 'An interesting book.' He coughed. 'Has Louise said she's coming?' He named his first wife.

'Yes,' David said. 'She'll be here.'

'Is she happy?' Vernon asked, offhand. 'Would you think?'

'As ever she will be. She's busy, anyhow.'

Vernon looked lugubriously down at his shoes, so that Karen suddenly asked, as if from embarrassment,

'Will you do your own conveyancing for this new house?'

'Yes, he will.' Alison, quickly, in understanding. 'Or he and his clerk.'

'Do you specialise?' Karen, again, keeping talk undangerous.

'My boss, Albert Frankland, is an old-fashioned solicitor. Wants a finger in all the pies. That's the way one worked when he started. And he thinks it's best. These young men are all experts in, oh, commercial law or family law, and that is not conducive', they could hear David trying to imitate his principal's voice, 'to good legal practice, or humanity, which is as important.'

'Does that follow?' Karen.

'Not in my mind. But he would like me, or so he says, to be an all-round man. It's hardly possible these days, I think.'

'But you'll go along with his notion?'

'To an extent.' David stopped, looked round as if he feared he bored them. 'That's the reason he wangled me into the large room on the ground floor.'

'Why you, David?' Vernon, almost fatherly.

'The other people of my age are appointed to their specialities. Commercial law's more and more important, for example, so he advertises and gets an expert, Geoffrey Samson; he's just a bit older than I am, but he's been doing it successfully in Newark, and he wanted to join a larger firm. There'll be a partnership in it for him before

120

too long, because he's good.' David coughed. 'But Frankland doesn't like it, and thinks he'll have a last try at the old ways. And chooses me for the guinea pig.'

'But why, David, why?' Karen, squeakily.

'You mean why did he choose me rather than somebody else? I don't know. He watched me while I did my clerkship, and he knew the prof. at the university. I suppose he thought I was an old-fashioned sort, that I wouldn't turn up at work dressed in denim or without a tie, that I spoke standard English and didn't get my rag out too quickly. I look big and trustworthy.' David laughed.

'And are you?' Vernon.

'Big and trustworthy implies not very bright. But I can see as far through a brick wall as the next man. In some ways it's not worked out exactly as he envisaged it, and I expect I shall end up doing family law in a few years' time. But I do other things as well for the present.'

'There's not much sense in his plans, then?' Karen asked.

'I don't know. Perhaps he sees me at the head of the firm in twenty or thirty years and thinks that a specialist won't be quite as qualified, let's say, to appoint people to other specialities or decide which way the partnership's inclinations should be directed. Or it's maybe that he just likes me, and trusts me, and wants me about near the front door.'

'Do you do court work?' Karen seemed interested.

'Not much. We have quite a lot of it nowadays, and it's done by another youngish man, with the possibility of further appointments next year. But I go sometimes. We don't much care for court appearances, not because we don't like public speaking, I do, in fact; I'm a bit like Dad here, but because you can never be sure of time. You can be kept sitting about in corridors waiting for your case to come up. But it's all part of the learning process as far as I am concerned.'

'Is the firm successful?' Karen again.

'Very. Don't get the impression that Frankland's a fuddy-duddy. By no means. We're well established and up to date. We know our way about. If I were in serious trouble I'd run to Lambert and Partners. They'd sort it out, if that was possible.'

'Murder?' Vernon asked.

'Murder.'

David smiled and said no more, so that the others were left waiting in vain for an example.

They talked on until midnight, hardly drinking. They spoke of Louise again, and Albert Frankland's wife and her desertion, about George and Polly, some tale of George's flying from Gander to Iceland in horrendous conditions. Vernon spoke little of his own work, but sat back encouraging the others to entertain him.

When they finally rose, Karen, rather out of character, pronounced,

'This is a happy house.'

It came oddly old-fashioned from the painted lady.

Vernon himself said it had been long enough since he'd spent an evening so enjoyable.

'It made me feel your age again.'

Alison, guests gone, said she was tired.

'You've done most of the work.' David held her close. 'And so very well.'

'Your father's intriguing. He's very much quieter than I expected. But even when he's saying nothing he seems a somebody.'

'The television bestows charisma,' he intoned. 'On the undeserving sometimes.'

'You don't think he is out of the ordinary, then?'

'I'm absolutely certain he is. I might find it difficult to say exactly why.'

'Did you feel that as a child?'

'Most small children look on their fathers as extraordinary. But what I most clearly remember is the time when he began to be away. But he could always keep me entertained.'

'And your mother?'

'She resented his success. She had to stay at home with me while he met interesting people and visited exotic

122

places. She thought she was cleverer than he. She's never got over her better degree.'

'And was she?'

'By no means. At university she worked on what the dons thought suitable. You know what you're like. "What I don't know isn't knowledge." Vernon would study and spend his time on things that would never appear on examination papers and if he brought them in would be considered either irrelevant or unintelligible.'

'There we stand condemned.' Alison, mockingly, shaking her head.

'Not you so much.'

'But a bit?'

'Yes. You think your students are ignorant, but that's partly because you set the boundaries of study, and don't consider matters outside.'

'Example, please?'

'Well, if, let's say, you set an essay on Coleridge or Byron or Browning and the student included a long disquisition on or a comparison with Mozart or Schubert you'd be inclined to mark him down . . .'

'I should be delighted if . . .'

'And you'd do it on the grounds that he'd made some elementary mistakes or omitted some basic considerations about the poet, and until he had those fundamentals straight, you'd claim he'd no right to be off on to fancy-work from another discipline.'

'There's some truth in what you say. But you wouldn't be too pleased if a barrister you briefed made a brilliant speech but failed to grasp the point of law in question. And I guess that your student's Mozart would be as flawed as his Coleridge.'

They argued, pleased with each other, until they had cleared up, straightened the kitchen, put the best crockery back.

'Vernon's livened us up,' he said.

'And made you argumentative.'

X

David, appearing on Monday morning, was met by his principal.

'Could I have a word?' The finger uplifted matched the sweetness of voice. 'Sit down. I should value your advice.' David guessed for himself what Frankland would want to know: what reggae was, or heavy metal. 'I have discovered my wife's address.' He allowed that to sink in. Now would come the awkward questions about Alison's visit, David's silence, his sense of loyalty. The younger man felt no apprehension. He had not mentioned Eleanor to his senior. He felt no moral obligation there. Frankland nursed clasped hands between his knees.

'I won't go into detail how I found the address. Suffice it to say . . .' He broke off as if annoyed at himself. 'I have let her know through my daughter that I now know where she lives, and have since learnt that she does not wish to see me, at least for the present.' Why that face-saving phrase? 'I, therefore, mentioned that I would like to send an emissary to make sure that she was faring, well, er, comfortably.'

'Wouldn't your daughter tell you that?'

'No, David. I do not think she would. She may not approve of what her mother is doing, may even consider that Eleanor's living in comparative squalor, if so be it she is, is no more than she deserves, but Jennifer would not consider it her business to call me in unless matters were desperate. Now, David, I want you to visit her. I shall obtain permission first, of course. If Eleanor says no, that will be the end of the matter. But she has met you, and you made a very favourable impression. You will be my "nuncio of more grave aspect". Frankland smiled at his inapposite quotation. David neither placed it nor saw its sense. More grave than who? He'd need to ask Alison.

'You want me to persuade her to come back?'

'If you can, if you can.' Frankland sounded positively jovial. 'But I don't think, from what I hear, that that is likely. No, I want you to go and look about you, judge her surroundings, her state of mind, ask if she is financially secure. Your remit, that is the modern word, is vague. Will you do it?'

'Yes.'

'Then I will try to make arrangements. Many, many thanks.'

As he ushered his junior swiftly through the door, his secretary appeared, her face bright with the morning.

When David walked out of his office at one o'clock Frankland stopped him again. These accostings by chance seemed barely believable. He kept his voice low.

'If you don't mind, what I would really like from you is an account of how my wife is shaping up to the change. Is she comfortable? Or eating properly? If she raises other matters, then you have my permission to pursue them with her. I think you understand.'

He gently patted his assistant's sleeve before he slipped away, to the amusement of a colleague on his way out to lunch.

'The trouble with Frankland is that his confidential manner has become a habit. He can't tell you it's a fine day without making it a state secret,' Geoffrey Samson said in the street.

'Impressive, though?'

'And sharp. I don't deny it.'

That evening David telephoned his grandfather's house. Polly reported that George was sick-visiting and that Vernon had returned to London.

'Are you busy? No? Come round to see us for an hour. George won't be away long. He can't stand Joe Stanley, but feels he ought to call on him. They just sit and grumble at each other about their aches and pains.'

'Do they enjoy it?'

'It's likely. But come on round and let him grouse to you about Vernon.'

George Randall, already back and ensconced in his shabby armchair, waved his grandson into the one opposite to him.

'Visitors have gone, I hear.'

'Yes. Saturday morning.'

'Have you heard from them?'

'Yes. Karen rang and thanked us. I've formed a very favourable impression of that girl.'

'Good.'

'She said that the break had suited Vernon. Certainly he stayed longer than I expected. Usually if he manages to stop overnight we're doing well. But she said he seemed rested. Nobody had been bothering him for a week, and that's just what he needed.' George looked up. 'He seemed very taken with you and Alison. Especially Alison.'

'Did Karen say that?'

'No. I did. That day up at the university really settled him down. She gave a marvellous lecture seemingly.'

'Are you surprised?'

'The trouble with your beloved father, David, is that he thinks he's heard and seen all he's going to find up here. Oh, he likes it, he says. The people are salt of the earth, and he enjoys looking round his old haunts. He waves his arms and tells me that my garden and orchard here are the ideal places of retirement. Close to the world, but cut off, if you want it, from everything except wind and sun and rain. He loves the idea of coming back. But half way through the next day, he's fed up. People are limited, keep to the same blinkered notions or words.'

'As compared with?'

'Presumably London. I question him about it. He meets a wider range of people. In television studios, I should think, or his pubs and clubs and restaurants. They're different, more lively, less liable to prejudice, more stretched by their environment. We're a crowd of old buffers or glue-brains. Even the young people.'

126

'Is it true?' David asked, smirking.

'One thing I'll say just before I answer that. He went to hear Alison, not expecting much, but smiling because she's a good-looking girl, and then she delivers this knock-out lecture that catches his interest, tells him something he doesn't know and makes him believe it's worth knowing. Again, he's like these smart alecs in town. Here, in the provinces, he finds somebody doing something outstandingly well. He'll tell himself that Alison's from London, and Oxford, and the rest of it, and that it won't be long before she's as dull and mediocre as you and I are. Or has packed her bags to leave us. Now what the hell was I talking about?'

'Whether we were boring compared with the metropolitan crowd.'

'Oh yes. We always argue about it. It usually has the effect of sending him packing.'

'But not this time?'

'No. This heart trouble or whatever it was has set him back. He wasn't quite so cocky. If you're likely to get knocked off any minute you're not quite so sure that your opinions are as important as all that.' Grandpa George rubbed the arm of his chair with the flat of his hand.

'You got on with him well enough?'

'Oh, we soon annoy each other. But this time there were other distractions. Your Alison. His Karen not allowing him up very early. And so on.'

'Are we dull?' David asked, after a pause.

'You decide for yourself. What your father doesn't see is that when he's up here, he's on the margin of people's lives, or more accurately right in the middle of them.'

'Make your mind up.'

'And none of your cheek, young man. What I mean is he sees and briefly speaks to people on their way to and from work, or shopping, or doing weekend chores, or following humdrum pleasures. In London he calls to him, or has his people search out, those who have just been appointed to some political or military or scientific office, or who are concerned in some notable event or case, and of course they and he are full of it. But I wonder what they'll be like cleaning their shoes or drying the pots, I beg their pardon, dishes, if ever they get round to doing that.'

'Vernon surely understands that?'

'But does he?'

'Yes, because when he calls us dull he means we aren't capable of becoming secretaries of state or ambassadors or trades union leaders or scientific discoverers.'

'Or wouldn't want to?'

'Isn't that the same thing?' David argued pacifically. 'I, you, we, haven't that inside us that drives us on to great state positions. Therefore, *ergo*, says Vernon, we're dull.'

'I'd judge people,' George respected his grandson and put forward his argument carefully, 'on how they react to the great events of existence.'

'Which are?'

'Birth, copulation and death. Wasn't that some poet? Such as marriage, or love, or rejection. But mainly daily work. Even friendship. Or care.'

'Your politician looks after thousands with his legislation, while Joanna Soap just cares for her aged mother.'

'And you'd call the second dull?' George spoke forcibly, calling his class to account. 'In my view, it's mind-numbing. It's no wonder she doesn't come up with some magnificent speech or epigram. All the poor woman can do is cry if you question her. But she's not dull. She's a volcano of passion as well as a mountain of stoicism.'

'Vernon wouldn't deny that. That poor daughter just couldn't express herself easily in words. Vernon, put to it, could give you two or three minutes of her on screen that would tear your heart out for you. He'd use her tears. And her weariness. And her love, even hate, and her inarticulacy, even. But television programmes are like poems or novels. They're performances. Done by actors of sorts, who mustn't mumble and stumble. And with a chance of revision. That's why Vernon finds us dull. People earning their living concentrate on that and not on making speeches or public acts of entertainment out of it.'

'Now you're coming round to my side.'

'Or,' David said, pleased both with himself and his grandfather, 'offering an explanation of what my famous father means by "dull".'

'There's just one thing,' George said, cagily.

'And that is?'

'He makes it an excuse to dodge off back to London as soon as he can.'

'That's not surprising, now, is it?'

'No. Up here the few people he meets can't see the research- or camera-crew behind him; properly so because it isn't there. In his studio, or whatever you call it, the people he's picked regard him and his screen as a means of publicity, and so they pull the stops out, give a performance. Up here they're impressed with him; they're goggle-eyed at any dolt who appears on telly, but they mostly feel inhibited and don't put on a show, so he writes them off as dull.'

'Is that true?'

'Is what?' Grandfather snapped.

'I seem to read about men outside nightclubs having a crack at athletes, at boxers even, just to show how virile they are. We defended one such last week.'

'They're probably drunk. I'll say this for Vernon, he doesn't booze much. But while he's here he doesn't visit the bereaved, or the heartbroken, or the soul-shocked, or the suddenly successful.'

'But if he did,' David intervened, 'wouldn't he find them dull in their griefs as well as their high moments?'

'Certainly. In so far as they don't give a polished actor's performance. But that's not to say they feel any the less. There's no way of measuring emotions, but I can't for the life of me see why a poet should feel more strongly than a plumber.'

'I'm not so sure about that. The poet investigates emotions, describes them, searches for the words for them, tries to understand and use their variations. The plumber looks at stopcocks, and cisterns, and radiators.'

'But, David, if his wife dies?'

'He can't describe it or think about it or even sublimate it in the language of plumbing. It's quite possible, in fact, that though he's very good at his job, he can't describe his own daily operations very clearly. He's not there to explain, but to do. And a verbal expert like Dad finds that dull. Except when his bathroom's flooded.' David held up his hand. 'But I guess Vernon does think we're stereotyped. Our opinions don't change much; our ways, our occupations, conversations, lovemaking, job-seeking, they're all predictable.'

'But I guess that's so in London.'

'Yes, but the mix of stereotypes is greater. And thus the opportunities for change. In the sort of circle he lives in.'

Polly entered with tea for George and coffee for David.

'You two aren't half arguing,' she said. 'I can hear you all over the house.'

'We're enjoying ourselves, woman,' George said.

'It doesn't sound much like it.'

She put down her tray, began to arrange crockery, pour.

'When Vernon first left here to go to Oxford, he'd be eighteen, nineteen. He'd been abroad a bit on his own. But he'd had enough of home and school. It's not surprising. Some of the children who'd been in the infants with him were getting married by that time. Most people have had enough of their parents, want to kick over the traces. And he'll never come round to it again. Any more than he'd have liked to stay in Oxford for eighteen years. So he has to justify his own choice by maligning us.'

'You've stuck it?'

'I am dull. In any case I had the war. Of course what I tell Vernon is that the place doesn't matter, it's what goes on between your ears.'

'And is that true?'

George rubbed his chin at David's question. Polly paused with the cream jug poised, waiting for his answer.

'It ought to be.'

'But it isn't?' David, keenly.

'For most of us, no. No. I'm afraid not.'

'So Vernon's vindicated?'

130

Polly bent to kiss the top of her husband's head.

'You two,' she said. 'It's no wonder Vernon earns his living interviewing people.' She laughed as they picked up their cups together like puppets. 'Is your work dull, David?' she asked.

'A great deal of it is routine. But we do meet people in trouble, at the extremes. Not too often.'

'Do you talk about cases. Amongst yourselves?'

'Yes. Now and again. When we have time.'

Polly touched David's shoulder, indicating that he should look at her husband, who sat, whistling almost noiselessly and tunelessly, concentrating, well away.

'In a world of his own,' she said.

'It's these mathematicians.'

'I can hear the pair of you,' George growled, but late.

'A penny for 'em.' Polly.

'They aren't worth it.'

George suddenly laughed out loud, almost crudely, but collapsed into paroxysms of coughing, his cheeks bulging and scarlet. When he had recovered David described Susan Bailey, the university mathematician, about whom both Vernon and Alison had talked to him, and her strangeness.

'I suppose women are taking over there as well,' a recuperating George said.

'In oddity or mathematics?' the grandson asked.

'Mathematics, you dolt.'

'Isn't he polite?' Polly.

They all laughed at George's assumed classroom ferocity. David left soon afterwards, kissing hostess and host both, unusually, and thinking how happy that house was. He imagined Polly's bustling last chores, George's grumbling progress upstairs, the pair and their pain in a double bed.

Strangely elated, he drove home singing.

XI

Eleanor Frankland invited David inside.

She looked smart, spoke briskly, offering tea or coffee. When Frankland had finally handed over her address, David had learnt with surprise that Mrs Frankland no longer lived in the street where Alison had been taken, but had moved to a smart maisonette built in the garden of one of the Victorian mansions higher up the hill. Albert had twice, though briefly, advised him about his mission, as if he feared the young man would be seduced into reckless admissions or agreements. Amused, David tried to play on Frankland's fears.

'Suppose your wife suggests a meeting with you?'

'Yes?' Smooth, smooth.

'You would be willing, I take it?'

'I see no insuperable objection.'

But the older man had frowned as if he expected his junior to start teaching him his business. He had sighed, politely if impatiently.

Eleanor's room glinted bright, brand-new with November sunshine, while to the old forest trees at the far side of the lawn a few rags of leaves still clung. When she appeared with a tray Eleanor expressed satisfaction at his appearance.

'I suppose you have a good number of visitors?' he asked.

'Some of my friends, yes. Not many young men.' She showed no dismay at the admission. 'I do, by the by, owe your fiancée an apology. I ought to have given her my new address and invited her round. She came with me to the old flat one afternoon. I greatly enjoyed her company. Did she mention it?'

'Yes. She was pleased to talk to you.'

'Did you say anything to Albert about it?'

'No.'

'Why not?'

'I understood from Alison that for the time being you wanted your whereabouts kept hidden, and that he could always get in touch with you fairly quickly in an emergency through your daughter.'

'I wonder if he knew that you knew.'

'I don't suppose so.'

'You didn't have any inkling that I'd left him?'

'Oh, yes. He told me one morning. It was soon after we visited you.'

'I see. You surprise me. He actually told you? What did he say?'

'Alison and I wanted to invite you both round to my house. He felt bound to explain why he, you couldn't accept.'

'Did he seem embarrassed?'

'Not really. Whenever he's talking to me, or anyone else for that matter in the office, he has this diffident manner.'

'Is it assumed?'

'Yes. I guess so. He has a considerable knowledge of the law. And it makes his expertise acceptable if he delivers it without force.'

'But that's what', Eleanor objected, 'you go to a solicitor for: a clear opinion of what the law says about what you've done or propose to do.'

'You'd be surprised. We've some pretty high-powered clients who resent the law being laid down to them, especially if it gets in their way. And their dislike comes over to the messenger. And his style.'

'They'll be relatively few, won't they?' Eleanor spoke easily. 'And having an unwelcome message mumbled at them rather than shouted won't make much difference?'

David laughed at the acuity of his hostess.

'You'd be surprised. It's a little theory of mine that people who get on in the world do so because they are in some way personally vulnerable and make it up to themselves by chasing success.'

'Quite the psychologist, are we?' Her hardness surprised him.

'I try to explain people to myself. Not very successfully. What does for one person won't do for another.'

133

'And what does Alison say about it?'

'Oh, she believes in the enormous complexity of individuals.'

'You talk about these things?'

'Sometimes. We ask each other questions, about our work and so on.'

'I'm not sure,' Eleanor said, sitting very straight, 'that Albert was very interested in people. I sometimes think he quenched such sparks as he had. I mean, he'd say that Mrs So-and-so was embarked on some course because she hated her father or wanted to impress her children but that if she persisted she'd run foul of the law. He never seemed to grasp that satisfying yourself, getting your own back or your side right was more important to some people than acting legally.'

'But that's not his function, is it?'

'Oh, I knew you'd say that. But with divorces or wills it's often important, isn't it, to know this other side, the drives, the motivation?'

She poured out more coffee, saying that she was not only enjoying the conversation, but reading it as a sign that she was approaching normality again.

'Normality?' David mused. 'Is that going back to your husband?'

'You young people are always in too much of a hurry. I know this chat of ours is in the firm's time, but Albert can afford it.' She beamed. 'No. I'm relishing my taste of freedom. So far, at least. It's lovely to come in, and slip my shoes off, and know I've only myself to please.'

'It can also be lonely, can't it?'

'Nothing's perfect.' She laughed. 'Especially at my age.' She straightened her face. 'Now, what are your instructions?'

'Well, now.'

'You can speak quite frankly.'

'He wanted to make sure that you were comfortably settled, that you didn't need anything.'

'He'll know my financial position to within a few pence.'

'I see. But he wished to be certain that you liked the place, that it was what you would have chosen if . . .'

'Why', Eleanor's face seemed mischievous, 'would he want to know this?'

'Yes.' He pulled a comical face. 'Our amateur psychologist will have to make a guess. I imagine he still feels under some obligation to you.'

'In spite of my behaviour? He's a conventional man. He'd consider that I had not done right by him. He would think that if I had reached my fifties, which I did two years ago, without pulling up sticks, then I'd no right to start now.'

'You must have quarrelled?'

Eleanor thought that over.

'For two or three years things weren't right. I was dissatisfied,' she said.

'In a way that was not so before?'

'That's a good question. We talk about the change of life, and it makes a difference I suppose. In my case, it didn't affect me too much physically. But the children were out of the way, and Albert was more immersed in his work than ever. He's slaved for that place, even before he became principal. But he enjoys it. It's what he does best. But at home. We visited a bit, and entertained. We went to a concert together, a few formal dinners, the theatre now and again, that sort of thing. I had my friends. But it didn't seem enough. I felt on edge, too ready to complain or criticise.'

'Unreasonably?'

'You could say so. Let's give Albert his due. He consulted me to some extent. If I made suggestions, he fitted in with them provided I gave him plenty of notice. But he'd no interest in me. And I'm not speaking of sexual relations only; I mean my ideas and opinions. We must seem ancient to you but I'm fifty-two and he's only fifty-five. He seems older, doesn't he?'

David made no answer so that Eleanor continued.

'I guess there'll be a good many couples of our age who've reached that stage and are satisfied with it. It's convenient to live and eat together, to take a holiday, to say a word or two about decorating the house or rearranging the garden, to entertain children, grandchildren, friends, legal luminosities in our case, now and then. I see to it that his shirts and sheets are clean, and he makes sure there's enough in the bank.' She looked up sharply 'That's so, isn't it?'

'But it didn't suit you?'

'No. It seemed not to.'

The mildness of the answer surprised him. He gestured her on.

'I felt I ought to do more, to make more of my life.'

'Did you mention this to your husband?'

'I suppose I did. But not with any force. We didn't listen very carefully to each other. He'd advise me to take up painting or music appreciation classes, or give some time to charity work, Oxfam or Relate or the Samaritans or English for Asian Women. That was sensible, but not what I wanted.'

'Did you try any of them?'

'Not really. So I don't know, do I? And it's not toy-boys I'm after, either.'

'Did you try that?'

'You're thoroughly wicked, I can see.' She laughed, comfortable with him.

'May I ask you something?'

'Go on. I don't guarantee to answer.' Eleanor's eyes wrinkled warily now.

'Have any of these longings of yours, if I may use the word, been satisfied since you left your old home?'

'No, I don't think so. But I've had to come to terms with the uprooting, the living in two new places, the facing criticism, implied or stated, from the family, from some friends. That's occupied me sufficiently. Now we are reaching stage two, in which I hope the new environment,' she coughed at her word, 'will encourage me to novel, bold ventures.' Her eyes squinted, almost closed. 'You think my language gives me away, don't you?'

'I don't quite understand you.'

'I'm overstating the case because it's so weak. "Novel, bold ventures." You'll be expecting "fresh fields and pastures new", won't you? "Smite the sounding furrows"?'

'I see.'

'You look stern. Like a schoolmaster. I'm not taking this seriously enough, am I?'

Again David thought fit not to answer. This time she was in no hurry with her excuses.

'More coffee?'

'No, thank you.'

Eleanor helped herself.

'We shall have to see,' she answered.

'Is there anything,' he said, after a pause, 'that you'd like me to report to your husband?'

'Such as?'

'You don't want to see any more of his emissaries, say? Let's have the organ-grinder not the monkey? Oh, dear. He's to come here? You'll visit him in your old home?'

'You're very polite. Your little quips. Young solicitors are usually very pompous when they're talking to older people. Especially older women. If I were in your shoes I'd report that I was physically very comfortable, but that I hadn't yet sorted out any of the great problems of life. I probably shan't. And it's my own fault.'

'That's an admission.'

'You mean,' she said, pleased still, 'that I've left home and husband with all the subsequent fuss and bother, and all to no purpose.'

'Something like that.'

'But surely I'm learning something about myself?'

'And your husband?'

'He can do without me, you mean? And he might want to make it permanent?'

'You don't, I take it? Want to make it permanent?'

'To be brutally honest with you, I've never even considered it. I'm on leave from my old life. I guess Albert can cope. I ought to have considered that more seriously, perhaps. But I didn't, and I'll have to pay the, take the consequences. Do you get on well with Albert?'

'Yes. He's been very kind to me.'

'Do you think highly of him?'

'Yes.'

'He's not an old fogey?' She laughed outright. 'I see you're hesitating.'

'He knows his way around.'

'Diplomatic. If I were you I'd give him a close account of our conversation, missing out all the bits that weren't very complimentary to him. Has he changed, in any way, do you think, since I left?'

'I hadn't noticed. He looks and acts as he always did. Does he cook his own evening meal?'

'I doubt it. He'll have his main meal at midday at his club, and something out of a tin or between bread in the evening. He's a decent sort.'

They talked for a quarter of an hour more, mostly about David's father whom Eleanor admired. Vernon's success, his heart trouble, his recent stay in Beechnall were discussed.

'Are you like him at all?' Eleanor asked.

'Nothing like so bright.'

'Yet your mother left *him*?'

'She was on her own a great deal. Looking after me. While he pursued his career. It didn't suit her.'

'And has she made anything of herself since leaving him?'

'She earns a living by academic work. Some part-time lecturing at London University and WEA, a bit of editing, one day a week. She's produced two books, one on Edward III, and one on *Shakespeare and History*. I've read them. They were well reviewed, as far as such things ever are.'

'But she's never married again?'

'No.'

'And no cuddly professor in the shadows?'

'Not that I have noticed.'

'Did you live at home until you came here?'

'In the holidays from university. Yes. We make out quite well, though she's not satisfied with life.'

'She'll be here for your wedding?'

'I think so.'

'And your father's present wife?'

'Karen? I approve of her. We hit it off. The few times we've met. My father was quite famous when they first came across one another. She worked for the Beeb, floor manager or something of the kind. I'm not sure she still does it. She works at something, I believe. I ought to know, but I don't. She doesn't talk much about herself.'

'No children?'

'No. And they've been together nearly nine years. Vernon will take some looking after.'

Eleanor and David parted, each pleased with the other.

It was late afternoon before he managed to have a word with Frankland; he reported the conversation without frills or comment.

'She looked comfortable, you'd say?'

'Yes. And was most pleasant.'

'With plenty of room?'

'For one person. She could put up a visitor or two.'

'She showed you round the flat?'

'No. I saw the sitting room and the kitchen.'

Frankland asked his short, prosaic questions. David answered as briefly. At the end of ten minutes the principal laid his white hands on the polished top of his desk.

'Was she at all awkward? Did she resent your visit?'

'The very opposite. She made me much at home.'

'She was lonely?'

'I couldn't say. She seemed not unhappy. I think she felt quite proud she'd made the effort. Though there was no bravado.'

'She had no intention, you gathered, of coming back?'

'Not for the present. But I don't think her mind was closed. That's only my opinion. Nor did she say anything about your visiting her.'

'You raised it?'

'Indirectly.'

They talked on. Frankland seemed to want to extend the conversation, repeating the questions, almost begging for comment or elucidation. It was a performance out of character, so that David was relieved when the secretary brought in letters for signature. Frankland thanked him gravely. Mrs Wakefield, waiting further instructions, smiled at them both. She, in neat two-piece and blouse, fingernails palely polished, teeth perfect, had recently divorced her husband, not without pain.

The three played their polite parts. Marilyn Wakefield, for all of Frankland's corridor confidentiality, would know what they discussed.

Frankland unscrewed his gold-topped fountain pen.

XII

Alison visited Jane Southall to talk about the wedding. Her friend was waiting with her own piece of news.

'Have you heard anything about Henry Corbett?' she asked. Alison was barely through the door. 'You knew he was going to be married? Well, it's all off.'

'Why's that?'

'I've no idea. I had it from the friend of a friend, so to speak. The girl was involved in a car accident.'

'Were the two connected?' Jane seemed determined to make Alison prise information out of her.

'I don't think so.' A long pause. 'Did you know her?'

'What was her name?'

'Rosaline Douglas. Something like that.'

'No. What did she do for a living?'

'PA to some bigwig at the Fenwick Corporation. A hunting type, according to my information.'

'And why have they . . . ?'

'Decided against it. That I don't know. You'd have more idea than I have.'

'I've never even heard of her.'

'No, but you know the egregious Corbett,' Jane answered, grimacing.

'Henry has his faults. But he'd make a respectable husband for the right wife.'

'If such exists.'

'There'll be plenty. Henry's not untypical, I should guess, of husbands. Job and status are important. And as long as his wife acknowledges this, he'll be courteous and attentive. There'll be many worse.'

'That's not the way you talked at one time.'

'It was my fault as much as his.'

'Could you have made something of it? Something permanent, I mean?'

Alison considered this.

'I doubt it,' she answered. 'I doubt it very much. But I was the wrong woman.'

She enjoyed these wry conversations with Jane, whose own marriage had lasted only eighteen months, but which had provided her with this house.

'How many people are living here now?' Alison asked her.

'Six. And all decent. Four girls, two men. I'm making a bomb. I'll always say a good word for ex-husbands.' She laughed. 'Eleven years next Friday since we parted.' She pulled her face about. 'And how's David shaping up to his impending doom, if you'll forgive the cliché?'

Alison thought that Jane, at thirty-four, had never outgrown her student days. But Alison was grateful, impudently suggesting that her friend should take up with Henry Corbett.

Next morning she was surprised to receive a note at the university from Corbett himself.

Dear Alison,

I think I ought to let you know that my intended marriage to Caroline Douglas-Hart is off. I see now that it had little chance of success.

I hope that all your plans are coming to fruition and that all is well with you.

> With every good wish,
> Yours sincerely,
> Henry Corbett

Alison found herself strangely shaken. The printed letterhead, Henry's large, well-formed handwriting in black ink, the simple formality of his phraseology all seemed typical of the man, mildly pompous, half-hearted, vulnerable. She wondered if the note made an appeal to her. But to do what? To confess her own affairs were unsatisfactory? To return to Henry? What was the force of the verb 'ought'? Why ought he to write to *her*?

141

She decided at once not to reply, but felt herself slightly ungenerous. Three times she read the note that morning before she stowed it in her handbag. From this she removed it again, to hold it up to the light to look at the watermark. Satisfied on this count, Three Candlesticks, she did not understand herself.

Before making off for coffee after a lecture she reread the lines. Was Corbett asking her to take up again with him? She decided not. He'd cover his uncertainty, if that was the case, with a bluster which demanded her return straight out. Alison, now more sure of herself, composed the letter for him. 'Now that we have both tested the market, the waters, we ought at least to acknowledge that we could begin to take up again with each other where we left off two years ago.' She could hear his voice, but felt unsure that she had caught his manner. He might well have been plainer. 'I beg you to come back', or 'Before we make another bad mistake, will you marry me?' She wondered why she practised these ridiculous exercises.

In the common room she met the professor, Jack Ryder, who had also received a letter which mentioned her from Rupert Melluish in America. He had accepted a tenured professorship there from the next autumn term, and suggested that Alison replace him at Beechnall. The OUP had some time ago asked him for a report on her book which he described as the finest first piece of criticism he had read in the last five years and the best account of the topic he knew, and he advised Ryder not to hesitate but to appoint her at once if she were the slightest use in day-to-day departmental work. If, however, for reasons of his own Ryder did not want her, then he was to tell Melluish *sine mora*, without delay, and he would see to it that there was a job with good prospects waiting for her in his university. 'Alison Hunter is the most scholarly post-graduate student I have known,' and this book and the two articles on Wiat she had sent him and which he had published demonstrated that she was maturing as a scholar and critic at the highest level. 'You've probably the finest Renaissance scholar in England on your hands, and she's moreover young and energetic and sensible. For God's sake give her a job, and when you go back to Oxford, take her there with you. Though she'd be better off in America, by a long chalk.'

'When's the book appear?' Ryder asked.

'Autumn next year.'

'They're not hanging about too much?' He stood up. 'I'll get you a permanent job here, Alison, if it kills me. We'll have to advertise, of course.' He sat down. 'By God, Melluish sounds impressed. An odd man. He didn't ever see me as a real scholar. Rather a bright knockabout comedian of literature. He once told me that my books were readable and had some effect. "Good for students and general readers because they were brilliant and showed you'd read and remembered." And then he'd shake his head. "But there's more to literature than co-ruscating paragraphs or breathtaking comparisons." I was at my best in *The Sunday Times* or the *TLS* or the *London Review*, scintillating to my mind's content but nowhere near the philosophical heart of the matter. And I guess the dour old bugger's right.'

Alison disagreed, but in her instant delight could not bring herself to praise her senior, even justly. If she were to obtain an appointment here it would be on her merits, not the result of diplomacy.

When Ryder left, he called back so that all the room could hear him,

'If you've a spare copy of those Wiat articles Rupert mentioned, I'd like to read them. Always willing to improve my mind. Look 'em out, will you?'

He waved, like a victorious general to his shock troops.

Alison smiled patiently, because she'd already presented him with copies.

That night when David called in at her university flat she showed him Corbett's letter, asking what the man meant by it.

'He's a typical barrister. They're like surgeons; they hate losing. And it damaged his self-esteem when you walked out on him. Perhaps he could never quite believe it.'

'He's very uncertain of himself. Have you ever seen him in court?'

'Not recently. He's all right. In the particular case I saw he knew the law better than the judge, though that's not always saying much. And he put his points clearly, and cross-examined to some effect. But it was all a bit what you'd call mannered. He tends to orate, whereas now the fashion is towards an easy conversational manner. That puts the jury at ease, and makes the occasional change to something more incisive or even eloquent more telling. Or that's the theory, I'd guess.'

'Is it right?'

'I'm not sure. The judge and the barristers are all there dressed up, and various people take an oath, and everybody has to stand on the judge's entry and so on. So perhaps the jury wants, or expects, formality of language. And our courts are confrontational. To exaggerate, they're tennis matches not investigations.'

'And you think that's wrong?'

'Not really. I don't know. Any system will have its advantages and consequent drawbacks.'

'Don't you wish you had been a barrister?'

'I wouldn't have minded. But I like the law. The legal side; what the books say. And I enjoy the back-room work. Barristers do that, of course. They give "opinions". But they are usually about mere *law*. That sounds like a contradiction. There's a lot of drudgery in my office, I tell you, but sometimes I come to the conclusion that I'm applying common sense rather than legal options.'

'More often than a barrister?'

'I'd guess so. I'm at the beginning of a legal process. They're more usually at the end. Or that's the interesting part. I quite enjoy my bit of court work, Albert Frankland likes me to appear now and again, but there I seem to be dealing with the stupid and disadvantaged more often than not.'

'Henry wouldn't be any good as a solicitor?'

'I can't judge. He'd be careful. But I guess he'd miss performing in the higher courts. And he must have had enough encouraging money behind him to keep him solvent when he started.'

Alison now reported Melluish's praise and Ryder's promise.

'I tell you,' David said after some discussion, 'where your great strength is, Ally.'

'Go on.' She was amused at this immediate reaction.

'Though you're a very hard worker and you seem to have chosen a line that suits you, you know when to knock off.'

'Expand.'

'Too many academics seem so concentrated on their work that it takes precedence over everything else.'

'Not only academics,' Alison objected. 'And not too many of them.'

'Oh, sure. Not that I know too many either. But I'm talking about outstanding ones. I'm just influenced by the last case I dealt with.'

'John Calderon-Jones?' She named a colleague, a notable psychologist, whose recent and late divorce David had handled.

'None other. When it came to his work he lacked all proportion. Outside that he seemed decent enough, even well intentioned. But everything must take second place to his research and his papers and his conferences. I can see he had to fight for his place earlier on in his career, he told me a good many tales of jiggery-pokery in this university as well as others, and he'd grown into habits of hard grind and caution, but he'd never consider his wife's needs.'

'And should he have done?'

'Yes. I know that businessmen work hard, and that those who do well are not just nine-till-five clock-watchers, but they need a break, have to learn to lay off. And they should appreciate the part their wife has played. I should have thought a professor of psychology would have cottoned on to that.'

'Oh, that's not his sort of psychology. He's a mathematician, a statistician.'

'I've never come across such a selfish being at the core. Self-centred to the verge of paranoia. And I kept asking

145

myself, "Is it necessary?" I suppose he's a leading light in his field, is he? And his studies are important? I tell you he didn't convince me. He wrote me off as a typical idle young hooligan. Why must he work such long hours? Why must his papers be put above all other considerations? It's not as if he were a Darwin or an Einstein or even a Freud . . .'

'One never quite knows. Really bright high-fliers must act as if they were.'

'What he needed was one week in every four off, holidaying, pleasing his wife, visiting his grandchildren, sitting on the beach twiddling his toes, doing crosswords, keeping sand out of his ice cream, and then he'd begin to see things in perspective.' David paused for breath. 'He didn't want to leave his wife, you know.'

'Go on.'

'I mean apart from the hassle and the time wasted talking to unappreciative blockheads like me. I gathered he genuinely thought highly of her.'

'She wasn't just another pretty feather in his cap?' Alison argued.

'No. It went deeper than that. She put him where he is. Encouraged him. Pressed him. Kept the family worries out of his way. He said all this. He was grateful. But now they'd come to a full stop. And she'd decided she wanted to be something other than a housekeeper to a prospective heart case.'

'Like Eleanor Frankland?'

'Yes. Exactly. Except the four people concerned are utterly unlike. Both men, you're right, haven't paid enough attention to their wives.'

'Is your father like that?'

'Tremendous grafter, yes. In my mother's case I don't think she understood why he made such progress in the eyes of the world and she didn't. Even when I was a baby she did a bit of university teaching and quite a lot of research at her medieval history. She was starting her book on Edward III then, I think. But basically, she just could not really believe that what she did equalled his achievements. If you had questioned her she would have sworn that serious historical work was of much more value than ephemeral interviews with politicians or personalities on television programmes. That would have been her argument, but she just couldn't bring herself to believe it. There was Vernon with his photograph or his profile in the newspapers; there was his bulging pay-packet and the invitations and social successes and the jaunts abroad.'

'Is that what she wanted?'

'No, I don't believe it was. But she was uncertain. The best she could expect would be a few grudging paragraphs of a review from some professor who couldn't bring himself to encourage her rival theories. Or perhaps an invitation once every blue moon to lecture to some provincial university or obscure historical society.'

'Did Vernon understand this?'

'Oh, yes. And he praised her and supported her. Or so he says now. Within his limits. But he didn't stop making his way in the world. And that was the real snag.'

'And Karen? Is she the same?'

'I hardly know her. But she came later in his career, when he was already famous. She must have noticed what she was taking on. And she's bright enough not to misunderstand. For all I know she believes the delays and the broken engagements and the failures to remember her birthday or her mother's or whatever are the prices worth paying. She realises that he'll put his job before any convenience of hers, but is steady or self-regarding enough not to make a crisis of it. And he might have come to depend on that. They've been married eight years now. They seem to be doing well enough. I like her. They've been married longer than Poll and Grandpa.'

'What's that to do with it?'

'Polly's another who's got the length of the bowling weighed up. George can be awkward, but she's strong enough to put up with it. Of course he's old and needs looking after. But she's learnt how to do it. She doesn't patronise him.'

'Why should she?'

'It's a big temptation when you're helping somebody out.'

'You're clever sometimes, David Randall.'

'Don't count on it too often. No. I think of Grandpa in his aeroplanes on mission after mission. I think of his flying into a wall of ack-ack fire. He'd know all the dodges, I guess, if there were any, but one moment you were flying along perfectly evenly and the next, psst, all the control of your machine's disappeared, the plane's on fire, the man next to you is dead. And all inside a second. You knew it was dangerous, and then, the waiting's over, you're licked, done, dependent, if you have time, on the parachute. This is what happened to a large majority of those young men. The casualty rate was ghastly. George survived. He had some near squeaks, very near, but every time he managed to keep control. But it was luck and he knew it. A piece of shrapnel twelve inches to one side or the other and he'd have been killed. What must have been the effect on him? And he had to fly back again and again.'

'Does he talk about it? Now?' Alison asked.

'Yes. Or he did when I was younger; he'd sometimes say something. Nothing very startling, even when he described someone's death.'

'Was he afraid?'

'Often, or so he says. But he put it from his mind. Then and afterwards. He took to teaching mathematics year after year.'

'Did he enjoy that?'

'He had some bright pupils and he made his own little niche. Flight Lieutenant George Randall, DFC, became Mr G. T. Randall, M.Sc. But I wonder how often he thought of those flights when one minute you held a beautiful piece of machinery steady in your hands, thousands of feet up in the freezing air and the next found yourself stranded there, tippling over, staggering down to death.'

Alison watched him.

'Have you often thought about this, David?'

'Not really. He'd be my age, no more, when the war finished. No, I've never said anything about it to anyone before. You make it easy for me. But I look at him and tell myself he's been tested as I never shall be, I hope.'

'And does that make a difference?'

'Again, no. It perhaps explains his bursts of bad temper.'

'Does Polly realise all this? Does he talk to her about it?'

'He'll let a bit drop every now and again, I'm sure, as he did with me when I stayed with him and Gran in the summer holidays. But some incident in the mess, or some anecdote from his time as an instructor rated just as high as his bombing missions.'

Alison remembered all this when three days later she called in at The Orchards to consult Polly. The back garden gate was locked so that she had to walk the long loop of road to the other side of the house. George was just stumbling, tousle-haired, out into the yard with a wicker basket of washing as she appeared.

'She's given me my orders,' the old man said. ' "There's a wind. Hang those shirts out." '

'Yes?'

'You're looking for Poll, are you? She's in the kitchen. As usual.' He grinned. 'She's plans for turning the whole house upside down for your wedding. Talk about spring cleaning. I shall be lucky to end up in a tent in the garden.'

Polly, hearing voices, appeared at the door.

'Oh, Alison. I'm so glad to see you.'

'She's about the only one I'm ever glad to see,' George trumpeted.

'Thank you.'

George Randall had something of his grandson's solidity. Not so tall, and now slightly bent, he had a look of David's honesty about him. You could trust him, she thought, then dismissed the conclusion as naive. Vernon, the man between, was more slender, delicate, perhaps vulnerable. George stumped off towards the washing line.

'I was just thinking about you,' Polly declared, leading Alison indoors. 'I've had a letter from Karen.'

'Is there a connection?'

'Oh, yes.' They took to stools in the warm kitchen. 'Listen to this.' Polly donned glasses, opened a letter taken from her apron pocket. ' "We're looking forward to the wedding. Vernon's cleared five days. I tell him he's in love with Alison".'

Polly waited. They heard George bang the back door, but he did not join them.

'And what does he say?' Alison asked since Polly was not forthcoming with information. 'Does she tell us?'

'It must be nice to be admired like that,' Polly said, pushing her glasses up her nose as if to read further. 'Especially by someone like Vernon, a cut above the rest of us mortals. But. Just listen. "He laughs, but I guess he knows, in some sense, it's true, and it's had a curious effect on him. He won't do anything about it. He won't say anything to her or even write. But *you* can tell her. She seemed a level-headed, clever girl, but I expect she's like most of us, in need of praise. So just you tell her, Polly, what I say. Now, you'll be asking, if you're curious enough, or she will when you tell her, what this effect is that I mentioned." You know when I reached that spot, I didn't read on. I checked my eyes. And I tried to guess what the effect would be.'

'And your conclusion?'

'Oh, daft things. Like singing in the bath. Or wearing bow ties. Or quoting poems.'

'And were these right?' Alison asked.

'Nowhere near. Now you guess.'

'That will waste time. I hardly know him. I'd say he'd just work harder, draw the attention of more people to himself.'

'That's exactly right. She's not written to you as well, has she?'

'No. But I wouldn't call it curious. If ambitious people are thwarted in some way, they'll make up to themselves by winning plenty of what they can get.' Polly sat wide-eyed. 'But go on. Tell me what she actually wrote.'

Polly now adjusted her glasses, breathed deeply in.

'Here we are. "He's slaving away like a madman. He's in the studios early in the morning, and works all hours. Sometimes he's exhausted at night. I say to him, 'You're killing yourself, and it won't impress Alison. She hardly looks at television.' And he said, 'You're right about that, Kari, but I can come to terms with my own inadequacies. That's the beauty. I prove to myself that I'm a somebody.' " Then she goes on about how frightened she is, and how he should take it easy. He never will. She's tired of warning him.'

'Do you get on well with Vernon?'

'We don't meet very often. He's the same age as I am. George and I have been married seven years and I've never been so happy. Vernon came up for a few hours for our wedding with Karen.'

'What did she do for a living?'

'She was some sort of manager, managerial assistant in television. I don't understand what these people do. It doesn't mean anything to me. Studio manager? Floor manager? Are there such things?'

'Is that how she met him?'

'I expect so.'

George Randall barged in, clearing his throat.

'Who's character's being assassinated now, then?'

'Not yours,' Polly answered.

'Is the wedding all arranged?' he asked Alison.

'We haven't mentioned it yet. We've been discussing Vernon.'

'Vernon. Vernon. I might have guessed. You women love him.' He grinned at Alison. 'I'll go and get on with my life's work.'

'What's that?' Alison.

'Doing nothing in slow time.' He rubbed his not-very-well-shaven chin and swerved conversationally. 'I hate these dark days. Mark you, not much more than a month and it's the shortest day, as well as your wedding. I hate it most in the bad months, January and February, and especially when we have the odd mild, sunny day and I walk out and think spring's begun, and then by tea time it's dark. I hate night.' He glared indignantly as if they were responsible for his unease. 'Anyhow, I'll leave you women to sort the big day out, long or short.'

'He'll be making lists,' Polly said when her husband had clapped shut the door on them.

'Of what?'

'Plants for the garden. He has to have help in now. He hates that, too. But he has to have all his fish meal or bone meal or sprays there ready.'

'He's very efficient, is he?'

'I suppose so. In small things. I'm a muddler.' Polly grinned. 'Will you tell David what Karen has said?'

'I've never thought. I suppose I shall, if I come round to it.'

'Will he be jealous?'

'It's possible. He's usually prepared to make allowances. He spends all day advising people who are either in trouble or making unusual or first-time decisions. Like buying a house or making a will. And so he's learnt to stand back. And it carries over to his own concerns.'

'Is that good or bad?'

'Good, on the whole,' Alison replied. 'I was in a mess when we first met and he steadied me down. I'm grateful for that.'

'George feels things very strongly. He's overwhelmed sometimes. I shouldn't say this but I don't think he's really got over Edna's death. His first wife. We're happy enough, but he's . . . missing, somewhere. He'd like her to lean on.'

'He's lucky to find you.'

'He'd want both of us. Typical man.'

When at the weekend Alison gave David an account of Karen's letter, her fiancé frowned and chewed at the end of his thumbnail, out of character. The Sunday afternoon was bright, and their street full of cars.

'I had a letter from Karen yesterday,' he said.

'And?'

'She's worried. You'd better read it for yourself.' He stood up to fetch the envelope from the next room. As he held it out, she asked,

'What does she say, David?'

He looked stunned, as if she had flatly refused to accept and read the letter, but spoke without restraint.

'She's very worried about him. A friend of his, a radio man, had his contract terminated after . . .'

'Is that Keith Harwood? I read about it in the *Independent*.'

'They're old friends. Started at much the same time. And from what Karen says Vernon admired Keith. Did you ever hear him?'

'I think so. I must have done. He's Radio Four, isn't he? Though I've heard him on Three.'

'Apparently Vernon greatly admired him. Said that he was the best broadcaster in the business. And they just sacked him.'

'For any particular reason?'

'Apparently not. In their wisdom they suddenly decide that change is necessary, give you a handsome lunch, and that's it.'

'Had he known it was coming?' Alison asked.

'For some little time. Vernon was furious. Talks about grey men, useless administrators, people who can't tell quality from dross. And so the best, the most talented communicator they employ is pushed out, not because of something he's done wrong, not because he's useless, not because his powers are declining, Vernon in fact said he was innovative all the time and never satisfied with himself, but merely because they want something different. Something worse, he claims.'

David passed the letter across, as if he'd said enough. Alison read solemnly; Karen had written with a straightforward brevity to express her anxiety about Vernon. Clearly she did not consider that David could do anything about it; she was not asking for legal advice about ways to protect her husband. She wanted to say plainly to somebody else what troubled her. Alison admired the short strength of the letter, said so.

'There's nothing we can do?' she asked.

'Asking them up. Going down for a day.'

'They'll be up in three weeks for the wedding. I imagine Vernon sees himself condemned by what happened to Harwood? He fears he'll be next?'

'Exactly. They sign a short-term contract so that both sides can change their minds. It's worked in my father's favour so far, in that he's been able to move or demand a higher salary. But as soon as someone in power takes against him, he's out and no redress.'

'He won't be unpopular with the administrators, will he?'

'One or two of his programmes have caused trouble, brought the politicians down on the back of the BBC though also won them favourable publicity. Journalists have backed Vernon, but that's not to say they will always. I imagine competition is pretty cut-throat at his level.'

'If Vernon is sacked, what will he do?'

'For a start there'll be plenty of offers. Journalism, again; a hardback or two; travel. He's thought to be influential. But, and I speak without my book here, the numbers he reaches on television, even at his rarefied, intellectual end of the screen, are very much larger than those the printed word affects.'

'But he always says, doesn't he, that they pay no attention?'

'They know his face. They see him every time something important's happening in the world, talking with the great ones as an equal. It's a heady brew, Ally, once you've become addicted to it. You don't give it up without wounds.'

'Would you like to be famous?' she asked him, simply, testingly.

'I've often thought about it. Because of Vernon. I've wondered what it would be like not to be able to go out into the street without being recognised. People will treat you as if they know you. As in a sense they do. I'd hate it. I'd like to be known as a good lawyer, especially amongst other lawyers, but . . .'

The pair went out in the car, drove out to Hardwick Hall, walked hand in hand in the park, did without lunch, young people in love.

XIII

At lunchtime on Monday David was summoned to consult Frankland.

'I won't keep you a minute.' The principal looked about him, though he knew his secretary was out of earshot. 'I've seen Eleanor.'

His eyes seemed bright in the cleanly, pouchy face.

'I'm glad.'

'We met by arrangement at her house.' He tapped his lips. 'I stayed for perhaps an hour and we talked very amicably. She spoke highly of you. We shall meet again on Friday.'

'I see.' David would give nothing away.

'We came to no permanent agreement, but that was to be expected. She appears to relish her freedom. And that maisonette flat of hers seems most comfortable, if small. I think we both enjoyed the exchanges.' He frowned at his word.

'She said nothing of coming back home?' David asked, hurrying the proceedings.

'Oh, no. There was nothing . . . precipitate.'

'She did not mention divorce?'

'Not a word. No. We had a cup of tea and explained how we spent our time. It was all very pleasant. I felt quite cheered.'

'And your wife?'

'Yes. She was not unhappy. I can't claim that there has been any radical alteration to our situation, but these matters are better not rushed. But I thought I'd do well to keep you informed. Your visit perhaps had some bearing . . .' He allowed his voice to trail off, meaning once established. 'Is all, er, thriving, with you? Your wedding?'

'Thank you.'

'I thought perhaps on Friday I might raise the matter of the invitation with Eleanor. If, that is, it's not too late, if your final arrangements aren't unalterable.'

'Ineluctable? Easy. The reception's at my grandfather's. We'll be glad to see you both.'

'Thank you.'

David ducked rapidly out. Pleased that Frankland was pleased, he grimaced at the unexpressive voice.

Back in his office, he had decided against lunch, he opened his *Times* and read a short paragraph headed 'Death of well-known broadcaster'. Mr Keith Harwood had been found dead in his car in his Hampstead garage yesterday, Sunday. The police did not suspect foul play. Mr Harwood, who was extremely well known for his regular *Morning Forum* and *Speak Your Mind* as well as many highly praised feature programmes, had recently, it is believed, terminated his contract with the BBC. His wife, Miss Deborah Miller, the actress, was at present in America.

Vernon's friend.

David turned to the obituary page, to the announcement columns opposite, but in vain. He looked at the top at the Scriptural text, today a verse from the Psalms, advising him that the law of the Lord was perfect, converting the soul. He'd had to learn the Nineteenth Psalm in the first form, but the version here seemed different. He wasn't sure. Vernon sometimes recommended study and learning of passages from the Authorised Version in all schools as the beginning of the mastery of language, if not of wisdom. That and the acquisition by heart of lines of verse. His son wondered if he had incantations ready now for the death of his friend.

Alison rang. Had he seen the papers? Was he going to write to or call Karen?

'I will. Not that I know what to say.'

'They'll be glad to hear from you, David.'

Unwillingly he telephoned his father's house twice in the afternoon but found neither Karen nor Vernon at home. He left a noncommittal message on the answering machine. Later in the evening Karen returned the call.

'I saw in the paper this morning about Dad's friend, Keith Harwood.'

'Did you know him?' Why did she ask that?

'No. I never met him. I wondered how Dad was taking it?'

'He knows. He's very angry. Especially with those who terminated the contract.' Karen paused. 'He's working too hard. Foolishly.'

'When does his contract expire?'

'Eighteen months or so. He's nothing to worry about yet, on that score at least.'

'But is he worried?'

'Vernon hasn't got where he is without spilling some blood. And he's fit enough, or so it seems, to keep going. Or so he thinks. This heart trouble frightens me. The snag is that he won't take a holiday. I've insisted that he keeps visiting the doctor for tests, and he goes, but I'm not sure that that does any good.'

'You're coming up for the wedding?'

'Yes. He's cleared his diary for five days. We'll stay with his father and Polly. But he always says that, and after a day they've clashed, and he's packing our bags.'

'Not last time,' David answered.

'No. I don't know if I ought to mention this, but he fell in love with Alison, and that kept him there. Has Polly said anything?'

'She told Ally who told me.'

'Are you annoyed?'

'I think, as far as my thoughts go, and that's not far, that most fathers fall in love with their daughters-in-law, don't they?'

'Is that the case with George and me?'

'I shouldn't be surprised. If George doesn't consider himself too old for such foolery.'

'Was it so with your mother?'

'I never noticed anything when she and my father were together. After that, George was included in the outright condemnation of all the Randalls. She'd come up to dump me on them, but she couldn't bring herself to be pleasant. I don't think my grandmother, Edna, ever had much time for her. So even before Louise and Vernon divorced there was some strain. As soon as she left the atmosphere changed in The Orchards. Even I cottoned on to that as a child. Louise didn't like Vernon-worship.'

'George wouldn't be averse to criticising his son.'

'No. But it didn't throw him into my mother's arms, her good graces or anything else.'

'I'm not suggesting there's anything sexual in Vernon's feelings for Alison.'

'How can you know that?'

'I suppose I can't. You're a very cool customer, David Randall. Is it the law? Nothing shocks you.' She laughed, not confidently. 'George is very short of temper, and Vernon's all nerve-ends, and here's the third generation steady as a rock. Why is it?'

'I don't imagine it is so. Or if it is, it's because I've not been sufficiently knocked about. George at my age was expecting to be killed in an aeroplane every time he went on a bombing raid; Vernon opted for jobs with no security and even an element of personal danger from time to time. I sit on my backside dully sorting out people's humdrum problems.'

'And are about to marry a girl they both fall in love with?'

'I'm lucky.' They paused, a great distance from their real topic. 'No chance of dragging him up here for a day or two?'

'I don't think so. He's just crowded his schedule. It's as if he's demon-driven all the time. Must do this; must master that. And though he runs himself and his kind of work down he's a thorough perfectionist. You know Keith Harwood left your father a note?'

'No.'

'Your dad had told Keith that he'd now have the leisure to write a book or two, to put down some solid memorial, and Keith wrote that he was so depressed that he believed that print was as impermanent as television and radio programmes. And he said that when old, bookish types like Vernon and Keith began to think this, it really was time to pack it all in.'

'He was a nice man?' David asked.

'Nice? I'm not so sure about that. But. He was a homosexual. Yes, I know he was married. Don't understand that. Bisexual. He could be most unpleasant to those not doing their job properly. He was ruthless, and made a lot of enemies. He was not very attractive, physically. He owed the world a grudge. He could be envious; of Vernon, for instance. He felt unappreciated. But. He was the best in the business. There was no doubt of it. And yet these administrators stopped him from doing what he did better than anyone else.'

'Did they think, perhaps, that they could stimulate him by the sack?'

'They didn't think at all. Radio's small beer, on the whole. Ring the changes and you'll be regarded as an innovator, whatever the quality.'

'You sounded really angry then, Karen.'

'Shouldn't I be? I know these people. And I think of the effect on Vernon. He's devastated. Don't misjudge your father, David. I know that there are those who say he's a mere front man, handsome appearance, with smooth or sharp talk tailored to the occasion. He's intelligent, David, interested in his work, a judge of what's good and what isn't in a line where either stuffy tradition or shifting fashion rule the roost so that one's never sure.'

'And is he good? In the Harwood class?'

'Yes. I think so. Yes.'

Karen spoke softly, very diffidently, as if he had no right to ask that question.

'Come up for a day or two before the wedding.'

'Thanks, David, but it's not on.'

'Isn't this an emergency?' Then, kindlier, 'The sight of Alison might settle him.'

'He's very taken with her, David, and I'll tell you why. She's very beautiful, but so quiet, so relaxed, so much in control of herself. She doesn't need to do anything or say anything. Her existence is sufficient in itself. She's there. That's the way he talks.'

'God help us.'

'But.' Karen seemed fond of this emphasised monosyllable. 'He heard her lecture, and that really impressed him. This goddess was a superb instructor. She drew the audience into an unknown subject, made them understand it, and then showed its relevance to their concerns. It caught the students' imagination, but Vernon reckons that Ryder

159

found himself equally engrossed. Ryder, the professor, by the way, says she's by a thousand miles the best teacher in the department because of her judgement. She knows how to talk to this person as opposed to that, whose behind to kick and whose brow to stroke. And as well as that, she's apparently a real scholar.'

'She works very hard, certainly.'

'Ryder's going to move heaven and earth to find her a permanent job.'

'I hope so. So he should.'

'Vernon says he was surprised that Ryder wasn't in the least envious.'

'Why should he be?'

'Because she's better than he is.'

'He won't think so. He's very sure of himself. He knows his place in the world. The grey men won't strangle him. He's too slippery by half.'

Both laughed, then paused, unwilling to give up the conversation.

'What's it like to be about to marry such a paragon, David?' she asked.

'You ought to know.'

'Very diplomatic, young man. I see I'll get nothing out of you.' She laughed. 'Do you know what I thought when I first saw you, David?'

'Go on. Tell me all.'

'How big you were. You were taller than your grand-father and Vernon then.'

'I was sixteen.'

'And still growing. What are you now?'

'Six feet four.'

'And big with it.' Karen hummed pleasantly, though he could not recognise the tune. 'Is Louise, your mother, coming to the wedding?'

'She is.'

'I've never . . . I think Vernon's a bit, just slightly, appre-hensive. I've never met her, of course. Not even seen her.'

'There'll be no trouble from Louise. She's doing now what she always wanted to do; that is: some university teaching, some editing, plenty of research and a book now and again. She has enough to live on. I think Vernon still pays her a small allowance, but hedged against inflation. She's lonely, I expect. She complains. The professor is idle; her editor-in-chief is ignorant of medieval history. But she's tied her life up in a bundle the shape she wants, and though it's not perfect it's by no means unacceptable.'

'What does she say about the wedding?'

'Nothing.' David made faces at the telephone in the pause. 'By that I mean she's made all the right noises, said how glad she was, that Alison sounds perfect.'

'Has she seen Alison?'

'No. Every time we've offered to appear for inspection, the occasion,' he coughed, 'has been inconvenient. She does travel about a bit.'

'David,' Karen said, 'it only takes you a couple of hours to London.'

'I know. She knows. But she hasn't made much effort. And neither have I for that matter.'

'Do you not get on?'

'Yes. Quite well. She doesn't make a great fuss of me. And vice versa. She's come to terms with life, and doesn't want the equilibrium upset.'

'You'd think she'd be curious to see Alison.'

'That's not Louise's sort of curiosity.' David delivered his judgement without malice. 'I've sent her a photograph of us together. She was very complimentary. You don't think she sounds human, do you?' He hummed now. 'She's reached a stage where she's satisfied. She doesn't want dragging into other people's lives, however pleasant. I think that's why she does medieval history. There are no newspaper cuttings. And the bits of scandal that are extant have survived by chance. And aren't contradicted by ten thousand others. I guess there are plenty of imponderables still, but they're manageable. I'm speaking without my book, of course.'

'Did she never think of marrying again?' Karen asked.

'Not to my knowledge.'

'Anybody else would be a comedown after Vernon?'

'I don't think that's it at all. She used to tell me, time after time, when I was too young to know what she meant, that she had a better degree than Vernon. She felt her mind was superior to his. It had just happened that he'd taken up with some modish career that in our uncritical, thoughtless society earned better money than that of those who really pushed the bounds of knowledge wider.' He laughed. 'Herself, for instance. Or her brother, some sort of fancy physicist in America. Vernon might well have been a professional football star or a successful bookmaker. Both made plenty of money, but neither was to be admired.'

'Poor Vernon.'

'Not at all. I think he encouraged her to argue like this. For her own good.'

'And what do you think?'

'Difficult to judge between one and the other.'

'Come off it.'

'I'm on Vernon's side. He's cleverer than she is; he has greater gifts; he's a more rounded human being. There's much more to him in pretty well every way. She ploughs a narrow furrow. Though I don't doubt she does it well. In fact I'm sure she does.'

'Did they quarrel? When they were together?'

'Yes. They tried to hide it from me. But my ears were sharp. And my memory's good.'

David had enjoyed this sprawl of conversation with Vernon's wife, but moved thoughtfully away from the 'phone. To him now both father and mother were shadows, abstractions, stereotypes dictated by his convenience rather than flesh and blood. He wondered why this was so. It was true that in the past three years he'd spent little time with either, rang only rarely, and wrote even less frequently. He had abandoned them. That was perhaps unfair. Vernon was always run off his feet, not to be reached, while Louise emerged rarely from her foxhole. He, the only child, ought to have made a more concentrated effort, bombarded his parents with coloured postcards and interesting messages. Both would have wondered, he decided, what was wrong with him.

At least he had told them about Alison.

He wondered what Louise would make of Karen, or even of the present Vernon. When he'd mentioned this to Polly she said that champagne would improve their vision.

XIV

On the evening before the wedding, a Friday, David Randall sat with his grandfather and Polly in their sitting room together with a smiling Vernon and Karen. They expected Louise to appear at any time, and then, slightly later, Alison with her mother.

Arrangements for tomorrow, they all knew, were complete.

'I could have gone to the station to pick Louise up,' Vernon was complacently grumbling.

'So could I,' Polly answered. 'In fact I offered to, but she wouldn't have it. She'll come in a taxi and disturb no one's life.'

Vernon and George looked heavenward in concert but said nothing.

Karen had rung at lunchtime to see if it would be inconvenient if they arrived in the afternoon. Vernon had finished his day's work by eleven against expectation and they were ready to start. They'd eat a gigantic lunch on the way and would need very little else by way of food. They had, however, not appeared until six o'clock, to George's annoyance. 'They're always behindhand. He'd be late for his own funeral if he had any say in it.' Now they were settled and comfortable. David, who had taken the afternoon off work to do 'any fetching and carrying' had found himself unemployed and had spent the time half-cleaning his carpets and polishing furniture.

He and Alison were not leaving for the honeymoon immediately after the wedding feast, but planned to stay Saturday and Sunday night in his house before travelling to the home of a friend of Alison's in London on Christmas Eve and spending the rest of the holiday there. Alison had organised the toings and froings, complicating matters according to David.

'You ought to be a lawyer,' he mocked.

The bride was to have the last night of her single life in her flat on the campus, then drive over in the morning to Polly's, where she would change and cross the city again by ribboned taxi to the church which was close to the university. David and his best man would prepare themselves in the bridegroom's house and had been warned that they were to be early at the church. 'Traffic is thick on Saturday morning. Leave yourself plenty of time.' David had been surprised to find Alison so nervy. Her father and his present wife would dash up for the ceremony and back later in the day. Alison's mother and stepfather had decided to stay in a hotel, but at the last moment, Frederick Payne had been called abroad, leaving the mother, a non-driver, to spend the night with her daughter. This had been a nuisance, Alison admitted, because Madeleine was bound to give a performance. Freddie would have smothered this. Alison had hoped to enjoy her vigil and wedding day and until her mother had been escorted safely on to an evening train there was little chance of tranquillity. Alison had been, in David's view, ruthless in making sure that her mother did not stay overnight until Sunday. 'You don't know her,' she warned him. 'You just don't know her.' Again he heard the jar in her voice.

David, new suit, white shirt, sedate tie, dark socks, polished shoes ready in the wardrobe back at his house, felt slightly deflated as he looked over the company at his grandfather's. Vernon had been expansive, a lord of creation, facetiously asking after the state of preparation and of mind, demanding when the stag party would begin. Karen pressed hand and arm, kissing him, friendly and slightly overpowering. Her manner suggested that weddings were important, serious, never quite to be understood, a high human gamble, whereas her husband enjoyed it as a joke, a piece of oddity, a best-bib-and-tucker comic occasion. Tomorrow was the most important day in his life, David had decided, but then wondered how a sober lawyer could reach such a conclusion.

At this minute Vernon was describing an occasion when he had been detailed to interview a painter in his London studio. The man's house was Victorian and by no means large; his studio was in the tall narrow stable. Why such meagre premises boasted a stable at all seemed unanswerable. The first tenant had more likely been a milkman than a carriage-owner. But upstairs the visiting party had traipsed, carting heavy equipment, by exterior stone steps, to find the artist, an undersized man in workman's overalls, dabbing at an enormous canvas, his naked model sprawled on a draped couch. As he painted, Edgar Partridge chattered, not very sensibly but at enormous speed, the flying spill of words contrasting with the slow, infinitely alterable beauty he was creating on the canvas. Sometimes the model, no goddess, rather fleshy with dyed hair, interrupted, contradicting or correcting him. The little man would gulp in breath, try to counter her arguments, but all the time working with his brushes, head cocked like a sparrow.

'Was the interview successful?'

'We needed ten minutes. Damien Brookes, our producer, greatly admires Partridge, has bought some of his pictures, the value of which will be increased, cynics say, by exposure to television. One never knows. And the naked lady was a bonus.'

'Is he any good?' Polly asked, bringing sense to bear.

'I think so. And the galleries are taking him up. He's quite expensive now. Beyond my means.'

'Rubbish,' Karen said. Vernon bowed to her sarcastically.

'And to make it worse, he's painting huge canvases, quite useless for anything under the size of a castle. I suppose he has museums and the like in mind.'

'And who was the naked lady?' Polly asked.

'No idea. Her name was Pamela. She spoke her piece.'

'Will she appear?'

'That I don't know. Quite possible. But one has to be careful. I remember, but this is donkeys' years ago, the trouble my cameraman had with an item on a naturist colony.'

The door bell rang. The back door.

'That'll be Louise,' George said smugly. 'Clean the conversation up.'

They did not speak as Polly went from the room. After a time they heard her calling out, over-loudly, perhaps to make sure they were prepared, 'Leave your cases here. We'll just go in and say hello to everybody, and then I'll find you something to eat.'

Louise entered, calm in the high light. She wore a dove-grey, very elegant coat and her hair, done up into a bun, was slightly mussed. The three men stood, George last and stumbling. Karen, now on her feet, was introduced. Karen's dark-eyed, blonde-haired beauty, the healthy redness in her cheeks, her bright clothes sparked garish and lively against, David thought, his mother's choice grey, her cool slimness. Louise kissed the three men solemnly and sat down when invited.

'Make yourself at home,' George said.

'Is Alison not here?' Louise asked her son.

'She'll come later. With her mother.'

'I'm looking forward to meeting her. I read a long article by her on the Renaissance in Italy. It was very impressive. She's very learned.'

'She is.' Vernon, with gusto.

Louise looked at him slowly, head to foot, as if to dismiss his qualifications to stand in judgement.

'You're quite ready for tomorrow?' she asked her son.

He outlined the proposed course of events. She sat, taking it all in, knees together, pale, long fingers clasped. When this was done, all questions answered, she turned to George, enquiring after his health. He tendered details, and she replied with the name of some new emulsion that eased rheumatic pains.

'Don't tell me you're a sufferer?' George blustered.

'Fortunately not.' She supported her view of the product with the opinion of some consultant friend. She had acquired a convincing jargon.

Polly returned to announce that Louise's meal was ready.

'If you'll excuse me,' Louise said, to Karen alone.

George coughed, after the shutting of the door.

'Exit Madame Ice-Arse,' he grunted.

'And very superior,' his son added, 'indeed.'

They laughed, then looked over at the uncomfortable David.

'Is she nervous?' Vernon asked.

'I expect so. She'll feel out of it.' The son sounded tired, discouraged.

'Don't see why she should. We make you welcome, don't we, Karen?' George huffed.

'Of course you do.'

'The trouble with her,' George continued, 'is that she regards this place as the back of beyond. A provincial dump. Nobody here does or says or discovers anything interesting.'

'And what's the real truth?' Vernon, with mischief.

'You're as bad as she is. With what you or your pretentious pals think is culture.'

'Come on now, Dad. Answer the question. What happens here that's so interesting?'

'People are born, grow up, marry, bear children, die.'

'In that case everywhere is just as interesting as everywhere else. Isn't it what people make of, write or say or compose or paint about these events that matters? Culturally speaking, at least.'

'I found, though you'll deny it, the opinions of some of my colleagues just as interesting and as well informed or expressed as those spouted on the telly and the radio, or written up in the serious newspapers and magazines. And this in one provincial grammar school. There must be dozens like it.'

'Why didn't they find their way to the media, then, and to wider influence?'

'They saw what they were doing as sufficiently satisfying. Don't you go equating ability with ambition. They may cleave together; they may not. I'll be willing to admit that as governments allow teachers to sink financially, and society, market forces, call it by what name you will, erode their status, more will tend to leave the profession and become barristers or politicians or media pundits.'

'I can't say that I noticed these paragons while I was here.'

'They were too busy instructing you.'

'Then they ought to have done it more interestingly. The majority of lessons were dull and mediocre.'

'They believed,' George said, 'that their pupils should be taught the basic principles of their subject whatever their gifts. Your television expert talks as if his audience could be in command of the subject, some large part of the subject, inside a few minutes. But you know, at least, they can't, and you won't or can't, therefore, attempt to set any real foundations.'

'These programmes are mainly introductory, to catch interest, to see that some light is thrown on the very many dark corners we all have in our knowledge. Then it's hoped some few will pursue the subject further. The majority will not be entirely ignorant. If you want the sort of teaching you outline then you should look at Open University programmes. But you must remember there's a great deal of old-fashioned paperwork expected behind them. We can't hope our viewers will show that sort of dedication or assiduity.'

'Assiduity. What a bloody word.'

Vernon laughed out loud at his father, who after a few seconds joined him, and sat grinning, hands on knees, ready for further exchanges.

'I'll leave you two to your cudgels,' David said. 'I'll go and talk to Louise.'

'Does it annoy you to hear us banging on like this?' George asked, surprisingly.

'Not at all. It does you both good.'

'You think that this sort of argument doesn't take place at television headquarters?' Vernon, head cocked, put his question disarmingly.

'I guess,' David answered slowly, like some puzzled sage answering a simple question from a *chela*, 'that like lawyers, you're too immersed in what you're doing to question the system inside which you work. You perform as brilliantly as possible within your short half-hour or so. Schoolteachers know they have a much longer time at their disposal, so that they can go back and correct errors and repair omissions and that at the end of the term or year or course the pupils will be examined by someone outside and, one hopes, objectively. We have a verdict, but it's often too rushed, and the juries can wrongly be influenced. You,' he turned to his father, 'have ratings.' David raised his hand. 'I can see all sorts of holes in my argument.'

'Shall I point them out?' Vernon's politeness was exaggerated.

'No. You battle on with Grandpa. It's meat and drink to him. I'll go and talk to Louise and Polly. Are you coming, Karen?'

She stood immediately.

'And we are left without beauty,' George said, in mock solemnity.

'Thank you, kind sir,' Karen said, genuflecting.

Outside in the corridor, with the door shut, Karen asked if the two would be all right.

'Yes. They enjoy themselves. George wants to make out a case that grammar-school teachers were important, and that Vernon has no right to put on airs at their expense.'

'But he doesn't, David.'

'I know, I know. And George is as proud as he could be of Vernon. You let any outsiders come in and suggest that Vernon's a flash ignoramus or a blabbermouth or that any Tom, Dick or Harry could do the job as well, my word, they'd soon have the rough edge of Gramps's tongue.'

Karen took her stepson's arm and squeezed it.

In the kitchen Louise sat at the end of the table, a substantial plate of beef casserole, with piled potatoes and broad beans, in front of her.

Polly, on her feet, seemed to be engaged on the tag-end of some culinary operation. She immediately offered them coffee. Karen volunteered to make it.

'You sit down. No, not at the table, David. Your mother doesn't want you parked there watching her eat. She wants you and Karen to tell her about the world.'

'When's Alison coming?' Louise asked.

'Any time. But she has her mother. And Madeleine takes a bit of sorting out. Ally will just nip in to check up that we're ready for tomorrow.'

'And are you?' Karen, socially.

'As far as I can see. We lawyers are always prepared for snags. Cases drag on. We kick our heels in corridors.'

'The story of my life,' Polly said.

Louise ate heartily, congratulating her hostess, but refusing pudding. All four had talked, and Karen and Louise, to David's amazement, had exchanged reminiscences of their wedding days to Vernon. Polly was deep into her own first ceremony, conducted by a bishop, no less, when the door bell rang and she had to break off.

Polly ushered Alison and her mother, Madeleine, into the kitchen. Mrs Payne seemed overcome by David's size, said little at first. On this, their second meeting, he tried to find resemblances between Alison and her mother, but failed. Their build, colouring, manners all differed.

'My husband sends his apologies. He has a conference in Paris from which he can't escape,' Madeleine Payne said. 'I'm not so sure he's not relieved, really. Domesticity isn't his line.' All men seemed condemned. Conversation was momentarily hindered, but Polly filled coffee cups and directed the party towards the sitting room.

'There'll be blood,' she said.

In fact, George and Vernon sat easily, almost as if one or both had just woken from a nap. Neither was speaking, and wineglasses glowed full and untouched. The men stood for introductions. For the moment the room appeared full, packed with a crowd, modestly marking their territory, speaking quietly but all at once, all unsure, suddenly becoming strangers, differing from everyday selves. George bent over, hung his head. Vernon held himself straight, smiling, inclining regally, not saying much beyond the barest greetings. David towered above the others; he felt like a ringmaster in slightly unexpected circumstances, quite hopeful that all would right itself inside seconds. He could see Louise's aristocratic head, and Alison's eager face. Karen and Madeleine smiled with lipsticked mouths, spectres at the feast. Only Polly moved, spoke reasonably, seemed at home, waving the decanter.

The coffeepot was emptied, the wineglasses replenished. People talked, asked questions, but did not immediately break into groups. It looked, to Alison, like a stage performance with everyone co-operating, parts learnt. Her mother sat queenly next to George Randall, a judge in court. Her hair, her own, was not unlike a wig.

Polly called on David to outline programmes for the morning. He did so, clearly, quietly humorous and without mistakes. Madeleine asked foolishly about other people's arrangements, but David handled her with care which left her smiling, sure of her own important place.

Louise asserted herself after perhaps half an hour by questioning Alison about the language of scholarship in Elizabethan England. The mother-in-law advanced the view that Latin had been for centuries the medium of cultural exchange throughout Europe, had been so as late as Milton and Newton, and that, therefore, was it not a possibility that the most important arguments about religion, philosophy, literature, history, science, life were put forward not in the vernacular but in the tongue that would be understood throughout Europe?

Alison listened, without fuss, reshaped questions for Louise, but did not accept the thesis. Englishmen, those who knew Latin, who had embraced the new Greek learning, wanted on the whole to instruct their fellow countrymen, the widening audience whose interest in words had so enlarged, strengthened an already flexible English. And these people, not the academics, were those who had made this an important country in the history of ideas, who had forged the translation of the Bible, following Tyndale, into a masterpiece, had opened the way for Shakespeare's brilliance amongst the many talented.

171

Not yet convinced, Louise probed to know if we thought like this because modern scholars could read Sidney or Shakespeare or Jonson or the Authorised Version but did not know enough Latin, or bother to use it if they did. Strange names were flashed: Julius Caesar Scaliger, Bodin, Ficino, Joseph Scaliger. The skill of Gabriel Harvey or Milton in the classical languages and Italian was used by both women, though here Alison seemed, to mouth-opened listeners, to have the advantage. Louise argued quietly, she had recently read some book, but in the end she came nearer Alison's pro-English view, though with the usual scholarly provisos and demands for advice on further reading. Alison sat, still and easy, spoke without force, but gave the impression she had spent the last few days preparing not for her wedding but for this viva. She did not once grow excited, but had, it seemed, a whole library of reference in her head.

The rest listened, though they were allowed to interrupt with questions. David noticed how neatly Vernon cleared difficulties with his brief interventions. But however often they were stopped neither Louise nor Alison lost the thread of their argument. It was a marvellous twenty minutes for the listeners.

In the end Louise admitted that this was outside her real period, though the Middle Ages did not stop in 1453 or 1485 but continued, old supporting as well as splintering the new. When she congratulated Alison on her superior knowledge, the younger woman with becoming modesty said that she could not deny that there was force in the other's argument even though few were willing to claim that the many Latin poems of the period were the equivalent emotionally, intellectually, verbally of those of Shakespeare and his contemporaries.

Vernon was quickly in with a question here.

'Why is that?'

Alison looked at Louise first as if to allow her to answer but was courteously given priority.

'It's a matter of personal taste. It must be. But put that consideration aside. We've had nearly four hundred years of Shakespeare, who's been studied and admired in periods that differ considerably, socially and emotionally, have different, even opposite criteria of judgement, and yet in all these ages readers have found things to approve of or marvel at.'

'Because of the universality of the poetry?'

'Universality? Not of an age but all time? They *all* found something good. Yes. Yes. Sometimes quite contrary virtues. I sometimes despair of my profession of critic. We look on Shakespeare as a learned poet nowadays, who'd read a great deal, listened, been delighted with new knowledge, but the likes of Dryden and perhaps Ben Jonson or Sam Johnson would have considered him as unlearned but naturally gifted, fancy's child.'

' "Murmuring his native woodnotes wild." ' Vernon, murmuring.

'If people know a great deal about what we know or judge important then we call them scholarly.'

'What chance is there that the people who think that the Elizabethan Latin poets and scholars are the glory of their times will win the argument?'

'Very little,' Louise said, suddenly breaking off.

'Very little. Though we never know. Not many people study Shakespeare or even Dickens in these days of compulsory education. But just imagine the task in hand for one who sets out to demonstrate to us that some Latin poems are more relevant or telling, a superior form of writing, than *King Lear* or even *Romeo and Juliet*. How do you judge and how do you convince somebody who doesn't even know the language? Could one make an Englishman, for instance, think that William Williams Pantycelyn or Miklós Radnóti wrote greater poems than Tennyson or Ted Hughes?'

'How would you convince me that Hughes wrote better than Tennyson?' asked Vernon.

'Not easily.'

The argument grew lively, more trivial, but David, next now to his growling grandfather, took little part. He felt pleased, not only because it supported George's theories

173

of a lively provincial culture but because Polly and Karen, those representatives in the young man's eyes of the great world, those women with both feet flat on the miry ground and both eyes steadily on the vagaries of the human race, seemed to be enjoying themselves listening to this scholarly farrago. Wrong word. Alison had made him look it up once, a jumble, a confused mess, from a word for mixed grain in Latin. That such sorting out should take place on the eve of his wedding seemed a bonus, but he sobered himself with the thought that if they had been talking about association football he probably would have been equally delighted.

Alison sat next to Vernon, modestly upright. She spoke with practised care, but easily, not attempting to shine, now merely offering her opinions as starting points. She smiled. Louise, on the other hand, seemed glum, or uncertain, as if she had been caught out trespassing. When earlier Alison had said, 'I take it you've been reading J. W. Binns?' she looked guilty, nabbed with a pocketful of scrumped apples. David had thought Alison's quiet question had been a disguised form of praise for the breadth of Louise's researches, but he remembered Vernon saying solemnly to father and son together the last time he was over that academics were odd, indeed, and that if you wanted a really malicious brawl all you had to do was to set one doctor of divinity against another.

The only person not enjoying herself, to judge by appearances, was Madeleine Payne, Alison's mother. She sat uncomfortably between Poll and Karen, playing awkwardly with an empty coffee cup rattling on a saucer. Twice Polly had tried to relieve her of it and twice she had drawn huffily away as if her hostess should have understood that some precious dregs were being preserved for magical use later. 'Look at their mothers first,' George had warned David once, when he had described on holiday his youthful lady-loves to his grandfather, 'because that's what she'll be like in twenty or thirty years' time.' Except for eye-colouring Alison had nothing in common with this rather nervous, frowning, well-dressed lady, who fidgeted with boredom or indigestion or lack of appreciation. Louise, except for her pallor, would have made a more suitable mother.

George nudged him, pointing at Vernon with his head. 'Look at him. He's in his eyeholes.'

Certainly he now conducted the conversation like a TV programme, encouraging questions, glossing them, face alight with enthusiasm. David, who seemed to himself to be unusually sensitive this evening to gesture and facial expression, noticed how polite, even subservient he was to Louise and how he never allowed Madeleine to be left out of the talk, to her own thoughts. All this he did without condescension. Here was a master of his art.

At about ten thirty the company drank the health of bride and groom, proposed by Vernon, seconded by Madeleine, and the company broke up. Within five minutes the house was clear.

In the December darkness of the closed yard they called to each other to take their fill of beauty sleep to be ready for the morning. Weather gripped bitterly cold under a sky without stars. David kissed Alison briefly. Watching her retreating back Vernon took his son by the elbow, whispering, 'That one small head could carry all she knew.'

'I know,' David returned.

'I'd be sorry if it was anybody else but you she was to marry,' Polly said.

'Oracular.' Vernon, nudging stepmother.

Two minutes later the yard stood bare, damp, empty, with light leaking in a wedge from one margin of the kitchen blind. Cars on the road, the other side of the house and the high wall, faintly interrupted silence. A snowflake or two flickered down without threat. The north-east wind was tamed in these few square metres, but nobody was there to notice.

XV

The wedding ceremony worked to perfection.

No one arrived late. Traffic thinned out to allow the limousines and taxis to draw up minutes early. The grey sky gloomily scattered small snowflakes during the photographic sessions, cut short by the cold. The choirboys performed lustily but the rest of the largish congregation in winter coats showed no taste for singing. Alison, breathtaking in white, seemed bemused, her mouth smilingly closed as if she preserved some secret. David, stolid colleague Geoffrey Samson at his elbow, took pleasure staring round the austere beauty of the church, its leaded and leaden windows, the grey serenities of Norman and Gothic imagination, the splash of flowers, of a banner, the dark polish on the wood of the screen. He toyed with the notion that long-dead masons had fashioned these shapes over some hundreds of lost years to complete his delight on this day, that an architectural providence governed his present success. When the rector, after Alison's arrival to the majesty of Jeremiah Clarke, strident trumpet cannonading round the walls, called them 'Dearly Beloved' and Alison glanced suddenly up at David, the words became believable instanter, and St Paul, who commended this estate as honourable among men, an unlikely but not unwelcome guest on the Randall side of the aisle. The bride's hand was delicate, ivory pale, as her husband invested it with the ring, but warm, freshly alive as spring, the finger enriching the gold, touching her man into a goodness, into a certainty, an order momentarily angelic. He nodded at his insight, the lawyer's mind first denying before granting approval.

Their little world was static and utterly clear as they marched out, man and wife, this time to Purcell himself arranged for giant pipes and cathedral-wide spaces. David had expected a blur, but he could have described in detail colouring and expression on the faces of approving friends, though he felt above all the hand in his, the flowing presence at his side. He noticed Henry Corbett, bride's friend, standing, breath held hard as if for his last appeal to the jury. Alison smiled on all.

In the vestry handshakes and hugs, incoherences and clichés, above all tears convinced them of all the world's approval. Madeleine wept as she had throughout the service, sometimes noisily, but tears spilled in silence down Polly's cheeks and Karen dabbed at her eyes, spoiling her make-up. Madeleine signed the register with a flourish, Louise with a neat, superior signature. Vernon looked much as God would have done, had he deigned in flesh to appear. George Randall lurked in the background, saying nothing, grim, putty-coloured. This morning he appeared to limp badly to the ceremony as if his hips denied him the happiness of the dancing day. David made a point of leading Ally across to the old man.

'Give your new granddaughter a kiss, then,' he ordered.

George obeyed; he had shaved unusually close, had his hair trimmed.

'Wish you every happiness,' he mumbled. Alison hugged him. 'Edna. She would have . . . I'll show you our photograph some time.' Polly had come across.

'He looks a credit to you, doesn't he?' she shouted, tears still on her face.

'Waterworks,' he growled. 'I feel like crying myself.'

'Why so?'

'Just look at her, woman. Just look at her. She's a picture.'

Polly's tears welled again so that Ally kissed both.

'You smell delicious,' she told the grandfather.

'Some stuff she made me put on. Scent.'

'Don't you like it?' Alison held his arm.

'Do you?'

'Oh, yes.'

'Good enough for me then.' George pecked at the cheek, awkwardly, beside him, beside himself, stood proud.

In time they made for the porch, were marshalled for photographs, quickly, by an artist in a mackintosh who bent double to signal them to places.

'What colour would you call his coat?' David asked Alison.

'Dirty,' Polly replied, overhearing. 'Greasy.'

The juxtapositions in the crowd delighted them out of the corner of the eye: an elegant Eleanor Frankland next to Professor Ryder, his hair, what was left of it, as if he'd been pulled through a hedge backwards; Geoffrey Samson's twin girls in straw hats for the occasion; Louise, Madeleine and the coated photographer with his lank long locks, and then, suddenly seen, on his own, Vernon, husk-thin in his tailored suit which looked too big for him, his face white and drawn with cold.

'Can't you get him inside?' David asked Karen.

'Not a chance.'

Her firm bravado instructed him that she had already tried and failed. Vernon noticed their concern and grinned, saluting left-handed. 'Let's not loiter about,' he ordered strongly. 'We'll be frozen.' People obeyed; even the photographer recognised authority.

It was warm in the hired Rolls-Royce. Now the roads were more crowded, and narrowed for repair behind red-and-white ribbons and bollards; the newlyweds sat still, inspected by passengers in other cars, waved at by children, smiled on by a policewoman, courteously allowed precedence by three motorists. By the time they had reached the Randalls' back lane and made for the garden steps it was snowing quite hard, large flakes tumbling. As they burst in the back door, brushing at their clothes, Polly welcomed them, overwhelming with congratulations.

'You made good time.' David, in surprise.

'We started before you did. We've turned the heat up. Wasn't it cold outside that church?' She altered her worried face. 'You'd like a cup of tea, love, wouldn't you?' This to Alison, and immediately a waitress in a white overall, large spectacles, a tightly belted waist and highly wrought hair presented a tray.

'Thanks,' David said.

'Heaven.' Alison, sipping. 'Heaven.'

'You don't take much pleasing,' Grandfather said.

'Come on, George,' Polly admonished. 'Drink with and to the happy couple.'

Randall reached for his cup. Now he had removed his overcoat they saw his light-grey, striped suit hung brand-new, on for its first outing, its stiff perfection contrasting with the withered neck, the weathered cheeks.

'God bless you.' He almost shouted.

Other guests had begun to arrive, reporting that the snow had stopped. The caterers were ready for them with scalding cups of tea to warm them in preparation for the wine.

The noise rang incredibly under the ceilings so that one had difficulty hearing one's neighbour, though now and then, by a freak, some voice cut richly through. 'I never patronised them again, I can tell you,' from a woman, and then from a senior man at Lamberts, 'He could not have been more than fifty feet above the ground.' The best, source unidentified, in a soprano certainty claimed, 'Love is eternal.' These rose like sudden islands and were submerged at once in the main of chatter.

The waitresses, unobtrusively in spite of the difficulty of movement, cleared cups and offered wine. By this time groups had formed. Grandfather Randall occupied a Windsor chair in the drawing room, with Ryder standing at one side and Eleanor Frankland sitting to the other. George offered them a lumbering commentary, to judge from appearances, directed from a lowered head towards his knees. Karen and Madeleine Payne entertained Frankland. Polly moved about, mistress of ceremony, a white rose in her hand.

'This'll be something worth remembering,' a man washed up by the crowd to David's elbow spluttered. David did not recognise him, but the white-toothed arrival of Frankland's secretary Marilyn Wakefield placed him: her next husband, Somebody Bolderstone.

A university group roared with sudden laughter, so loud that many heads turned. In the centre Vernon posed modestly, satisfied with the effect of his witticism.

Alison's father, Julian Hunter, and his present wife, Peg, approached David, now separated by a few feet from his bride. The Hunters congratulated him. They had arrived at the church at the same time as David and had introduced themselves in the porch, and later had exchanged felicitations in the flurry of the photographic session. The father reminded David of Alison, though it was difficult to say exactly how. Perhaps it was the shape of the face, the delicacy of movement, the concentration on his interlocutor, the precise hand movements. He looked younger than his fifty-two years, hair untouched by grey, his body carrying no undue weight, footsteps light. A schoolmaster, he spoke without force, making no show. David wondered how this man had come to marry the exigent Madeleine, but guessed that her beauty, now almost completely dissipated, had made her eccentricities, her volatility, her excessive demands understandable if not reasonable. Madeleine had taken a position by Alison now, determined to be at the centre of events, speaking with authority and, it appeared, success, her colour high, the sullen expression gone.

Julian Hunter's wife, Margaret, Peg, was an elegant woman in her thirties with thick ankles and wrists, her eyes dark blue in a pale, perfect complexion. She smiled but did nothing to thrust herself into prominence, though she surprised David, when her husband had turned away judging he'd taken up sufficient of the bridegroom's time, by saying in a deepish voice, 'He's pleased.' David understood her to be talking about her husband. She laid a beautiful hand on his arm, the nails were pink and regularly oval. 'This is his idea of a paradise.' Peg waved towards the window, now steamed up. 'Inclement weather outside. Snow and cold. And inside light, warmth, security, society and a happy event. This is perfect for him.'

'Why do you think that is?'

The violet eyes widened; the well-modulated voice wavered not at all, but continued. 'The world's a dangerous place. He's a kind of Wind-in-the-Willows character, with a bolt hole. He was bombed out of his house as a little boy.'

Alison had not mentioned this.

180

'No, nobody was injured,' Peg continued, as if she read his mind. 'His father was away in the army, and Jules and his uncle and grandmother were in the Anderson shelter. The house was demolished. It rained bricks and debris all over the garden, but they were far enough away to be safe.'

She stared across at her husband who now hovered on the outskirts of Polly's group.

'I always supposed it was that,' she said. 'I was born years after the war, but I sometimes feel rather that way. I wonder if it's not common. In ancient Greece or the Dark Ages or even much later death was always in wait for you just around the next corner, with violence and killing illness, but we are protected, aren't we, in a way they never were? Until we have to die.' She smiled calmly, her face unmoved, her hands beautiful. 'You'll think I'm morbid, talking like this on a wedding day.'

David lowered his head.

'I'm sorry we never came to visit you,' he said, 'before the wedding.'

'We didn't visit you, for that matter. "Madeleine will want their spare time," Jules said.'

'Nor did we go to see Madeleine what with one thing and another. Nor Louise, my mother.'

'Which is she?'

David pointed her out. She was in serious conversation with some man from the university, a musicologist with a red face and yuppy's striped shirt. Both were nodding.

A young jack-in-the-box with a camera appeared, making space for himself.

'Look up,' he called. 'And all pleasant. Cheese.' The flash startled. He thanked them, and pushing people aside, greeted his next victims.

'Who's that?' Peg asked.

'No idea. The photographer's assistant. Or somebody Polly's brought in to capture the moment.'

'I'm glad. Will you have an album made up?'

'We've not thought of it. Or I haven't. It's a good idea. Have you met Alison quite a few times?'

'Yes. She's stayed with us once or twice when she was in London. She looks happy. A year or two ago she thought she'd made a mistake coming to Beechnall. Or at least she gave us that impression. Jules was worried.'

'She's got used to the natives,' David answered.

'But you come from London, don't you? According to my sources.'

'One of the rejects.'

'You wouldn't want to go back, then?'

'Not unless there was a really interesting job. I think I've just about hit my level here.'

'And if Alison has to move?'

'We'll think about that when it comes. It's quite likely, I guess. I shan't stand in her way.'

'Even if it means living apart?'

'Exactly. As if I were in the merchant marine. And that makes you want to ask about children?' He kept the tone light.

'No. Not now.'

At this moment Madeleine Payne appeared, to shower David with congratulations, on the ceremony, the reception, his appearance. He thought from the exuberance of her delivery she'd shortly praise him for the snow, divine confetti. She spoke loudly, perhaps the general racket made this necessary, and totally ignored Peg, who did not, however, move away. 'Do you know all these people?' Madeleine demanded. 'But of course you can't. Some will be Alison's university colleagues.' She went on to describe a conversation she had had with a 'crazy' lecturer about deserts and birdsong. In the middle of this, and clearly she had learnt little, she noticed Peg and stopped.

'You're Margaret, aren't you?'

'Yes.'

'We haven't met before. I'm Julian's first wife.'

'Madeleine.' Peg put out a hand. Madeleine took it briefly. She seemed flustered, fidgety, in need of something to say.

'Is Julian keeping well?'

'Thank you, yes.'

182

'Very busy?'

Peg inclined her head. Madeleine, casting round for a subject, remarked that this seemed quite an occasion, if noisy. They murmured agreement.

'But,' Madeleine's voice struck stridently, 'I can't see any children. These affairs seem curiously imperfect without childish voices.'

Polly passed.

'Where are the children?' David shouted.

'They're all in the butler's pantry.' She pointed, not stopping. 'They're drinking lemonade and watching videos.'

Madeleine now advanced the argument that cutting the young generation off from their elders reduced the enjoyment and value for both. Neither Peg nor David argued. Madeleine breathed in deeply, not discouraged.

'It seems remarkable,' she said, 'that we appear to congratulate you and Alison on your wedding day, and yet with both sets of parents the marriages broke down.'

'That sounds as if you wanted us to live in sin,' said David, nettled.

'Nothing of the kind. Though, if I understand it right, you have been doing so. No. It's as Dr Johnson said, the triumph of hope over experience.'

'And is that good or bad?' David, as Peg hid her smile with a polite hand.

'Oh. I was concerned to criticise us, the parents, if it is a criticism, rather than you. The older people were found wanting.' A waitress filled her theatrically held glass.

'I have only married once,' Peg said dully.

'Opportunity, my dear, opportunity.' She raised her glass. 'Your good health, your happiness, in spite of precedent.'

Madeleine left them, elbowing her way towards the bride.

'Bloody hell,' David said.

'Exactly.'

At that moment Polly clanked a huge handbell to announce that the buffet lunch was now ready and that they should start to queue. When they were replete there would be a reading of telegrams and one or two short speeches. She disappeared to ring and shout in the other rooms.

'I'll leave you to Alison,' Peg said. 'Come and visit, won't you?'

Now people stirred themselves to form a double crocodile in the hall. The caterers dipped and dashed, guests reappeared with piled plates, but the queue did not alter much. The temporary cessation of noise was over; voices again banged metallic pleasantries, laughter squawked; one young man from the university made balletic movements with his arms, watched wide-eyed by two middle-aged women in sensible dresses. Madeleine now harangued Alison and her entourage. David waved to Vernon who had come in from the other room. His father wove across.

'How are you?' Vernon asked his son.

'Bedazzled.'

'Alison's a picture. I wonder if her mother looked as well on her wedding day.'

'You wonder no such thing.'

Vernon aimed a laughing punch.

'Have you talked to Mum today?' David asked.

'Not yet. I shall do my Christian duty before the day's out. Actually, I think she's not unhappy. She's roughly where she wanted to be, independent and doing quite well in her own line. She knows what she's talking about. I thoroughly enjoyed the argument between her and Alison about Latin.'

'Are you making a speech?' David asked.

'No. Not a word. Karen and Poll decided that. You and the best man. That's all.'

'Pity.'

'You said it.'

They made for Alison, took her towards the queue in the hall. At that moment Grandfather Randall appeared to look the line up and down.

'What,' he roared. 'The bride and groom queueing on their wedding day. That won't do. Stand back.'

People obeyed.

'It's all right,' Alison objected, very quietly.

'It might be for you but it isn't for me.'

'It's all right, Grandpa,' David said pacifically. 'We're going to listen to Vernon's fatherly advice as we stand here.'

' "Man shall not live by bread alone." ' Vernon.

'Back in line then,' George shouted. 'Three ranks.'

The fallers-back re-formed. George joined his son, pleased with his performance.

'I just want to listen to this,' he said, but immediately a young woman snatched him away to help Polly out of some difficulty in the larder. He stumped off, grumpy and delighted.

'As he gets older,' Vernon said, 'he's more and more like the boy in the back streets he was nearly seventy years ago. In his prime he was very much the schoolmaster, middle class and stiff-collared as you like. Not now. He's the huckster on the market stall or the man flogging fruit from a barrow.'

'There's something remarkable about him,' Alison said.

'And what do you think it is?'

'He seems very much alive. Young, even. Against appearance. I know he has these aches and pains but he's not giving up.'

'No,' Vernon answered. 'When my mother died I thought that would be the end of him, but it wasn't so. Within a year he'd married Polly.'

'Very sensible.' David, sharp.

'Oh, I don't deny it. She's ideal for him. She keeps him interested. My mother was a different kettle of fish altogether. You remember your gran, David, don't you?'

'I was seventeen when she died.'

'As old as that?' Vernon pulled a televisual face. 'She knew her mind. She was ladylike. Always ready with the best china cups for her Earl Grey. Straight-backed. She could speak plainly, if there was the need. I can't help wondering about the time I don't remember, when I was very young, and Dad was in the RAF. To be at home with

185

a baby, knowing that you might hear at any time that your husband had been killed. That's one thing I resent about the last war: all those bright, fit, clever young men trained up to the hilt and then knocked off like skittles. The nation's best. It's a bloody disgrace and I suppose it was worse in the First War. Flower of a generation.'

Vernon's voice grew slower, weaker, running down, matching the lines on his face.

'This is boring,' he said, tone crisp, 'especially on your wedding day.'

'Not at all,' Alison answered. 'It's fascinating. I'm one of the family now.'

'Do you ever talk to George about the war?' David asked.

'Not much. The last few times we've been up here we haven't exactly hit it off. We have words, and I just pack my bags and skedaddle. Cowardly, but I don't want to hurt him. When I was a boy I'd question him and he'd always answer, and my impression is that he did it quietly without either boasting or shuddering.'

'Did he never tell his classes about his exploits?' Alison.

'Not as far as I know. And not like some of the others.'

'What do you quarrel about?' Alison, again.

'Anything. The day's news. Public waste of money. Litter. Holidays. Television especially. It doesn't take much to get him going. Basically, he just can't find it in him to approve of what I'm doing. And this aggressive provincialism of his gets on my nerves. You mention something that has happened and he'll immediately give you two better examples from not a mile away.'

'What about genocide?'

'He's not cracked, David. He doesn't claim that somebody's running an Auschwitz in the next street. And there's an element of truth in what he says in that there's plenty of interest going on here. But it really boils down to the fact that he can't believe that I deserve the salary I earn, while I think I give value for money. So we're on edge, ready to argue about, oh, the right time on the kitchen clock or the rector's name.'

David was amazed to find his father speaking so frankly within earshot of other people. Strangers recognising Vernon usually cocked an ear even if he merely ordered a newspaper or a cup of coffee. Perhaps today's racket would drown the voice. Vernon spoke frankly in honour of Alison, David considered, and he felt uneasy.

By the time they had filled their plates George Randall had returned and conducted them to a small round table with a starched white cloth, where magnificent in the middle the wedding cake towered.

'The seats of the mighty,' George pronounced. 'You eat in full view today, so Poll says. This is where the speeches will be made so that people in the hall can hear as well as those in the room. She's organised it all.' He whipped up two printed cards, 'Reserved', from the chairs.

Vernon, dismissed, disappeared. George, duty done, attended elsewhere to the inner man. All the time the young couple ate, friends strolled by to interrupt with congratulations. Upstairs Polly had now laid the presents out for inspection, grouped round the piece of furniture, the early-nineteenth-century sideboard which Vernon had given and which had now been buffed by George into a miracle of polished grain, golden metal. 'You should see the back,' George had told them. 'It'll never look anything, but I'll need another month's work on it at least.'

'It's perfect,' Alison had admitted.

'He likes nothing better than playing with old wood,' Polly told them. 'He's a real genius.'

'There's workmanship there,' George said. 'It's worth spending your time on.'

After the meal, and it took long enough, the speeches were short. The waitresses poured champagne as Geoffrey Samson rose, read telegrams. Under orders, he claimed, he toasted both bridesmaids and bride together. He told one story in his dry lawyer's voice, about the horse which taking a couple on honeymoon twice collapsed in the road. On these occasions the groom dismounted, restored the horse to its legs and warned, 'That's the first time,' and again, 'That's the second time.' When the horse next dropped, the groom took down his gun from the cart and shot the animal, with the brief explanation, 'That's the third.' His wife, shocked by the inconvenience or the cruelty, remonstrated with her new husband as they tramped along the road lugging their cases. He listened politely until she had quite finished, then looking her straight in the eye, poked out a finger and said: 'That's the first time.'

A brief silence stabbed, then uncertain, finally hearty laughter. Samson scowled at his listeners, and asked who was issuing warnings today. If his own marriage was anything to go by, it was Alison. The point was inappropriate and mismanaged at that, but delivered, as it were, from a distance, like a piece of printed matter that could be read or ignored from choice. He cheered his voice and facial expression to praise Alison and wish her happiness. She also had chosen well. As the crowding guests, mostly standing, prepared themselves for more pleasurable warmth the speaker raised his glass, invited them to join him in a toast and, that accomplished, sat down, in mid-flow, pleased with himself.

David spoke even more succinctly. He thanked them on Alison's behalf and his, claimed that was why he was on his feet. He recalled that on his first court appearance Albert Frankland had instructed him to make sure the magistrates knew the facts and the law and to leave it there. He murmured that he proposed to take the advice today.

'But did you win?' a voice challenged. David glanced briefly up.

'No, we did not.' He ignored laughter, and hecklers. 'I can't tell you how I feel at this moment. "Happy" by no means describes it.' He looked down solemnly at Alison, who lowered her eyes. ' "Overwhelmed" is nearer the mark. By my good fortune.' He paused, teeth together, rapt. When he began again his voice was clear, quiet. He thanked them all, for their presence, singled out Polly and Grandfather for the use of their house, and all for the kindly good wishes expressed or felt. Again he paused. No one seemed embarrassed by these silences; they proceeded without interruption, like set prayers; the bridegroom wanted high spirits momentarily subdued and all agreed. He began again each time, carefully, not as if struck by inspiration but knowing his way. 'As Geoffrey here was speaking to you, conveying as he always does the exact thoughts of each one of you and us, givers and receivers, in his usual, deft, daft, throwaway manner, that's why he's such a good lawyer, he knows what you exactly want, and makes you certain that he does by expressing it in language you would never choose for yourself, I sat here holding Alison's hand, and wondering what I had done to deserve this,' he stopped, 'this lady, this fortune, this day. I am less excited than I expected, more overjoyed, though that word conveys nothing. I should use a word like "transported". Except that I am still here and wouldn't be anywhere else. I'm extrapolated. Projected into a new area of experience.' He glanced gently down at his wife. 'I even know the Latin. *Extra* and, I suppose, *interpollare*, and beyond that *polire*, to polish. Oh, I had to use the dictionary. And it doesn't mean polished up on the outside. By no means.' Again the pause as he lowered his head. 'I have never in my life felt as I feel now. And yet I cannot describe it even to myself. It's ineffable. I know now what that means. But. Louise told me once. I used to ask her about words. But. There is a word. And I use it in a religious sense. It's grace. Unmerited favour.' He paused again, thanked them on his wife's behalf as well as his own, bowed like a barrister, and sat.

They applauded, called for speeches from Alison, who smilingly stood and refused, from Vernon, who waved, said he dare not disobey Polly, and in any case would not be so foolish as to follow a speech of the quality of his son's.

Karen told him that night that a lawyer's wife had whispered to her husband that she didn't know what Vernon meant. 'David might be nice, but he's as dull as ditchwater, and Alison was very pretty, all dressed up, but she's just a little mouse of a woman.'

189

'What did you say?'

'Not a word.'

'You're as bad as she is.' Vernon's face blushed ugly with anger.

Outside after the speeches plates were collected, people began to take their leave. Madeleine was escorted queenly to her taxi as the sky darkened, holding off snow. Alison changed from white; Grandpa George threatened to take his tie off, but did not do so. Vernon spoke to everybody, caterers included. In the evening, with Louise, Karen and Vernon the only remaining guests, Polly cried, saying she'd like to have it all over again the next day.

'The most satisfactory wedding I've ever attended. By a long chalk.'

Her husband, short of breath, kept his mouth shut.

XVI

The Christmas honeymoon in London disappeared at speed.

In the mornings the newlyweds walked, mainly about the streets, but once in Regent's Park. In the afternoons they idled with their hosts, chattering, listening to compact discs of the music of Richard Strauss, John Banks's latest favourite, and twice in the evening they were taken out to the houses of friends. In the first they ate, drank and talked, while in the second they were required to play energetic games, charades, murder, blind man's buff, Dickens's Yes and No; the list seemed childish and endless. They all danced madly.

The hostess, a successful commercial solicitor, said she and her husband had determined, at first without consultation, that they would not spend this evening slumped in front of television screens. David enjoyed himself beyond belief; he lived for a few hours in another world where sophistication took on new guises. To dance 'Oranges and Lemons' and 'A-hunting We Will Go' ruffled hair, reddened faces, raised voices, loosened collars and tongues, left even the young breathless. Everybody was nobody; competition was reduced to infant proportions. They hadn't energy left for malice; laughter cracked sides, and, once, a tray of glasses.

When they returned to Beechnall, Alison said that the founder of the feast, a barrister, had questioned his grandfather about children's parties in the twenties and thirties. They reported this to George Randall.

' "A hunting we will go"! By God, I couldn't do that now.'

'But would you like to?'

'Yes. You held the girls' hands. And dragged them up and down.'

The old man's face brightened.

'What sort of people were at this party?' Polly asked David.

'Professional middle classes.'

'Middle-aged?'

'They wouldn't thank you for saying so, but on the whole, yes.'

'And they enjoyed themselves?'

'Oh, yes.'

'But why?'

'Surprise,' Alison answered. 'They hadn't expected what they found. They could take their shoes off to dance.' She offered the sentence as though it contained an explanation. 'It was energetic. They weren't expected to compete. They could drink . . .'

'And sweat,' David interrupted.

'But it was the element of surprise. It was different, and childish.'

'Murder wasn't childish in my day,' George said. 'Not the way we played it.'

'You were a dirty old man as a boy,' Polly rebuked. 'And those London people enjoyed themselves? It doesn't seem very likely.'

'I imagine they chose their guests.'

'Did you know them before?'

'Only by name. The Bankses took us.'

'We,' David answered, 'were on honeymoon. Everything pleased us.'

'I would like to have seen it.' George, jovially. 'Prancing up and down.' Then to Alison. 'And you'd be the most beautiful.'

She curtseyed; David said, 'By far'; Polly applauded before asking,

'Were they dressed for it?'

'Who? The guests? Casual clothes. But jackets and sweaters and tops came off.'

'And the women?'

'They wear more sensible things anyhow. But it was the enjoyment that amazed me. People glowed. With heat and with pleasure.'

'And did that include you?' Polly asked her.

'Of course it did.' George.

'Yes. Perhaps because one game followed another so quickly. We just danced and then acted and paid forfeits like five-year-olds. Though Tim Miles, the host, said in the one interval when we stopped to eat that he thought that young children enjoyed the organising as much as the game itself.'

'Is that right?' George asked.

'You were a schoolmaster.'

'A long time ago. I've forgotten.'

'They're all different.' Polly started on a tale about her own family. The moral seemed that they differed in childhood, had changed considerably as they grew older but had not become alike.

'Do you see the children in the adults?' David asked her.

'Hard to say. Sometimes. Fiona's obstinate still. Like her father. And Godfrey's a loner. I don't know. I think "Yes". But I could equally answer "No".'

For the rest of the holiday Alison worked daily at the university. She and David set out at the same time each morning, though he pressed her to start half an hour later when traffic had thinned. They cooked the evening meal together, enjoying themselves. Both were extremely occupied, and happy with it, with each other.

On the first day of the university term, Alison had left grumbling cheerfully, Geoffrey Samson called in at David's office.

'Are you and Alison still considering moving house?'

'We've talked about it.'

'That's what I thought. I've heard you. There's a nice place going in our street.'

Samson lived in a cul-de-sac of pre-1914 houses with large gardens.

'It's four bedrooms but not enormous. They've only just decided to sell, told me last night, and I mentioned you. It's not gone to the house agents yet. Interested?'

'I'll need to consult Alison.'

'Of course.' Samson wrote down the address, 'phone number and price. Expensive. David said so. 'Worth every penny, and more. Go and see it, but don't dawdle. It'll sell in a jiff, never mind the market.'

David, home first, began on the evening meal. The week's menu had been decided on Sunday. Alison looked glum, apologising for her lateness, throwing down her handbag, kicking off her shoes.

'Usual chaos?' he enquired.

'Not chaos, lethargy.'

'On your part? Or theirs?'

'All round.'

He handed her a cup of tea, ordered her to sit still, gave her his news about the house. She said little, but came soon into the kitchen with her empty cup.

'What do you think about it?'

'Worth a look. Geoff thinks it a bargain even at that price.'

'Isn't it big? For us?'

'A study each. A good investment.'

'And the drawbacks?'

'All these old houses need care. And there's a biggish garden, if the Samsons' is anything to go by.'

They talked, casually, in brief sentences, making no great attempt at serious consideration even when they were at table. Alison liked the idea of a garden, but feared her ignorance. He said they could just about afford the mortgage, but as he expected a substantial rise next year he was not worried.

'What are the snags as you see them?' she asked.

'It will occupy more time. If we stick here we'll always think we're on the point of leaving, and the place takes hardly any looking after. If you want to put a long day in at your desk, or I do, it's no trouble. If we're whacked when we come home, we can afford to go out for dinner now. A scholar like you needs time for her work.'

'A scholar like me would do well to consider other people.'

'Expand,' he chaffed.

'The more I work, the more I realise that my study is not entirely from books in dead and dying languages. It needs a knowledge of people, social conditions that can only be picked up in the home, the street, in the staff club, with your clients. I don't want to tuck myself away with mere learning.'

'Even when you're very good at it?'

'Even more so on that account. Literature demands understanding of people.'

'But surely people of the Renaissance thought, felt quite differently from us. Environment must have a tremendous influence, even if the basic feelings of love and hate and fear are much the same.'

'Their expression will alter, surely. I can't understand Shakespeare's admiration for euphuistic writing, for instance, but, but . . . I haven't sorted myself out on this. And when I do it won't do me any good academically. My colleagues don't want to know how my over-the-garden-wall chats or quarrels with my neighbours affect my view of Wiat or Henry VIII or Thomas Tallis or . . .'

'Shakespeare, the man himself.'

'Right. And yet in one way that seems the heart of the matter.'

'And so. What do we do now?'

'Go to see the place.'

David telephoned; the two reported at The Hollies, Oak Close, the next evening.

The house, double-fronted, in a pleasant local brick, stood last in a line; the other six were tall, majestically fronted semi-detached Victorian villas. At the end the street was blocked off by a brick wall with a small white gate and behind, darkly in wet winter, a copse huddled.

'It's quiet,' Alison said. 'And near the top of a hill.'

They stood with two minutes to spare, under an umbrella on the greasy pavement which was none too well kept, flagstones sunken irregularly and with clumps of grass in the interstices.

'Favourable, or otherwise? So far?' Alison asked.

'It's good. Even with leafless trees. And rain.'

An elderly man with fluffy hair answered the door. Very gravely he invited them in, offered his hand and his name, James White. They removed outdoor clothes, hung them in an ample cloakroom. By this time Mrs White, Margaret, had appeared, and was introduced. No one seemed easy.

White offered facts about the house, dated 1905, the size of the plot. He pointed to the strong solidity of the balustrade, patting the wood. Switching on lights he said he did not know where to start.

'Let's begin on the dining room.'

The room was plainly but beautifully furnished with an oil painting of a church, and large water-colour landscapes on the magnolia walls. Curtains were drawn; they would have to come by daylight to see the shape of the double-glazed windows.

'How long have you been here?' Alison asked Mrs White.

'Thirty-eight years.' The husband answered first.

'Our family was brought up in this house. They were small when we arrived.'

'We've never been tempted to change.' White again. 'But I suppose that tells you more about us than about the building.'

'I doubt if we'd have moved, but a cousin of Margaret's died and left us a convenient flat in the Park. Now we have to sell one or the other property. That's all on the ground floor. Intellectually it makes sense to move there. But we haven't quite decided. You'll have to convince us. I suppose it's not very clever commercially to talk like this.'

'Oh, I don't know.'

'Like that Roy Brooks man?'

That baffled the young people. Mr White took his time with his explanation of the house agent's advertisement of ruined mansions, cramped basements, falling towers, crumbling flats in the posh Sundays. He showed his yellow false teeth, pleased with himself.

In the end they were taken round the house, and little by little offered anecdotes from the White family sagas, shown the place where Jerry had fallen downstairs or had blackened a wall, now repaired, with an experiment with his chemistry set. No, he was not a scientist now: he was the organiser of a national charity. There Amélie had decorated and furnished her doll's house, now gone. The husband gave exact measurements of each room as they entered, with confidence, as if he had just done the calculations. Then followed the stories or an account of what could be seen from the window on a spring morning. When the inspection was over, White said that it would please him greatly if Alison and David would take, the word, coffee with him.

'We look on you,' Mrs White added, 'not as prospective buyers, but as friends.' She hurried away to her percolator. White mentioned Geoffrey Samson, enquired about David's position at Lambert and Partners and on learning that Alison taught at the university said that until a year ago an emeritus professor of physics had lived next door, a man called Stafford-Bates. 'Did you know him?'

'No. I've seen the name.'

'I believe he was quite famous for what he did, whatever that was. He was an odd man. He'd waltz down his garden and shout at the sun. Because it had dried out some favourite plant. You may think he would have done better to water or to shade the thing, and he knew that, but he had left it in his wife's care, and she sometimes forgot, and rather than reprove her he'd curse the sun. He had waved his fists about, really shouting. As if he wanted to draw the neighbours' attention.'

'Why was that?' David asked.

'Perhaps he was warning his wife, indirectly. Or it may be that he felt the better for the performance. He died a year or so ago. His wife went back to London to live near her daughter. The man who lives there now is a butcher. He's very respectable. And not without money.'

'And no eccentricities?' Alison asked.

'If he has he keeps them to himself.'

197

Mrs White returned with the coffee and made a ceremony out of serving it. She would, it seemed to David, do anything except pour liquid.

'This is a most convenient house,' she said, in the end, handing out cups.

'And beautiful.' Alison.

'I suppose it is,' White answered. 'Even in itself. But especially in the setting of the garden. Early summer is my favourite time. With the wistaria, and lilac, and the first roses on banksia and the broom and tree peonies. With the trees in full leaf. Then the house seems in its proper setting.'

'We shall be sorry to leave,' his wife said, 'but it's proving too much for us.'

'We haven't been able to manage the garden for some years. And though the man we have in is in many ways very satisfactory it's not the same thing.'

Mrs White provided chapter and desperate verse.

'My grandfather has been in his house since soon after the war.' David diffidently offered a few details of George's war service and the circumstances of acquiring his house.

'What did you say his name was?'

'George Randall.'

'Was he ever with the 424 Squadron at Watnall?'

'I don't know.'

White stroked his chin, poked out a finger, wriggled fantastically within his physical limits in his chair. His wife watched with concern.

'What is it, Jim?' she asked.

'Well, I . . . It might . . .'

Suddenly he made up his mind, rose stiffly to his feet and with a muttered 'Excuse me' shuffled out of the room. His wife's assumed expression of humorous incredulity conveyed nothing to the visitors, who sat silent. She began to talk about the trauma they had experienced in first hiring experts to fell a diseased elm tree. Her story moved by awkward jerks, not as if she had trouble in the telling, but as though they had difficulty in understanding without a wealth of detail. A moment after the tree had crashed, albeit safely, down they heard an illustrative smack from somewhere outside. Mrs White stopped, listened.

'Whatever is he up to now?' she asked. They listened to the silence. 'Oh, my goodness me. I wonder if I should go and see if he's . . .' They concentrated again on nothing. 'It's no joke growing old.' Her face, mask-like, looked comically askew, shapelessly grim, round, witch-like with wrinkles. No further noise disturbed them. The hostess now began to talk about a summerhouse at the far corner of the garden which had been repaired after a Pyrrhic campaign. The narrative was more broken than before, and during pauses she listened, not bothering to cover anxiety. In the end, before the tale of incompetence and racketeering was complete, she stopped, dropping her hands, head cocked.

'I shall have to go to find out what he's done.'

'Can I . . . ?'

'No, thank you. As you grow older you become clumsier. And you can't remember where you have put things.' She dithered. 'I'm sure he's perfectly all right. Oh, dear. I'm not sure.'

'Go and look,' said Alison, gently. 'We'll wait.'

Even so, Mrs White kept her position, moving her trunk as if her feet were glued to the floor. Sighing, she left with effort.

Alison and David did not speak for a time, expecting the immediate return of the old people, but the door remained shut.

'How is it that they are so certain about the price if they've not seen house agents yet?' Alison asked.

'Well, you can still get a free valuation. Or they may know a surveyor. Or White might be in the business himself. I don't think there's any trickery there.'

'But you think the price is high?'

'Yes. But we haven't seen the building by daylight. Or looked at the garden.' He smiled. 'You can't tell. They may be very astute business people for all we know.'

'And all this part of the plot?'

'It seems unlikely.'

'I shouldn't think so.' Alison expressed her own satisfaction. Both had spoken in whispers.

Soon they heard a small commotion outside. Mrs White bustled in, dusting her hands, smiling widely.

'I'm sorry we've been such a time.'

She was followed by her husband who carried a long framed photograph.

'I thought I was right,' he said.

'Here, let me dust it.' Mrs White had acquired a cloth with which she thoroughly cleansed the picture, laughing as she showed the smears of black dust to her guests. 'Now.'

White placed the photograph on a small table.

'What are your grandfather's initials?'

'G. T.'

White smacked his lips, scowling feebly at the picture before he laid a pointing finger on it. 'Flight Lieutenant G. T. Randall,' he said. 'Here. Come and look.'

Wife and guests edged across. Now White's finger was tapping the glass, almost irritably.

'That's the man. Is that your grandfather?'

All three took their turn, bent to peer at the young face under the peaked RAF officer's cap. An unlined candid expression, unsmiling, body stiff with a bit of swank, knees smartly together.

'Is that . . . ?' Mrs White.

Now the others stared at David, silently urging him to make up his mind. He looked at the black-and-white photograph. Four rows of uniformed men posed in front of a dark bird of an aeroplane. All the faces were young, almost childlike, as if someone had dressed up schoolchildren for the occasion. The set of caps, chip bags or cheese-cutters, varied from the pert to the prim, from riotous to regimental. Some stood to attention, others lolled; grins, smirks, proud heads, scowls spattered the rows; one had moved, blurring his head. The squadron leader, young as the rest, sat in the middle of the front row, shoulders squared, strong hands on knees, a spaniel at his feet.

'Is it your grandfather?' Mrs White again.

David examined the unlined, unsagging face, the dark eyes. It could well be. How thin.

'It must be,' he said, staring again. He scanned the legend. G. T. Randall. Then along the same front row to Flt. Lt. J. E. R. White, on the far side of the squadron commander, a slim, smart figure with a serious expression, wanting this over so that he could get back to his work. He wore no wing or wings on his chest.

'Would you recognise him?'

'I think I might. Just.'

'You haven't seen this photograph before?'

'No. Though I've seen one of him in uniform, when he was married.' David looked again. 'He wasn't wearing a cap, then.'

'What date was that?' Alison asked him.

'1941. My father was born November 1942. On Guy Fawkes Day.'

'What does your father do?' Mrs White.

'He works for the BBC. Vernon Randall.'

'He used to read the news,' she said in excitement. 'And chairs that political programme. We always watch it. We always watch it. He's very good. And that radio phone-in. What do you think of that, Jim? Mr Randall's father is Vernon Randall on the television. The man you like so much.'

'Yes, dear.'

White was still bent painfully over the photograph, a crooked finger assisting faded eyes. He straightened.

'A good number of aircrew personnel were killed.' He spoke into the corner, to himself, his mouth slightly open as if trying to recall the dead colleagues. Or give due weight to their shortened lives. To account for it all. His finger touched down on the surface after slow leaps, loops, marking presumably the dead. Now he nodded, finger held on some favoured chest in trembling immobility.

'He doesn't listen to a word I say.'

'No, dear.'

'That very bright-faced man on the television that you like so much, Vernon Randall, is Mr Randall's father.'

'Vernon. Vernon Randall.' He concentrated on the photograph, trying to form a sensible connection. 'G. T. Randall,' he read. 'He had a very good reputation. A fine pilot, afraid of nothing. Had a bit of a swagger about him, but not reckless in the air. Intent, you might think. Yes. We weren't together long. I was sent out East.' He sighed and straightened. 'But I remember him quite well. What did you say about the BBC?'

'That Randall's son and this Mr Randall's father,' she waved David into recognition, 'is Vernon Randall on the television, the . . .'

'*Questions Put and Answered*. I know, I know. A famous father? Is it a nuisance, eh? And the son of G. T. Randall. Is your grandfather still alive? What did he do in civilian life?' His face became stricken. 'He wasn't killed, was he? In the war? So many of them were. I was abroad, didn't hear. It's possible.'

'No. He's still alive. In Beechnall.'

'Some of them were boys barely out of school. And young fathers leaving widows with families. You say he lives in Beechnall. What did he do? He'll be retired, won't he?'

'He taught mathematics. At Highfield Grammar.'

'I would never have guessed it.' White picked up the photograph, held it close to his face. 'A little bit aggressive. Not unduly so. Some of them were unbearable. No, that's unfair. When you consider the strain they worked under.' White jerked his head up, back to the present. 'Give him my regards, will you? James White. J. E. R. White. I was concerned with the interpretation of photographs. I had to learn it, of course. When one is younger, one can acquire new skills in no time. It had its problems.'

Mrs White prised her husband away from the photograph. Her interest lay with television and Vernon. White spoke sensibly, haltingly sometimes, now and then at a loss for a word, but pertinently, occasionally with directness. He dissected Vernon's interviewing technique, explaining why, though it seemed ruthless, robust, it was acceptable to both victim and audience. 'He must research with real thoroughness.'

Once the coffeepot was dry it was clear the Whites wanted to be rid of their visitors.

'We mustn't keep you up late,' David said. It was ten past nine.

'No. We're early birds these days.'

The Randalls made arrangements to come again on Saturday morning to view the house by daylight. Until then the Whites would make no move towards selling the place.

They exchanged handshakes in the hall, before the door was opened to let the young people out and crabbed winter in.

'What do you think?' Alison asked, once they were in the car.

'Slightly overpriced.'

'Why is that?'

'They don't want to leave, feel that they have to be rewarded if they do.'

'What do you think?'

'I'd be inclined to buy, even though it's a buyers' market.'

'I liked the Whites,' she said. 'I know it's the house, not the occupants we're considering.'

'We'll get a surveyor in, see what he says.'

'Will your grandfather remember Mr White, do you think?'

'I expect so.' He might not, David thought. Memory played tricks.

On this unpleasant February night the streets were not short of traffic.

'I wonder where they've all been?' David mused.

'Out to change their lifestyle. Like us.'

'Well said, my girl.' They laughed together.

'You sound like your grandfather.'

XVII

Grandfather Randall eventually remembered James White. David gave some account of their attempt at house purchase, and when this was satisfactorily concluded with a quick-fire of questions from Polly, Alison said that White claimed to have been attached to George's squadron or wing. The three looked at the old man who sat there apparently making up his mind whether this needed an answer. He pursed his mouth, then stuck out the bottom lip comically and wetly. Polly laughed, copied him. Finally he breathed deeply in, rolled in his chair, grabbed a fistful of his trouser-leg in his left hand and spoke.

'What did you say his name was?'

'James White. J. E. R. White.'

He screwed his eyes and blubbered his lips again.

'Where at?' The words were short, almost as one, biblically antique.

'I think he said Watnall,' Alison offered.

George Randall now stroked his chin, deliberately slowly, before he committed himself.

' "Chalky" White,' he said. ' "Jerry" White. All Whites were "Chalky". All Millers "Dusty". A hangover from the days when the RAF was part of the Army. "Jerry" from his initials, I imagine. He must have been quite a bit older than I am.'

'He's eighty-two,' David answered. 'He told us.'

'Ten years. Has he worn well?'

'He looks rather delicate now.' Alison. 'You can tell he's old.'

'Tallish, thin man. Used to pull on his specs when he did his work. Didn't like wearing them.'

'Was he married then?' Alison asked.

'Can't remember. I never met his wife. Or if I did I've forgotten.' He frowned, rocking. 'He lived in the mess, I think. Didn't have a billet in the village.' Again the ferocious concentration. 'I'm not sure. No. Anyway, what does it matter?'

'He said you were a very good pilot,' David said.

'How would he know?'

'From what other people said,' David suggested. 'Or from the photographs brought back. Your accuracy on target.'

Grandfather Randall looked pleased, smirking.

'He used to attend briefings,' he said. 'I didn't have a great deal to do with him, personally.'

'But he remembered you.' Alison.

'How could he forget?' Polly, mocking.

The young Randalls reported this back to the Whites, who showed them round their garden on a bitter, bright morning, frost still lying in the shadows over the lawn. In the course of an explanation of his scheme of planting trees, White asked,

'I wonder if he'd like to meet?'

'You'd have plenty to talk about.' Mrs White, socially amenable.

'I'll give you his 'phone number.'

'Yes. Thank you. Is he married? I mean is your grandmother alive?'

'No, she died eight years ago. George married again. A very nice woman.'

'Younger than he is?' Mrs White.

'Considerably. Nearly twenty-five years.'

'She's able to look after him? Yes. It could be sensible.' She coughed. 'Just remember that when I die, Jim.'

'I shall go first. I hope I shall.'

They completed the circuit of the garden, then slowly round the house again, White interpreting. Again the slow coffee ceremony delayed them as the host explained to Alison exactly what his war work had been. He spoke rather hesitantly, with a frog in his throat, and with pauses as if he gathered his wits. Yet his account was clear, even interesting, though he made no attempt to conjure atmosphere. He mentioned death, but as a statistic the listener could construe as she pleased. He described a remarkable accident: a plane failing to touch down after an exercise actually rolled along on its own bombs and thus preserved the lives of its crew. He described the excellent meals provided for the airmen, who would be served three new-laid eggs when none was to be found elsewhere in the country. 'They didn't eat powdered egg, oh, no,' he said.

'Mrs Randall won't remember that,' his wife objected.

'Do you?'

'No. I've heard my grandmother talk about it.'

Once the young people were outside Alison asked her husband what White had done for a living.

'I believe he was in some sort of family business. Dyeing, bleaching, finishing. Or perhaps the manufacture of clothing. I ought to know. But I don't.'

'He doesn't talk about it. I mean it was all about his war service.'

'That's because of George. He's pigeonholed us as RAF types. That's our real connection with him, he feels.'

Alison giggled.

'Well?' he asked.

'We're discussing James White instead of the house.'

'Is that good or bad?' David sounded delighted.

She looked puzzled, gently straightening her hair with the tips of her fingers.

'Would you like that house?' he asked, seriously.

'Can we afford it?'

'Just about.'

'Oh. Ought we to wait a bit, then? For something more within our range?'

'If you're really taken with it, we'll have it.'

'That's not the sort of advice I expect from a solicitor.'

'Oh, solicitors are like everybody else. If we see something we really want we're willing to pay over the odds for it.'

'Then we're buying it?'

'If you really like it.'

'I really like it.'

'It's as good as yours,' he said, and kissed her in the street.

'What are we standing here for?' she asked. They were still on the pavement.

'Well, I was just wondering whether to give you the little lecture I give my clients about their house being the most valuable possession they're ever likely to have.'

'You give them this talk when you've only owned one little box of a house in your life?'

'I pontificate about divorce, and I haven't tried that either.'

'Don't.'

They kissed again, hoping that nobody watched but not much concerned.

At the beginning of March, coming in this year like a lamb, Grandfather Randall told them that he and Polly had, on invitation, visited the Whites.

'Success?' David queried.

'I quite enjoyed it,' Polly answered. 'I was curious, for one thing, about the house you were going to buy.'

'Did you like that?' Alison.

'Yes, it's beautiful. And you'll be able to decorate it and furnish it just as you wish.'

'We shan't be able to change much or afford furniture. Or not enough to fill the house.'

'You've got Vernon's sideboard. That'll half-fill a room,' George said. 'I reckon you bought the house to accommodate it.'

'Tell us about the Whites.' David brought the meeting to order.

Something of a quarrelsome silence marked the demand, then frowns, sniffs, coarse breathing from Grandfather.

'George and Mr White didn't altogether hit it off,' Polly ventured, lamely.

'Grandpa.' David wagged a finger.

'He's a miserable old devil,' George said. 'On about welcoming death, and all that sort of claptrap.'

Another pause. George seemed disinclined to say more.

207

'I thought you encouraged him when you looked at those photographs. "He was killed over Hamburg or Bremen or Wilhelmshaven or somewhere." The pair of you.'

'There was a high casualty rate in Bomber Command,' George said, mildly for him. 'That's a fact.'

Again the hiatus, the awkwardness, the sense that more was at stake than mere conversational exchanges. George, rousing himself, was the first to break in.

'I didn't like it. He kept saying that they'd had the best of it. These young men, David's age, and some a lot younger. Knocked off like flies.'

'He wasn't very well himself,' Polly objected. 'And it perhaps made him worse raking up these old memories. And perhaps he felt guilty. That he was alive and they weren't.'

'He should not expect me to subscribe to his rubbish.' The old schoolmaster.

'I don't think he did, George. He seemed to be talking to himself more than to us half the time.'

'Had he changed much? Would you have recognised him?' David intervened.

'Long streak of misery,' George glowered. 'No.' David could not tell which question the word answered.

'They made us very welcome,' Polly told them. 'They weren't very fit, Mrs White had a terrible cold and sore throat, and you could tell that they were upset about leaving the house. But they said they couldn't look after it properly, and how pleased they were you'd taken it. You were just the sort of people they had in mind. You'd know how to treat it. But I guess they felt low, poor old souls.'

'No reason for his behaviour,' George growled.

'Weren't they hospitable?' Alison.

'Yes,' Polly answered. 'They went out of their way. But Mr White, oh, told us some horror stories your grandpa didn't like.'

No more was said, but when David helped Polly to wash the crockery, she enlarged. 'He talked about having to shovel the rear gunners out of their aeroplanes after some raids.'

'I see.'

'And then he said something about the effect of bombing raids. You know, knocking down cathedrals and buildings that were priceless architecturally.'

'Gramps didn't like that?'

'When we were coming back home he grumbled. He was too occupied with flying and doing that properly, he said, to be concerned with consequences. And the fact that his life was on the line, that he could easily be killed at any minute, seemed somehow to balance the equation.'

'Don't you think he'd thought about this before?'

'I honestly don't know, David.'

'He never talks about it, then?'

'No, not much. But he was in London during the Blitz, I do know that. And he saw the ruins after the raids, and bodies being dug out. This was before he was a pilot, I think. So he must have had some idea.'

'He doesn't say anything now?'

'Very rarely. He'll tell you about his training and flying and so on.'

'It must have had some effect on him?'

'Must have done.' Polly's voice sounded clear, youthful, interested, but unconcerned. 'Mr White said, "You young men lived on the extremes of life," and George said, "They kept us at it." Just think of that. "They kept us at it." And on the way home he said one other thing. "Do you know, Poll, I was never once frightened?" and I said, "Was that unusual?" and he sounded very cross, "How the bloody hell do I know?" and I told him, because it doesn't do to let him have it all his own way, "You must know, George," and he said, "Some were, some weren't," and then in an out-of-the-way voice, "We're all different." It was as if he'd remembered something.'

'It's long enough ago.'

'That's what he said. You know what he can be like, all grum and gruff. But I'd sometimes thought of it myself in the same way that Mr White had, about these young men snatched out of ordinary life to live so dangerously and then when it was over sent back to be civilians again. It must have had its effect.'

'Do you think they'd become used to buckling their feelings back?'

'In some ways, but not altogether. George was terribly upset when he heard about Vernon's heart attack. He cried a bit.' She stood, a wet cup in her soapy hands, musing. 'Being a teacher must have been dull. I mean after all that excitement. And yet there he stuck, day after day, week in, week out, year by year with his algebra and geometry and trigonometry.'

'He and Gran went abroad for holidays?'

'Yes, they did. I don't think he enjoyed it much. He loved poking about in his garden. He still does. And when it gets beyond him, I don't know what will happen.'

'You think,' David asked, slowly, 'that his time in the RAF was the high point of his life? And that it's been downhill all the way ever since?'

'That's what he sometimes says.'

'And?' David laughed. 'But?'

'He was very successful at his job. His old pupils are always stopping him in the street and telling him how good he was. I know they wouldn't be likely to say anything else, but I'd guess it was true. He coached my two through O level and they weren't much good at maths. But it's the difference between murdering, being murdered and teaching people to solve equations.'

'Have you ever put it to him? As plainly as that?'

'Yes, but you know what he's like. He'll only answer what he wants to. Though one day he did tell me that quite a few of the people who taught him had been in the trenches in France in the First War.'

'Did they speak about it?'

'I think some of them did.' Polly shrugged as she packed away the final cups and saucers. 'But he said it made no difference that he could see. He couldn't tell who'd been in the war and who hadn't. Well, there you are.'

Polly unfolded and rebuttoned her cuffs.

'He'll be delighted in there, entertaining Alison. He dotes on her.'

'She's very fond of him,' David answered.

'He can't get over how learned she is, how much she knows. "And yet, she never throws her weight about," he says. I don't think he understands that sort of modesty. He's never known anyone as young as Alison who's such a master', Polly laughed in joy at her misuse, 'of her subject. She's not like his old colleagues.' Again Polly paused, stepped back, nodded. 'He really admires knowledge. Especially of literature and history. He reads quite a bit still. He belongs to that generation where the scientists were expected to know about music and art and poetry.'

'But not the other way about?' David interposed.

'You're worse than Vernon. I know these mathematicians are funniosities. I was quite good at school mathematics, but even there the teachers would miss two or three steps out and couldn't understand why they puzzled you. Why, that odd, old woman professor who came to your wedding. George had a word with her. "Couldn't understand a damn word she said. What she does doesn't sound like mathematics at all." He's always been a bit like that.'

'Is he keeping well?'

'Yes. He's seventy-two now. I suppose that's no sort of age these days. He's slower, but he can still go out and work in the garden. Hours on end.'

'Does he think about dying?' David asked, shocking himself.

'No. I don't think he does. I do more than he does. He's a lot older than I am, and I sometimes wonder what I'll do if he goes. But I don't think he's much concerned. He's not in a great deal of pain and he still has his wits about him. In small ways he's never got over Edna. It upset him when he thought Vernon could die. That didn't seem right. He's really proud of your father. I know they quarrel, and George says disparaging things, but he's proud.'

'Is life good to him?'

'He's not as energetic as he was. He's not short of money. He still has interests. His health's reasonable.'

'He has you.'

'Of course.'

'Is he different from what he would have been if he hadn't served in Bomber Command?'

'He must be,' Polly answered. 'But how can I judge? I wonder if it's left no more mark on him than, say, a hair-raising ride at Goose Fair. Except this one lasted for three years. But I guess, and it is only guesswork, that his personality was properly formed before he ever went up in an aeroplane.'

Polly took David's arm and led him lovingly back to the sitting room.

Alison and George were not talking but smiling. They looked up satisfied as the other two entered.

'Done all the work, then?' Grandfather asked.

'Yes. You two are very quiet.'

'We're thinking the more.'

'What about?'

George poked out a finger, half-closing his eyes, as if to a pupil who has raised some awkward objection but out of ignorance.

'Alison has been telling me about death.'

'What about it?' David, chirpily.

'Now then, young man.' George folded his arms. 'How people at different periods have looked differently on it.'

He said no more; Alison offered no gloss. The other two took to armchairs and entered the silence.

'Get yourself a drink, Poll,' George ordered. 'And one for David.'

'No thanks. I'm driving.'

'That's what Alison said. You can't both be. Is he a good driver, Alison?'

'Very.'

'Do you think you could fly an aeroplane still, Grand-pa?' David asked.

George pulled faces, clutched the clothes over his heart.

'Oh.' The single syllable moved from note to grunt to sigh. 'A year or two ago they invited us to some do, at RAF Wattersley, and they helped me up front in a Stirling. They had an exhibition. And I did begin to wonder if I could get it in the air.'

'And what conclusion did you reach?'

'It would have been very unwise to trust it to my tender mercies. But if the kite were already up and there was nobody else to do anything about it, then I probably could have made some sort of go of it.'

'Landing, you mean?'

'Yes. I'd done it so often. I'm slow now, and clumsy, and my co-ordination's not what it was, but if I had to put it down I reckon I'd be in with a fifty-fifty chance. It's forty-six years.'

'How did you feel to be in the pilot's seat?' Alison asked.

'You mean, was I excited? Or felt as I did when we were off on a mission? No. Not exactly. Far from it, in fact. I'd had to struggle a bit to get there, as I never used to even when I was all dolled up in my flying suit and three pairs of socks and the rest. But I was breathless. I knew I was an old man. Puffing and blowing. But I looked round the dials and knew what they were for.'

'Was there anyone there you knew?' David, hurrying him on.

'One old chap who said he knew me. I didn't remember him. I'd hoped my old navigator would have turned up, but he'd had a fall. He's a year or two older than I am. Very good man. We all thought he brought us luck.'

'Why, George?' Polly asked.

'He never had a scratch, even when his plane was hit. He was a decent stick, kept the lid on our pot. Cooled us down and gave us confidence. And we needed it sometimes. I don't think he ever got lost once.'

'Didn't that depend partly on information from others?' David asked.

'We all depended on somebody else.' He coughed. 'The foolhardy had to be pulled back and the timid pushed on.'

'What sort were you?' David again.

'Headstrong. Too much by half. But I learnt in time what I could do and what I couldn't. You had to. The consequences were dire if you didn't.'

George Randall became tired, dozing off once, and the visitors did not stay late.

Outside in the car the young Randalls summed their evening up, as usual.

'You don't get much out of him,' David said.

'You mean about his feelings?'

'Yes. He'll talk freely enough about the dials on the plane, or the instructors, or technical details, but not much about how he reacted.'

'And can you deduce something of his emotions from the way he talks, let's say, about the handling of a bomber?'

'I can't. No.' David spoke incisively. 'Ought I to be able to?' He received no answer as Alison sat waiting for him to pronounce. 'In my business people lie like mad to make their own side right. I was talking the other day about it to Donald Tait, the barrister, over lunch. "You have to try to judge, from what people tell you, how they'll react to some other matter you or they have never mentioned when the other side raise it in court." That was his line.'

'Does it happen often?'

'I shouldn't think so. It will depend what sort of case it is.'

'George was very good with me when we were talking about death. He was like a sixth-former with his questions. Eager.'

'And what conclusions did you draw from that?'

Alison pondered. David sat at the steering wheel, and they had not yet moved. Strapped in, they saw no reason to hurry their departure.

'Well . . . It was as if he'd considered this before, and here I was giving him chapter and verse for what he believed. We spoke about societies where there were duels, or about the many deaths in childbirth, when medicine couldn't save you from consumption. He asked me whether I thought the Victorians, for instance, grieved as much over the death of children, or if there were tragedies which one could never come to terms with, however common they were.'

'You told him what?'

'That I didn't know. To judge from literature, they did, but I can't say that that provides an accurate picture of

214

the rest of society. Dickens seemed never quite to have recovered from the death of his sister-in-law, a young girl who enjoyed an evening with them at the theatre and then suddenly collapsed and died. But he may have kept the wound open for his own purposes.'

'Literary purposes?'

'If you like. If you can divide the totality of the man into parts like that.'

'And Shakespeare?' David asked.

> ' "Grief fills the room up of my absent child,
> Lies in his bed, walks up and down with me
> Puts on his pretty looks, repeats his words . . ."

Shakespeare lost a young son, and will be making use of his own sorrow here, but the form is dictated by the literary conventions of the time. That's the way poets move people. Sometimes they extend these conventions, they have to, or brilliantly put those that already exist to their purpose. Ben Jonson and the poem on his son, his best piece of poetry. Bishop King and the Exequy on his Wife.'

'Don't know 'em.'

'I'll look them out for you.' She nudged him. 'Home, James. Don't spare the horses.' He set off, nodding. Once they were on the main road she continued the conversation as if there had been no break. He liked this, regarded it as a compliment. 'I'm always interested in what you make of these things. You've not had a literary background, or not much so, and it's fascinating to see what an intelligent but untrained reader finds in these verses.'

'And what conclusion have you reached?' David slowed for a cat, crossing the road, a low, swift shadow, black against the darkness.

'Nothing out of the ordinary. Just what you'd expect, in fact. One needs to learn, and to accept the validity of the convention before one can be really moved. And if one doesn't understand the mechanics of what's going on, one could easily find that the poet seems obsessed with the form to the detriment of the feeling.'

'Are some forms more suitable than others for one purpose or another?'

'You mean to express love or hate or grief or loathing? Yes, I suppose so. But it's impossible to be sure. There's no way of measuring emotion accurately. And one varies from day to day. What at one time appears unbearable one can easily put aside in other circumstances and ignore.'

They had arrived home. Alison opened the house, had the kettle on and the curtains drawn when he returned from locking the car away.

'Drink?' she asked.

'Bed.' He kissed her hair, pointed.

They made love. He groaned: his pillows toppled. When they had finished he held her naked to him. She seemed small, almost childishly dependent, very quiet, who a few minutes before had wildly commanded his climax.

'I suppose sex has its conventions,' he murmured, kissing her. 'And they vary.'

She did not answer, smiling with eyes closed.

XVIII

In early April Alison had an unexpected offer of a post in America for which Rupert Melluish, her former tutor, had recommended her. He had read her book for the OUP, had made sure the publishers knew its worth, and now wanted to see her established in the USA where she'd be 'appreciated'. He knew nothing of her marriage. He rang three times in a week.

'Don't be put off by stories of ignorant students. It's true they're less well prepared than English first-year people, but they catch up, and there's money about. But you'll have to make your mind up quickly. Our terms start earlier than yours.'

Alison consulted David and her professor Jack Ryder who, struggling with depression, seemed incapable of decision. The university had not decided whether to replace Melluish permanently, and in his present frame of mind Ryder would not fight for her. David, though supportive, was alarmed that she might be leaving so soon. He crept miserably about the house.

'If Ryder can't get you a job here, then you must take this American place.'

'I don't really want it, not now at any rate.'

'You must look ahead for yourself. Vernon spends a good deal of his time away from his wife, and that's considered proper. No, if Jack Ryder hesitates, you must be ruthless. I don't want to lose you, but I think you owe promotion to yourself, and it would be wrong for you to hang about here. Have one more go at Ryder, or I will, for you, and if he shilly shallies then you must pull up sticks.'

'It's not his fault, David. He'd give me a job if it existed. He's under pressure to economise. And he's so down, in every way.'

On the other hand the OUP had decided to change her publication date and Alison was already reading the proofs. This calmed her.

One morning, as David sat in his office, Frankland's secretary, Marilyn Wakefield, appeared with a long face. Sun sparked outside. Mrs Wakefield scented the room.

'Oh, Mr Randall, I've some bad news for you.'

He stood, fingers splayed on desk, head bowed, waiting.

'It's Mrs Frankland. She died in hospital in the early hours of this morning.'

'I'm sorry. I didn't know she'd been ill.'

'Apparently she has. For some months now. A gastric ulcer.'

'She looked quite well at our wedding.'

'She's been a sufferer for some time longer than that.' Mrs Wakefield sniffed. A large tear rolled out of her left eye. 'She had a massive haemorrhage.'

'Was she on her own?'

'No, her daughter was with her. She's apparently been staying with her mother for the last five weeks. Since her mother became so ill.'

'Mr Frankland hadn't mentioned this to me.'

'I don't think he knew. They kept in touch, you know, but not closely.' The woman now sobbed. David sat her in a chair, provided her with tissues and a glass of water. When she had slightly recovered, he asked if Frankland was in his office.

'Yes. He came in this morning at the usual time.'

As she staggered up, her face crumpled, and grabbing at him she howled like an animal in pain. David Randall enclosed her awkwardly in his arms. She was a solid woman, stronger and heavier than he had noticed. In time he returned her to the chair. She recovered quickly, apologising for her appearance.

'Is he still there?' David asked.

'I think so.'

'Has he any appointments?'

'Not until eleven.'

'I'll go across.' He straightened his jacket. 'You stay here until you're ready.'

Frankland's voice inviting him in seemed normal, but when David entered the room he found his principal standing by the windows staring into the folds of the lace curtains. He looked back.

'Ah, David.'

'I'm terribly sorry. I'd no idea Eleanor was so ill.' David could not bring himself to call his boss 'Albert', though he usually did so. The stiffly held shoulders, the neat, weary face and carefully combed hair, the well-cut, well-filled suit precluded intimacies.

'Yes, it's a shock to us all. She's been quite ill for some time. Jennifer has been staying with her this last month or so, and they've had a nurse in.' He looked down at his shining, nut-brown shoes. 'They didn't tell me.' His face seemed lifeless, drained, but he walked firmly across to his desk.

'Sit down.' He waved at the clients' chair, eased himself, straightening creases, into his seat.

'At the time of your wedding we began to see more of each other, and a reconciliation seemed possible. We visited, went out to meals together, enjoyed the company. But in the New Year we finally concluded it was useless, knew it without doubt. She said so. We did not decide on divorce. And then, I believe, she began to fail in health. My daughter, Jennifer, blames our decision for her deterioration. Jennifer is in some ways an unreasonable woman, but there may be some truth in her accusation.'

'How long is it since you saw your wife?'

'Over a month. In February. Six weeks. I arranged to see her as there were some documents to sign.'

'Was she ill then?'

'I thought so. She said not. We were very polite. She made it plain that she had no intention of returning to me. She said, "You have hurt me too badly." I blamed Jennifer for that. She had been working on her mother. At Christmas, why, we were utterly friendly.'

He talked about his daughter, a woman soured by her own matrimonial failures, who hated men. His sentences

219

were clear, without venom, offering facts. Frankland had nothing to reproach himself with as far as Jennifer was concerned, but she had deliberately turned his wife against him. 'It seems an unlikely scenario, David, but it is the truth.'

Suddenly Frankland tired of the conversation.

'Thank you, David, for listening to me. I'll leave Eleanor's will in your hands. It's quite without complications. I'll tell Jennifer to contact you.' He held his hand out, shook David's formally, led him towards the door by the elbow like a favoured client who needed comfort. 'Thank you, thank you. This has eased my mind. I am most grateful, most grateful. Now it's back to work.'

The door was opened; David found himself outside in the flagged passage. From the far end, at her desk, Miss Baines smiled sympathetically at him. His office was empty, Mrs Wakefield gone. He found Frankland's behaviour barely comprehensible. Later in the week, Hughes, a quite senior colleague, speaking of Eleanor's death and funeral, had muttered out of the blue, 'You know, of course, that he's been conducting an affair with his secretary for some years now.'

'Marilyn Wakefield?'

'The same.'

David felt suddenly helpless, ignorant. He had not known. She had divorced Wakefield. But there was another man, surely. Bolderstone? What did he think? Joe Hughes looked him over, lips pursed, the dry old stick personified. Why had Frankland, that pillar of society, needed this peccadillo, if that was the word. Had Eleanor known? Was that the cause of the rift? He tried to imagine Frankland, the lover, naked. Frankland needed a collar and tie to be himself, a background of law books or gracious living, a clubman's armchair or a seat on a committee. The sunshine mocked human endeavour. David took to his papers again with unaccustomed weariness.

Alison attended the funeral service with him. It was conventional to a degree; Jennifer Fisher followed the coffin on her father's arm, both faces hard, eyes lifted.

Black ties, black hats abounded. Mrs Wakefield sat two rows in front of the Randalls, dabbing at her eyes. The congregation sang the one hymn, 'Abide with Me', without fervour, in general embarrassment, leaving it to the organist, who obliged with constant variation. Expressions were solemn, as if people were not sure of themselves, of morality, of their judgements. Once people were outside the church, and the coffin and the close mourners away to the crematorium, life resumed, creakily, stiffly, with some shaking of hands, but with acknowledgement of the sunshine and the dart of spring wind among lilac bushes.

Jennifer Fisher rang David in his office.

'My father tells me you were to deal with my mother's will.'

David offered her his sympathy. She thanked him brusquely, made an uncomplimentary reference to her parents and continued.

'There will be no need for you to do anything. A month or two ago I took Eleanor down to see Tom Hooker and he made a new will for her.'

'Presumably your father didn't know?'

'He wouldn't have asked you in that case.'

She rang off. When David mentioned the call to Frankland, the principal answered, 'I'm not surprised. It won't make much difference. I arranged a decent division of the spoils when she first left. I expected her to outlive me. Jennifer would have urged her to cut me out, and now she's worrying that I shall get my own back in my own testamentary arrangements.' He laughed, not pleasantly. 'She needn't worry; I shan't leave my money to a dogs' home.'

Mrs Wakefield entered, carrying coffee. There seemed little warmth between the lovers, only customary, indifferent politeness. Were they acting their parts?

A week later David scowled at home. The Whites were moving out; his own house was up for sale, had been twice inspected by prospective buyers. Was it sensible to take over the new commitment when his wife was likely to move overseas. Contracts were now signed and exchanged. At least he and Alison could have a month or two together in The Hollies. He knew that the American academic year began and ended much earlier than the British so that she'd have a very brief summer vacation. He had tried not to dampen his wife's enthusiasm, had insisted, in his family lawyer style, that the house was a good investment even if he slummed it in the kitchen and one bedroom during her absence. Alison had remained cheerful; whether she emigrated or stayed to occupy The Hollies did not seem to have for her the gloomy importance he invested in the change. Their marriage would not last at this rate.

The telephone interrupted his misery.

'May I speak to Alison, please?'

He recognised the voice. Jack Ryder, Ally's professor.

'She's out. She's up at the university, attending some students' literary meeting.'

Ryder knew nothing of this. He wouldn't, idle bastard.

'I've some good news for her.'

David waited for expansion, received none, said nothing.

'I'd sooner break it to her myself, if you don't mind. Would you, please, ask her to ring me when she comes back?'

'Right. Many thanks.'

'Are you keeping well?' Ryder asked.

'Very.'

The broken exchanges did not continue long. David sat hunched by the 'phone, bent as if to ease a gripe in the guts. He wondered what Ryder's idea of good news was. Some doddering professor had whispered over his claret in an Oxbridge combination room that Alison's new book, read in proof, was the best thing of its kind since *Culture and Anarchy,* or *New Bearings.*

He stared down at the table, barely able to live with himself. That he could be brought so low surprised him, but gave no comfort. He had married, and now in August his wife would set out for America, leaving him to nurse his sorrow in a big, half-furnished house. He had never until recently taken the American venture as a serious possibility; it had been a well-deserved compliment to Alison's reputation as a scholar. And Ryder's good news? Perhaps he'd stirred himself and elicited a half-promise of a job from the authorities. David did not believe that, either. Ryder, for all his attractive attributes, could do nothing for them. He was weak, a yes man. It was even likely that he thought and would recommend the American move as the next and most sensible step in an ambitious career.

David's shoulders ached; his arms were weak.

He knew, he decided, how Vernon felt. Any minute the blow could fall, however well you prepared. For reasons unconnected with yourself the whole fibre of your life could be ripped apart. You watched it happen to a colleague, and then in turn you were flattened. It was no wonder that Vernon seemed to combine a spectacularly brilliant manner on screen with suspicious glances over the shoulder in private. He should have opted for a job like George's, with regular hours and pay, continuity, and, provided you kept your nose clean, a position until you decided to retire. That wouldn't have suited Vernon, who had recently been in the Middle East, then China, and only last week bringing a series of heartbreaking reports from the Horn of Africa. He needed to be on edge, nerves taut. He performed most masterfully when the ground slipped from under his feet. What the hell had that to do with him? David asked himself. And yet, yet, it was the work, the constant absence that had broken his marriage to Louise. Or so she claimed.

David pushed himself upright, examined his face in a mirror. It was his habit in a time of crisis. See if it has altered your face. He looked, tried a photographic smile. He appeared, as ever, healthy, sensible, bright-eyed, with smooth hair. With loathing he moved back from the reflection, and turned to face a print, quite sizeable, of rapidly dashed water-colour flowers, a marvellous lively design, tenuous and yet strong. Alison had bought it, 'for the space outside the painting,' she had said, donnishly.

223

He liked it, in its plain oak frame, for its bold vaguenesses. He wondered if she'd take it to Boston. They'd already decided its position in the new house, and the sort of wallpaper it needed behind it.

Rapping the surface till knuckles hurt, David pushed himself away from the table.

How did the young George Randall face the death of his friends? George, who'd stuck thirty-eight years in the same job? Your name was posted, he'd said, your briefing complete, you tested your plane, and in due course set off into the darkness, across flat land, black heaving sea, to bomb a place you knew nothing about. You might not return, and almost certainly one or two of those bright faces you'd sat with in the briefing room would be absent next day, burnt beyond recognition, bone-smashed in Germany, the Low Countries, the sea bed, at best prisoners of war.

David sipped coffee, tried whisky, failed again to work, laid the evening paper on his lap but did not open it. At twenty past nine, he had not even reached for the television switch, Alison returned, calling out.

He rose, put on the electric kettle. She joined him in the kitchen.

'Jack Ryder rang.'

'What did he want?'

'He had some good news for you.'

'Oh.' She waited. 'Well, come on. What was it?' Strain roughened her voice.

'He wouldn't say. Wanted to tell you himself. You're to ring him.'

'Tonight?'

'Tonight.'

Alison slowly removed her coat, and stood, garment dangling to the floor, indecisively.

'I wonder what it is.'

'Go and find out, woman.' George Randall's voice.

She threw her coat at him. He caught it adroitly, folded it. She slipped out. He closed her door not only to allow her privacy but to block him away from disappointment when it came. He opened up at the back, stared into the small patch of dark garden, the sodium lights above the walls. Cold dowsed him. Wind crackled from the northeast. It ought to be sheltered here with the flowering cherry trees and the many neat, convenient, expensive living-boxes like his own. He was a fool to loiter outside in his shirtsleeves on an April night. If Ryder's news had been bad he would have stood by Alison, face serious, ready with arm, advice, love, but as he expected nothing for himself and little for her in this call he had shut himself away and hung foolishly about in night chill. This admission sobered him. He stepped inside, locked and bolted the back door, switched the kettle on again, lined up mugs, coffee, milk.

Alison emerged perkily a minute later.

'It is really good news,' she said. He did not move, or speak. 'He's seen the VC and they're going to offer me a lectureship.'

'Going to?'

'It will be formally tied up on Friday.'

He stepped forward, threw arms round her, hugged her close.

'Congratulations.' They kissed. 'Are you pleased?'

'Of course. Steady, you'll break my ribs.'

'Shall I open a bottle?' he asked. She shook her head.

'No. Coffee will do.'

Alison explained the circumstances. The vice chancellor seemed keen to hold her now that the Americans had invited her. 'I'm informed,' he had said, 'that there's no one to touch her on your staff. Is that so?' Somebody, Ryder thought, had been at the VC. 'He remembers things, and he was in Oxford last week. Somebody had perhaps mentioned your book. Or somebody here had told him to ask about you. He loves to master the small print. To dazzle you with detail you didn't expect him to know existed.'

Wife and husband talked until midnight, too excited to make love until they went upstairs. This development needed lengthy talk. They could move into the new house. David, light-headed with happiness, drily discussed the date, the possibility of bridging loans, the possibility of speeding up the selling of this place. They kept their voices low but their marriage seemed secure. At eleven fifty they took to each other's arms and briefly danced their joy.

The next day brought further good news. Vernon, in with a short note saying he was flying back to Africa, enclosed a cheque for £5,000, 'to help furnish this new house'. It was not as much as he would have liked but he hoped they found it 'better than a poke in the eye with a sharp stick'. That evening they saw him in a television appeal among wasted African children, eyes terrified in old men's faces, strenuous flies invading closed lids. Though Vernon was moved, his voice warned strongly. He stood rock-solid among the scabby stick-legs, the ribs, swollen bellies, the flat empty breasts, the stricken-dumb burial parties, the ubiquitous dust. Now he spoke to the conscience of the western world, a voice crying in the wilderness to powerful effect.

The young Randalls compared their fortune with that of these broken souls and were silent. Both wrote cheques self-consciously.

On the following day Alison showed a colleague and her husband round the house in the morning, and by the afternoon they had decided to buy. As they lived in university accommodation and wanted a quick move, there would be no difficulties, no chain, speed. The husband knew his mind and drove straight off to see his solicitor.

David, delighted, rang Vernon's home, to speak to Karen, to thank her for his father's generosity. No one was at home. The answering machine was turned off. He tried two or three times in the next week, but contacted nobody. The George Randalls had no idea where Karen was, suggested that she had perhaps accompanied her husband to Africa. It seemed unlikely. In the end he wrote a letter outlining how he and Alison proposed to spend the gift, but received no reply.

XIX

On the first Monday in July, a morning sweltering with sunshine, the young Randalls moved into The Hollies.

Alison, still busy with end-of-term ceremonies and celebrations, at least had completed the marking and administration of finals papers. The move, both had taken the day off, was done with little fuss by professionals, so that early in the afternoon the pair sat alone in their new premises, in overalls, drinking coffee and eating ham sandwiches, almost straight.

The house sounded empty. Even the rooms they had furnished stretched enormous. David's stereo, whacking out Mozart's Fortieth, had resonated to advantage in the tall spaces.

Tired, and dusty, they perched delighted with themselves.

'It hasn't been nearly as difficult as I expected,' Alison said.

'We haven't had time to collect clutter. And we both have our own offices. Wait until we've been married twenty years.'

'Shall we last that long?' Her face was smudged with dust or cobweb.

'Enough of that sort of talk.'

Energetically they had scrubbed and polished and straightened. Polly 'phoned, then appeared.

'I knew quite well you'd say there was nothing to do, but I thought I'd better find out for myself. Anyway, George says you're to come to dinner tonight.'

Polly helped them vigorously for a couple of hours. Just before she left the three walked the garden together; David had been over twice a week since the Whites' departure to trim the lawns. Alison argued with him whether to employ a gardener.

'Ask George,' Poll advised. 'He knows what you need.'

'Are you sure?' David.

They laughed out loud by a concrete birdbath, ugly as sin.

The young couple cleaned up in the new bathroom, made love on the old bed, in the new amplitude, sauntered round their rooms, bare or not, hand in hand, children on holiday.

Polly met them at the back door, face serious. She ushered them silently into the smaller kitchen.

'George's had a 'phone call from Vernon. There's trouble between him and Karen.'

'When did he come back to England?'

'Two or three weeks ago. He only rang this evening. It's upset George.' Polly breathed hard. 'He likes me to listen in these days. "I'm so stupid," he says, "I might miss something." And he gives me a signal to go to the upstairs 'phone. I mustn't intervene, but I can take a note if I like. It's odd.'

'Well?'

'Vernon enquired how we were, and you and Alison. As usual. He talked a bit about his travels. Doesn't say much. Your grandpa told him we'd seen him rather a lot on television. It was the ordinary sort of conversation we have with him. He doesn't boast. And then, suddenly, he said, "Karen and I aren't getting on too well. In fact, we're living apart now." He was vague. George pressed him about the cause of the trouble, but all he would say was that they had got on one another's nerves. George spoke quite sharply, "But you're never in company together," and Vernon laughed and said that was perhaps the trouble. He didn't seem put out. A bit subdued, perhaps, but not much different from his usual self.'

'How long have they been married?' Alison asked.

'Nine years,' David answered.

'Yes. All of that. It was before Edna died. She went down to London for the wedding, though she wasn't very well. I don't like to guess at these things, but I think George connects their wedding with her and it's, I know this sounds daft, it's a slap in the face for her if they break up.'

'Has he said as much?' David asked.

'In a roundabout way. I can put two and two together. Anyway, he's very down in the mouth, so it's a blessing you've come. He needs somebody to cheer him up.'

In the large sitting room George Randall hunched his shoulders in his armchair, his red face shapeless with trouble. He acknowledged their greetings with a violent heave of his buttocks upwards from the seat and a grunt.

Alison gave a brief account of their move to The Hollies but he listened with impatience, furious fingers drumming on his knee, breathing stertorous. He made no attempt to offer drinks, or polite answers, but rolled uncomfortably in his chair. When Polly, almost immediately, called them in to dinner, he staggered to his feet.

'You've heard what this bloody fool of a father of yours is up to?'

'Yes. Polly told us.'

'What do you think then?'

'I was surprised. I hadn't known anything. Though I couldn't get hold of Karen when I tried to ring through.'

'It was a shock to us all,' Polly said pacifically.

'It was typical of him.' Grandfather growled to himself rather than at his listeners. 'He has to live like a programme on his bloody television. He can't settle. He has to stir the waters, shift everybody about, make it interesting. Nothing can last. If it goes on for more than ten minutes he dismisses it as boring.'

'He's been married nine years,' David mildly objected.

'Nine years. Nine minutes. That's about the time he was married to your mother. What are we standing about for, woman? These young people will be hungry.'

George ate vigorously as if to relieve his ill-temper by champing at his food. He greatly enjoyed his meals, they knew, but there was no pleasure for him this evening. Polly invited him to a second helping of meatballs and rice in a rich, reddish gravy.

'I couldn't, Poll. I'd choke.'

'You needn't eat fast. You can take your time.'

229

'My mother,' George said, 'used to call it "golloping it down". That's better than "gulp" don't you think?' He grinned at Alison.

'Are you having any or not?'

'You've twisted my arm.'

His anger had abated; he ate and leaned back. At the end of the meal he congratulated Alison on staying in the city.

'I didn't much care for your going to America. It does me good just to see you, even if we don't exchange a word. And I don't suppose I've much of life left. Once you get to my age, the slightest ache or pain might be the beginning of the end.'

Polly aped a cinema violinist at a tear-jerking waltz.

'You'll learn, my girl,' George told his wife, but without venom. 'And before too long.'

'You must come and see the new place,' Alison said.

'I've been. We went to see the Whites there.' He coughed. 'How are they shaping? In the flat?'

'We've not heard.'

'We ought to invite them here,' Polly said.

'Must we? I thought he was a miserable old devil.' He shook a warning finger at Polly, who giggled.

'You'll see it in its new, emergency state.' David spoke firmly. 'We haven't started decorating yet.'

'Very sensible. When we moved into this house we didn't do anything straight off, except keep the wind and rain out. It was in a hell of a mess, nothing done to it during the war. An old couple had it, and they practically lived in two rooms.'

'Did you enjoy setting it right? In the end?' Alison asked. He blew breath out.

'In some ways. It took years. We'd repair a room, then decorate it. A long campaign, and it's like the Forth Bridge. You need to start again as soon as you finish.'

'Did Grandma have ideas?' David.

'Oh, yes. Very much so. "I'm going to be here all day." That was her line. And she was a beautiful painter. Much better than I was. Basically, she was in no hurry. She'd prepare carefully. That's the secret. And later we had to replace the roof, and the windows, and have a new damp-course and central heating and double glazing.'

'You did all those things yourself?'

'You flatter me, Alison.' He clapped his chest. 'No. We had people in. I hadn't all that amount of leisure. I used to take two night-classes. We did it, a bit at a time, as and when we could afford it. When Edna's mother died that gave us money to play with, and we bought quite a large piece of the garden next door.'

'Did you never think of moving?' Alison again.

'Thinking was as far as we went. We talked about it. This house has its drawbacks. It's right on the main road that side. And it's old. Needs repairs and replacement. But it's roomy. Warm in winter now, cool in summer. And it has the two orchards and plenty of space. That's going to be a problem before too long. It's a struggle now. But I might well snuff it before it gets beyond me.'

'And what happens then?'

'Poll can sell it, or employ a gardener or find herself a toy-boy. I shan't put any restrictions on her.'

'Do you like this house, Polly?' David asked.

'I love it. I've only lived in convenient, modern places. It gives me something to occupy me.'

'You enjoy housework, then?' Alison.

'Not really. It has to be done. But apart from the lawns and flowerbeds, I keep looking round indoors, rearranging it, redecorating . . .'

'I can never find anything where I left it,' George grumbled.

'That's not right. I never touch your study or any of your outhouses.'

' "And the band played 'Believe it if you like' ",' George trumpeted.

The meal ended in laughter. When David said they ought to go back, George shouted,

'To see nobody's burgled it.'

'They won't find much.'

'What are we going to do with that father of yours?' Grandpa Randall asked at the back door.

231

'I'll ring him, shall I?' David.

'Yes. But what will you say to him?'

'That I don't know until I've heard his story.'

George blew out his lips in derision.

'Off you go home,' he ordered, 'before it rains.'

Clouds blew across the full moon. It might have been March or April.

Inside the next few days David's attempts to reach his father by 'phone failed. Taking Alison's advice he wrote short notes to Vernon and to Karen, offering to help if that was possible.

His stepmother replied first.

The letters, she said, had been forwarded. She did not mention when. Vernon was away, she understood, in Northern Ireland. This worried her. She had taken a convenient flat in Hampstead, and travelled daily to Earl's Court, where she was busier than ever. This was a blessing. She had no communication with Vernon, but he had readdressed David's letters. She was occupied, and passed her free days with friends or relatives. Their invitation to spend a weekend in the new house sounded most attractive, and she'd take them up on it before too long. She thanked them both for their kindness.

'She doesn't say anything about the trouble between her and Vernon,' Alison said.

'Perhaps she's giving him first shot.'

'Do you think she'll tell us about it when she comes here?'

'I don't know whether she'll come.'

Karen immediately telephoned Alison to ask if she could spend Saturday and Sunday with them. She would arrive, it was arranged, for lunch.

She ate heartily, drank two large glasses of wine, and seemed in no way uncheerful. They spoke mostly about their occupation of the new house, their plans, about the three weeks Alison had arranged to spend in Rome.

'It must be exciting,' Karen pressed.

'We haven't properly learnt to live in this house yet. We're both busy at our jobs. David has a murder trial on his hands. My book comes out this autumn.'

'Have you started another?'

'I've two essays sent off to editors to be published this year, both written in a hurry . . .'

'Both admirable,' David intervened.

'. . . and I've started thinking about a book on drama, and am making an anthology of Elizabethan and Jacobean criticism, and an edition, or rather a selection, of Skelton. These last two are commissioned.'

'I don't know how you manage all that and can still cook delicious meals.'

'David did most of it.'

'He's not like his father then.' The reference was made without difficulty.

'My mother wouldn't allow him anywhere near the kitchen.'

'He was in no hurry to invade mine.'

They talked at length, walked the brown length of the garden where summer burnt again, and where Karen said, only when asked, that she would like to see George and Polly, because she loved them.

'They seem very English. My grandparents were continental, and Jewish. That was colourful to me as a child, with a string of relatives dropping in with their foreign languages and odd foods and outlandish clothes.'

'Did you keep up any religious observance?'

'Not at all. My parents never went to the synagogue, even for burials. I attended school assemblies, nativity plays, carol services, the lot. But they kept their name, Lodtz, didn't change it to Lowe or Loder or Letts, and my brothers were both circumcised. My mother and father had English accents, thought of themselves as English.'

'Weren't they reminded of their origins by all these relatives?'

'I suppose so. And I imagine we visited the continent more frequently than most English children. I mean, not just a fortnight on Spanish beaches.'

Though Karen was fair-haired, her eyes were dark; the only exoticism the brightness of her neat clothes. The three sat in the drawing room watching sunlit leaves wilt

233

on the limes outside. They talked about David's work and then Alison instructed them on Montaigne and Florio, the subject of one of her essays, and Karen described the dull, necessary work she did at the television centre. David phoned to George Randall; Polly insisted that they attend for high tea at five thirty.

'She thinks you need feeding,' David told Karen.

'I'm slimming like blazes.'

'To good effect,' he said, courteously. She was thirty-five, looked younger.

Karen put a hand flat on each arm of her chair, straightened her back.

'I suppose you're wondering what the trouble is between Vernon and me.' David inclined his head as if acknowledging the wisdom of a client to speak frankly. 'It's all very banal, really.' She seemed to concentrate on Alison. 'It was this heart spasm, attack. I was busy at the time. The drama department had tremendously full schedules. Those three big Shakespeares, with no theatrical production behind them, and the Chekhov festival, and Part I and II of Goethe's *Faust*, though that fell through, and a Beckett cycle and six new plays, Potter, Bond, you've read all about it, I expect. It drove me mad, and then suddenly Vernon cracked.'

She paused, put hands between knees, dropped her head.

'You won't like this,' Karen continued, 'but I couldn't get the idea out of my head that somehow he'd managed, imagined, cooked up his illness to get in my light, to stop my working. He never thought much of my backstage administration; that's what he called it. It suited me; I had to deal with people, talented, wayward men and women who were used to their own way. Organising scripts and schedules and playwrights and directors and players and musicians at the right time so that all fuses together in the end is no simple matter. It's not creative; it ought not really to be necessary after the first shot, but it's my sort of work. I'm immersed in it; it fulfils me. And I don't think I'm exaggerating at all.'

234

'And you think Vernon deliberately. . . ?' David began. Karen quietened him with a hand.

'No, I don't. It isn't possible. He had this heart attack. Chiefly because he worked too hard, put himself under too much stress. I can't doubt it. Even Vernon, and he's a great actor when he thinks fit, couldn't sham to that extent. And yet, and this is the point, I could actually think, feel this because it came so inconveniently for me, that he was trying to obstruct my career.'

'Was he jealous?' David asked.

'Jealous? Not of the sort of thing I was doing. It was quite important, he'd admit that, and necessary, but anybody with a smattering of intelligence or common sense or care could do it. No. He resented the time I spent on it, and not on him. Or that was my conclusion.'

'Was it the truth?' Alison asked, bright-eyed.

'We lived a decent life, I'd thought. Did things together when Vernon was home, discussed our interests, talked about you two like good old-fashioned parents, though I'd no right to do it. We could combine well. We'd money and a well-stocked freezer and room to entertain. We complemented each other. We went out to meals together. Of course, we had rows. Everybody does. Differences of opinion. And I tried to slow him down, make him treat himself more easily, but I see now I wasn't serious, I didn't mean it.'

'Didn't . . . ?'

'No. Vernon had to do his thing, racing about the world, chopping and changing at the last minute, holing up in inconvenient and dangerous places. A colleague was killed right in front of his eyes.'

'Yes, we heard . . .'

'I thought he could stand it, take any amount of stress. Then when this attack came, I knew that if he didn't carry on as before he'd be under pressure from himself. He was obsessed with the notion that if you didn't appear on the screen you'd be forgotten. Ask people about the famous television names of twenty, or ten, years ago. Youngsters have never heard of them and those older people who have

235

are vague. So he pushed on, and I nagged and that put us at odds.'

'What should you have done that you didn't?' Alison asked.

'If I had given up my job and stayed at home to look after him, I think he might well have slowed down. That's why I say I wasn't serious.'

'That's not very fair on you,' Alison said. 'And wouldn't there be a considerable drop in income?'

'Yes, but we could have managed. But he was right when he thought I wasn't prepared to give my work up permanently.'

'Why should you?'

'Why indeed? But that's what marriage is about. Making disagreeable decisions to suit somebody else. And it's more often the woman who has to make them. The man earns more, usually. What makes it even sillier in our case is that there aren't any children. That would have altered the situation in my case. At least I think so. I felt guilty, I can tell you. And that made it worse, so that the quarrels, not about the real difference, but about all sorts of little things: meals, clothes, theatres, oh God, anything and everything. In the end I couldn't stand it, and walked out.'

'Did you feel guilty about that?' David asked.

'No. Intense relief. I feel a twinge or two now, I suppose, but not at first. Just to be out of his way. I went to a friend's, and then she found me a flat near hers. Vernon was abroad. I had a week.'

Alison felt the pang as Karen wept; her eyes brimmed, briefly overflowed. Her voice and demeanour otherwise seemed composed. They made her sit on a deckchair while David trimmed his lawns and Alison hacked away in the borders. She seemed comfortable enough, even dropping asleep.

Before five they went indoors to clean up. Parked in the back lane behind George Randall's garden, Alison, who had driven them, and sat with Karen, said,

'Well, here we are.'

Karen placed a hand on Alison's. She seemed fearful.

236

'Don't worry. You say what you like.'

'It's what they'll say that's worrying me.'

'No, no, Karen.'

'They won't tell me anything about myself that I haven't told myself.'

'It's Vernon they're likely to be rude about. Especially Grandpa. And that might be harder for you.'

Karen shook her head.

The back gate was not open so they grumbled and walked round two sides of a triangle of road. The kitchen smelt deliciously of Poll's cooking. New bread, sponge cakes, parkin, cheese straws.

'Are you desperately hungry,' Polly asked, 'or would you like Georgio to lead you round the estate first?'

'I'd like the walk,' Karen decided, as the other two gestured their deference to her. Polly hugged her again. To see the women clasped comforted Alison.

George Randall roused, stumbled up, to kiss Karen and Alison, said he didn't need a jacket because it was July and led the two women out together.

'We're forgotten,' Polly said to David. They let the others climb ahead into the garden; she questioned him about Karen and Vernon. He told her what he knew. Still in the yard, she listened, questioning.

'So she blames herself?' she queried in the end.

'That's so. At least to us. I'm never sure, of course. People are so mixed up that they can't be sure what's happening.'

'Don't they usually blame the other party?'

'Well, yes. But not always. I imagine this has been going on in small ways, for a considerable time. They wouldn't quite realise how bad it all was. And then comes the heart attack, and Vernon wants her to drop everything and look after him.'

'I thought she did. For a start.'

'I think that's right. But after a week or two she couldn't see any sense in hanging about the house waiting for the next attack. Especially as he was back at work.'

'Did money come into it?'

'She said they could live on Vernon's income. But she'd need a job if he died or was thoroughly incapacitated.'

They looked about once they were into the garden proper but could see nothing of the others through the thick foliage, nor hear their voices.

'My flowers,' Polly directed. 'George will be fine with his young ladies.'

She led him to the bed in front of the house, bright now with rock-roses, cistus, eschscholtzia, ladybird poppies, delphiniums, brilliant Kassel, Penelope and Celeste in superabundant masses. A sprawling buddleia alternifolia scented the whole garden, with lilies, pinks and peonies.

'Gorgeous,' he said. 'Are you out every day?'

'Weather permitting. An hour or two anyway. Especially this summer.'

'Does Grandpa intervene?' David asked.

'No, he's surprisingly tolerant. I was a bit anxious at first, but he said, "That's your province, my girl." Of course he makes suggestions. But he's old-fashioned. New things or very old ones reintroduced don't interest him so much. He encourages me to play about with catalogues and drive off to garden centres or nurserymen.'

She looked at two flat, saffron clouds of yarrow.

'That's a marvellous colour. So clean. And look at the size of those foxgloves.' These spired to nine feet.

'Aren't they wild flowers?' he asked.

'Not now. We're all growing our own cowslips. Sit down.' She pointed to a seat under a huge philadelphus, not yet blossoming. 'He's extended my province. I don't think your gran was very keen on gardening though she did come out here.'

'I think she knew a fair amount.'

'I see. I thought she was a hybrid-tea-rose lady.'

'Ought we to follow the others?'

'No.' Polly answered with firm alacrity. 'He'll enjoy every minute of their company, explaining how he can't do this and that, but boasting how much fruit we shall have in the autumn, and the cunning ways he's subverting obstacles.' She used the verb, lifted from her husband, without embarrassment. 'And I shall know how much he's enjoyed himself because he'll tell me all about it, drag it up at every verse end. "I was only saying to Alison when she was with me in the orchard the other night . . ." ' The imitation fell wide of the mark. Both laughed.

'He's full of life,' David ventured.

'Yes. But he's slowing down. I can see it. But he enjoys every day. He comes to terms with it, if you understand me. Even when you arrive at my time of life, you find friends and acquaintances dying off on you.'

'And? It worries you?'

'By and large you occupy yourself with something else. A girl who was my best friend at school died last week. Cancer. She was forty-eight. I can't help wondering how she felt. She'd want to live as much as I do. Unless there'd been too much pain or distress. I was surprised. I hadn't heard anything. She wrote a bit on her card last Christmas. Her daughter rang me. And they can do such marvellous things about cancer these days.'

'Where did she live?'

'Cheltenham. Her husband was a doctor.'

David mentioned Eleanor Frankland's death.

'What did she die of?'

'A perforated ulcer, I think. We went to the funeral. It was a drab affair. She'd separated from her husband.'

'But she was here with him at your wedding?'

'Yes. She'd been away some time then. Ally met her by chance in the Park, and I went to visit her for Frankland when she changed her address. At the time of our wedding they both thought or hoped there was a chance of reconciliation.'

'What was wrong with them, between them?' Polly lifted herself from the seat with straight arms like a child with surplus energy. 'You'd think that after they'd been married all that time they could have stuck it a bit longer.'

'Yes. It puzzled me. She seemed thoroughly respectable, compliant. Not an ounce of revolt in her. But she cleared off, with the help of her daughter. I can't see any advantage to her, unless she just could not stomach a minute more of poor old Frankland.'

'It took her long enough to find out.'

'But she had at least the wit to see he'd treat her decently. I'm not sure how much money of her own she had. The house certainly was in his name only. Odd, because we always advise clients to hold property in their joint names.'

'Would she have gone if she hadn't been financially independent?'

'I don't know. She'd have had to throw herself on the mercy of her daughter, and, as far as I can make out, she's a pretty unpleasant sort. She encouraged her mother to leave, but I don't think she would have been mad-keen on supporting her, even if she had the means. But if Albert was driving his wife mad, I mean beyond all reason, then she'd shoot off whatever the consequences.'

'What's wrong with him?'

'Dull.'

'I thought he was clever.'

'He's that all right. And thorough. A first-rate lawyer. But dull. He'd be a man of habit in the house. Pipe and slippers except he didn't smoke. And if it was a case of home on time or some piece of work to finish or some important client to see, home would lose.'

'Had he a mistress, David?'

'That's the office rumour. I don't know the truth.'

'But his wife? She went, didn't she? She'd had enough. Why?'

'I don't know.'

'Was it a warning?'

'If it was it misfired. She may have intended it that way, and then she found she much preferred being on her own.'

'What was their house like?' Polly asked.

'Beautiful. Spacious. Bigger than this. Always plenty to be looked after. Good furniture, polished to the nines. Pictures. And whenever I went, winter or summer, the place seemed full of cut flowers.'

'Bought?'

'They must have been, in the winter.'

'Was she a nice woman?'

'As far as I could tell,' David answered. 'I like Frankland for that matter. He does me well, and he knows his way round. And if he gives me a job he won't interfere.'

'Even if you're doing it wrong?'

'He's not likely to know, unless somebody makes a complaint at the time or there are unpleasant consequences for the firm.' David breathed the sensuous warmth and comfort of the evening. The sounds of traffic could be disregarded. 'I liked her. She seemed sensible and pleasant, motherly, but she walked out.'

'Was it the daughter?'

'She'd poke her oar in. And she'd be a feminist. Insist that her mother had rights. But Eleanor knew all that. If her daughter did influence her unduly, and I don't know that that's the case, it would only be because Eleanor was off balance already.'

They talked easily. Polly, asked about George, gave her opinion that though her husband spoke often about death, he never seriously considered it, that he was basically too well.

'I don't know what would happen if he was really ill.'

'He wouldn't be a very good patient?'

'I wonder if he'd want to live. I mean . . . Oh, I don't know what I'm talking about. After all he's survived all sorts of changes. Flying, then schoolmastering. He had to give them up. And bereavement. Edna died. But he was younger and more resilient. He's a survivor. Or lucky. He can't understand Vernon's heart attack. "At his age," he says. "He can't have been living sensibly." But I dread to think what he'd be like if ever he is properly incapacitated. He'd prefer death.'

Polly's face screwed with pain.

'You can't say that. We don't know.' David spoke calmly.

'I suppose not.'

She was tranquil again. A mechanical roar from close by ripped evening calm. 'The man next door,' Polly said, 'and his motor mower. His garden's about an eighth the size of this, but he's bought one of these machines he can sit on. I know the garden's mostly lawn, but . . . George thinks he's daft. "There's Sir Malcolm Campbell," he says. He's a funny little man. On a night like this, he'll be wearing a collar and tie and a trilby hat. And there he'll sit, arms stuck straight out on these handlebars, up and down the lawn at three miles an hour. "More like the royal bloody coach," George says.' She stood, dragged David upright by the hand. 'Come and have a look.'

'How old is this paragon?'

'Late sixties. Seventy, perhaps.'

'Does he have a little moustache?'

'How did you know?'

They crept, still hand in hand, through a rockery, past a soft-fruit cage, to the boundary where from behind weigela and berberis and a fence they could catch glimpses of the neighbour cutting his grass. He sat upright, glasses awry; the trilby hat was chocolate brown, perched askew. As he approached them, and they were no more than five yards from him, they could hear above the metallic din of his engine that he was singing. Words emerged; he attempted fortissimo, reedily.

> 'And the man at the wheel
> Was having a feel
> At the girl I left behind me.'

Polly clapped a hand over her mouth, eyes wide in unexpected delight. They waited for his next run past but this time he made infantile revving sounds to outsoar the even cacophony of his machine. On the next turn they caught only 'the girl I left behind' (three swanking syllables in arpeggio) 'me.' He stopped the mower in midcourse, removed his hat, and wiped his sweaty forehead with a dirty handkerchief. He had stepped down so they could see his baggy grey trousers, black polished shoes, buttoned jacket, collar and prim tie.

The voyeurs crept away, grinning, hot, satisfied.

'What do you think of that?' Polly asked.

'Does he usually sing?'

'I've never heard him before. But the words? I didn't think he'd sing anything like that.'

They moved towards the path by which they expected George to return with his escorts. No breeze disturbed the apple trees; a glowering cherry spread behind them, immobile, beautiful. The moving machine tore again at the still air.

'The old salt's off again,' David said.

'I didn't think he'd know such songs. And his wife's so very proper.'

'What did he do for a living?'

'I think he was a headmaster at a junior school. No wonder they say standards are falling. George despises him.'

'The singing lessons would be good, though,' he teased her.

'The dirty old man.'

Suddenly they heard George's voice laying down the law. The three appeared, both women laughing.

'Forward, ladies,' George shouted. 'We're hungry, Poll.'

'Has he behaved himself?' she asked Alison. 'You can't trust the old men round here.'

She explained herself to her husband who lifted comical twiddling fingers devil-fashion at each side of his head.

XX

Between them they persuaded Karen to spend another night in Beechnall.

She slept late on Sunday morning, loitered an hour in the garden, then took the hosts out to lunch. In the afternoon they drove to the Dukeries and walked in blistering sunshine across Rufford Abbey park and afterwards in the shadows of Sherwood Forest. Back home by seven thirty they drank tea, ate new bread sandwiches, talked out in the garden, swilling gin. David spoke about his murder case and how the barrister proposed to defend the client. Both were sorry for the youth; both were sure he would lose. Karen talked of the preparations for next year's work, and surprised them with her sharp sketches of an actor they all admired. Alison explained how she would spend her time in Italy.

'I feel exhausted and lucky. I've so much to do. People are beginning to hear about me.' Immodesty sounded the opposite.

'Quite right,' David said, fuddled already.

'Requests and commissions for essays and articles keep arriving, and I try not to let them stand in the way of the book I'm writing, so I have to divide my time sensibly. Sometimes David doesn't see me properly for days on end. But he's very good about it.' Alison stretched to touch his hand. 'He understands my compulsions.'

'And will you manage to complete all the commissions?' Karen asked. 'I mean, doesn't the teaching interrupt you?'

'It does. But it's part of my motivation. I like it. I like explaining matters to pupils . . .'

'Clever ones?'

'Yes, but not mainly. To see to it that some not really bright student can come to grips sufficiently with a tricky topic to score, let's say, a low 2.1. on it, I'm sorry to talk like this, is rewarding. But I regret the time it takes.' Alison paused. 'And there's one other thing.'

'Now the dirty secrets are coming out,' David said.

'I ought, I want to write a big book about my subject. It's all vague as yet, but it would roughly be about the effect of the Renaissance in Europe on England. Something like that. It would take me several years, even with sabbaticals.'

'Don't your bits and pieces, your essays and reviews and your lectures, help prepare you for this?'

'Yes.' She answered her husband gravely. 'But I have to write about what my immediate clients want, and that often means disregarding matters I consider important, but which would be irrelevant or beyond their scope. But . . .' She held up a finger.

The gin had affected them all. Karen giggled.

'Proceed.' David, raising his glass.

'I think it's the puritan in me, but these, these obstacles, detours, petty frustrations should in the end make it possible to complete the big book. Not because they give you a wider view, but because, provided they are not allowed to proliferate, they limit your time. And that, if you're really motivated and prepared, is the proper foundation for the long haul. You concentrate on essentials and this is most important in a large work rather than a small.'

'Why? If I may ask.' David again.

'You think a big definitive book is just a small book with more examples or provisos. It may be that. But I don't want mine to be. Illustrations, yes, but only when they're necessary to make my point.' She smiled, then allowed her lips to pout. 'That's what I aim at. Size is determined by scope.'

'It must be marvellous to have such an objective,' Karen said, admiringly.

'Yes. As long as I can keep a sense of proportion. The more I learn the more ignorant I realise I am. But I must keep firmness even about that, not let it deter me, or distract from the original scheme.'

'And won't there be modifications of the scheme as you go along?'

'Certainly. But you must retain overall shape. Otherwise you'll finish with huge slabs of information randomly processed, merely strung together.'

'Aren't there many books exactly that?' David asked, interested in the shift of pronouns.

'I'm afraid so.'

This exposition, shapeless itself, was repeated, giving pleasure. They laughed, loud as earlier church bells, basked relaxing in evening warmth and good company. The young Randalls were not unduly surprised when Karen put down her glass, and with a straight face asked,

'Tell me. Should I go back to Vernon?'

The young people did not answer immediately. David looked down deep into his gin, swirling the lemon slice.

'You advise her, darling,' he said to Alison after a long silence.

'If, as you claimed, you can't stand the sight of him then it wouldn't be much use, would it, however good your intentions? After a short time you'd be in the same quandary.'

'Unless you detect some change in yourself.' David.

'How would I know?'

'It can't be very marked if you don't notice it.' Alison, waspishly.

'You may see the change when you're back and putting it to the test.'

'Is that a lawyer's advice? Is that what you'd say to me if I was your client?'

'It's true that lawyers do hand out advice of that sort, but that's not really what we're there for.' David deliberately veered away from Karen's first query. 'It's our job to ask a great number of questions about financial arrangements, property and so on, to check the answers, and then make sure that the client hasn't done himself/herself irreparable harm by the method of running out or staying put. We deal with what the law says. We concern ourselves with a client's interests, because at a time like this, matri-

246

monial failure and break-up, there is invariably stress, of many sorts, and distress, and the person may, therefore, act foolishly. Agree to anything to escape the hated partner. I must make sure that the other side does not profit, or take advantage of this. This isn't always popular. You'll hear people claim that the break-up of their marriage became more hurtful because greedy lawyers insisted on extracting every pennyworth the law allowed.'

'Is that the truth?' Alison now, leaning back, arms chastely crossed.

'Sometimes. It's mainly women who have to be defended financially against husbands, and I know quite well that the probing can have distressing emotional consequences. But in my experience, and I admit that's small, very much more good than harm comes of it. I haven't mentioned children because you and Vernon have none. They complicate matters. But there it is better to have the whole business settled by outside parties, according to the law.'

'But this other sort of advice you give?' Karen asked.

'Yes.' David appeared serious beyond his years. 'Let me put it simply. Now and then we have to convince ourselves that what our client really wants is a divorce.'

'Don't they know?' Alison asked.

'Not always. Something's blown up. There's been a row. The woman, usually, but not always, feels a big gesture is necessary. And I act as the bogeyman for her. In the ordinary way one consults a solicitor only after a long period of quarrels, then compromises, domestic attempts to set things right. People on the whole, even in these days, hang on to their marriages.'

'Because separation might prove worse?' Alison.

'No. I guess people take marriage seriously. They mean what they say. I know you're going to tell me that one in three fails. That's true. And it's probably good rather than otherwise that the law makes this possible. But it's my impression that most people when they marry do so in the expectation of staying that way.'

'Is your impression to be taken seriously?' Alison teased.

'No. Nor is it quantifiable. And I don't know whether, say, Albert Frankland would have the same opinion. I'm a young starry-eyed newlywed and I see what I want to see. Frankland's old, and his wife suddenly left him, and then died. It makes a difference.'

Alison put out a hand in his direction, but he was now beyond arm's reach.

'And what about me? Am I serious about it, walking out as I did?' Karen asked.

'I'm in no position to judge. But I can well imagine that marriage to Vernon isn't a sinecure. His life's full; his job is utterly satisfactory in that it's fascinating, obsessional, highly paid and well regarded by society. And he has behind him a devoted team, or one that gives that impression. And he needs that at home for his few moments of leisure. He'll be selfish because he lives in a world where he must put Number One first; otherwise somebody else will clamber above him. Furthermore, he's not sure of himself.'

'In what way?' Karen, sharply.

'He from time to time can hear the voice of Grandpa Randall.'

'Saying what?'

'Suggesting that what he's doing is nothing much after all. That's what you yourself say he feels.'

'That,' Alison said, 'is because he's between periods. He believes that in the old days one could look back on the book, or the score, or the picture and feel some sense of achievement. In a few years' time it's quite possible that the video will be seen in the same way. But Vernon can't believe it.'

'Is that right?' Karen appealed to David.

'Yes. He realises that to do what Alison does, even Louise in her smaller way, requires a tremendous breadth of knowledge, of application, of intelligence.'

'And what does he need?' Alison, in tipsy mischief.

'You could argue for exactly the same qualities, but in his low moments he thinks he needs a handsome appearance, a persuasive voice and, worst of all, constant self-promotion. And his recent ill-health has made it worse.'

' "Thou fool",' Alison intoned. ' "This night thy soul shall be required of thee: then whose shall those things be which thou hast provided?" ' She laughed at herself.

'In part. Without religious overtones, I mean, that could apply if you'd just written *War and Peace* or the Ninth Symphony. No, he can't quite believe in what he's doing. We're all a bit like that, especially if we have any sensibility.' David turned to Karen, lecturing. 'Did you not notice that both Ally and I used the word "big" when we meant enormous, gigantic, exhaustive, definitive? A small three-letter word to show that we were serious, that we meant business, we weren't boasting.'

'Goodness,' Karen said, wide-eyed.

'Well, now, big chief,' Alison mused. 'We haven't answered Karen's question. Is she to go back?'

'Yes.'

'Another three letters. Let's have your reasons.' Alison.

'The fact that Karen has seriously considered it, thinks it worthwhile to ask our advice means she wants to try it.' He looked them over. 'There's more alcohol than logic in that. But I want her to. Vernon needs her. She's good for him. And like Grandpa I approve of my father. Vernon, with all thy faults I love thee still.'

'Should I ask Grandpa?' Karen murmured.

'Yes. He'll rave on about Vernon, and then tell you to go back. But consult Poll as well. She won't know, but she'll blather and you'll be able to pick sense out of her flounderings.'

'I like them,' Karen admitted. 'Both. In different ways.'

'What about George's marriage,' David asked, 'when he was in Bomber Command? That doesn't bear thinking about.'

'Don't they choose, nowadays, their astronauts and cosmonauts from among married men with children because they have so much to lose?'

They sat silent. Alison breathed deeply, in a small voice slowly quoted as if it was wrung out of her,

" 'In bombers named for girls, we burned
The cities we had learned about in school.' "

'Who said that?' David asked.

'An American poet, an academic, Randall Jarrell.'

'Randall,' Karen mused. 'Like all of us.' She smiled. 'Is he still alive?'

'No. He killed himself under a lorry.'

'Randall,' said Karen again. 'Randall.'

The telephone rang.

'You answer it,' Alison ordered David. 'I'm incapable.'

The women talked, not volubly, while David was out. At one stage Karen voiced the opinion that David seemed years older than his age.

'I had to keep looking at him to remind myself how young he really is.'

'Will you go back to Vernon?' Alison asked, when she disposed of David's gravitas.

'I'll think seriously about it. In my present state I couldn't go back to anybody. No. I'll talk to George and Polly. And decide. And ring him. Perhaps he won't have me.'

'Do you really think that?'

'I just don't know. As I sit here, with you two, in this house, I realise how little I know of Vernon.'

'Of anybody, for that matter,' Alison answered. 'Not just you. Everybody.'

Karen frowned, concentrated, rocked slightly in her chair.

'Has marriage made any difference to you?' Karen asked.

'The word I'd choose is "comfort". We're both busy. We go out early, and work late, at home or in our offices. We have Saturdays and Sundays more or less together. Mad with delight.'

'Sex must be exciting,' Karen said, with no embarrassment.

'Yes. Not new. Different, better. I think perhaps it's this house. It seems a privilege to live here together.'

'Don't you ever quarrel?'

'Not much. Not yet. I expect we shall. We don't see eye to eye on everything. But it doesn't seem to matter. We work on all day and yet we belong to each other. And this alters everything.'

'Your work?'

'Well, not basically, I suppose. I don't expect to come to different conclusions, let's say. But I feel happy, comforted. I read somewhere that Einstein said no one had ever made any great creative discovery in physics while he was unhappy.' They both pondered this, ostentatiously, intoxicated. 'Of course I can see it might mean that the physicist is so caught up with his problem, is working at it with such skill and sense of progress, such mastery, that he can't but feel happy, doing what he does best so well. But I don't think he meant that, I think he implied a happy life outside his physics, with love, or good health, success, right outside the brilliance of his performance of discovery.'

'He's a bit old-fashioned, isn't he? David?'

'In what way?'

'He talks about protecting women. As if they're helpless.'

'I guess that even in these days the man has most of the money, the better-paid employment, and that's why the woman needs help. I suppose it does perhaps suit his temperament.'

'Guarding the weaker vessels?'

They were laughing when David returned.

'Who was that keeping you so long?' Alison asked.

'A man from London called Owen. He said old Mr White had died.'

'The one who lived here?' For Karen's information.

'That's why he rang. Wanted to know if he could do anything. I gave him Mrs White's address and 'phone number. He'd been abroad and out of touch.'

'Was he a relative?'

'I don't think so. An old friend of the family. He still had this number in his book. Somebody had mentioned the news to him in a letter. Without details.' He turned to Karen. 'He was in the RAF with George. Grandpa didn't like him, but I suppose we'd better let them know.'

'He'd be past eighty.'

'Why didn't George like him?' Karen asked.

'Heaven knows. I think Mr White went on at great length about the pains and drawbacks of old age. It's all right if *he* does, but nobody else is allowed to.' David cleared a dry throat before continuing. 'And he took the line that those young men killed during the war had had the better of it. George said that was senile blether.'

'And Mrs White?'

David allowed Alison to answer.

'Ladylike. One of these women who needs protection from her husband.'

'Did she know that?' David enquired.

Alison shook her head.

'Feminist chatter,' she mocked him. 'She'd be happy. She probably knew exactly how to manage him at the same time as allowing him to think he ruled the roost.'

The next evening as the younger Randalls drank coffee Polly rang. Karen, who had set out on Monday morning at eight thirty when they left for work, had spent a very happy morning at The Orchards. George had dressed up, escorted her round the marketplace and, it appeared, into Woolworths, wearing himself out in the process.

'I haven't talked so much for years,' he told his wife that night.

'I'm glad you made the effort,' she retorted.

They'd taken a leisurely late lunch before Karen had started for London at about four thirty to miss the rush hour at the far end of the motorway. Spare time they'd spent in the garden. George had bustled about a bit at first, showing off, but he'd soon pulled the brim of his panama over his eyes and fallen asleep in a deck-chair.

'Ask her if Karen said anything about Vernon.' David instructed.

'My husband's interrupting,' Alison said. 'I'll see what he wants.' She knew quite well.

'Yes.' Polly answered his question. 'We talked a lot about him. George had praised Vernon while they were out, just as David apparently said he would. She told me a lot about how they'd first met and then about her two miscarriages.'

'Did Vernon want children?'

'He said so. But she wasn't sure. She was quite ill and he was away, abroad, at the time. When he was at home he was very good to her.'

'Did you know about this?'

'No, not really. In a way. It must all have happened soon after George and I were married, I think. We heard she'd been ill, in and out of hospital, but I don't think I knew why. George wouldn't ask, perhaps, when Vernon phoned. Or Vernon wouldn't tell him. We had less to do with them then, though they came up about the time we were married and she seemed healthy enough. I remember how handsome she looked, striking. "A bit different from Louise," George said. "She was a drooping lily." Though it seems Edna greatly liked Louise, and was very distressed when they divorced.'

'Did Karen say anything about going back to Vernon?'

'Yes. She asked me.'

'And how did you answer?' Alison looked up towards her husband, on the edge of his chair, all ears. Polly's voice was now so clear he could make out what she was saying.

'What could I? I told her to go back because I've always thought of her as Vernon's wife. She was, when I married George. Um. That didn't seem ever so sensible, and I said that. She put her arms round me. She's never made much of a fuss before; I always thought she was a bit standoffish, you know, but she isn't. Still, it's no good reason to go back just because it would suit me.'

'But what did she say?'

'She'd think about it. She'd talked it over with you, and you wanted her to. She promised she'd write first. Because she wasn't sure whether Vernon would have her back. I said George would ring him, but she was against that.'

Polly talked furiously on, repeating much but with snippets of new information. It was an ear-drilling experience.

In the end Alison handed over to her husband, whom Poll riddled with verbal grapeshot.

'How's Grandpa in the middle of all this?' He knew how to stop volubility in clients.

'Perfect.'

'My wife wouldn't describe me like that.'

'I mean he's well. Mr White's death didn't shock him. Old people seem pleased rather than otherwise. They've hung on a bit longer, I suppose. And he likes young women. He feels quite proud marching Karen or Alison, Ally especially, through the streets in full view of all.'

'And how do you feel about it?'

'About his pretty young ladies?'

'No. About Karen's going back. Do you think it's on? Does she want to go, for a start?'

'I can't answer that, David. I don't know them well enough.'

'After all these years?' He mocked her.

'It's all very fine for you to say that, but we don't see them often. And Vernon's the one making his presence felt. Not Karen. I guess she wanted to go back, but I couldn't say why.'

'Perhaps because you told her to.'

'I don't know how your wife puts up with you.'

Towards the end of August, over a month later, Polly telephoned again. Alison had returned now from Rome where she had been for three weeks. David had visited the George Randalls twice. They had heard that Karen had gone back to her husband and that she and Vernon had spent some pleasant days in Paris. Cards of the Sacré Coeur, the Mona Lisa, Michelangelo's 'Slaves', the Winged Victory, the Pont de la Concorde, the Pont Alexandre III, the Luxembourg Palace decorated their mantelpiece. 'She must have spent all her spare time collecting and writing these,' George muttered, but he was touched that Karen had taken such trouble to keep them informed or happy.

This time Polly announced that all four had been invited to Hampstead for the day on Sunday. David said he would drive. George demanded an early start.

254

'Get them up early,' he had ground out. 'It'll do them good.'

The Beechnall party started before nine, found the motorway comparatively empty. George nodded off even at this hour of the day.

'The co-pilot's away,' David told the ladies in the back.

'You watch the road,' George murmured.

When they arrived they felt slightly constrained, uncertain. The coffee tasted delicious; the furniture was polished; the house had been thoroughly cleaned, everything put away, piles of magazines squared up. George commented.

'Don't worry,' Vernon replied. 'We've been up all night killing the fatted calf.'

'Not for us, surely?' Polly asked.

'The gaffer gave the word.' Vernon, in a short-sleeved blue shirt and resplendent tartan slacks, grinned. Deeply tanned, his arms were muscular. Karen wore a simple cream dress about which the visiting women questioned her. She had bought it in a Beechnall shop on her last visit and wore it in their honour.

'It's beautiful,' Polly said. 'Isn't it, Vernon?'

'It's what's inside it.'

He sounded mealy-mouthed with satisfied domestication. They walked, sat about in, the garden, not large, but completely in the care of a professional who came twice a week.

'I ordered him to have it spick and span,' Vernon told his father. 'That an expert was coming to look it over.'

'I bet he was all of a tremble,' Polly said.

'Does he make a good job of it, Grandpa?' Alison asked. David could not remember her calling George by that title before. The old man squinted content.

'Neat. Well kept. Planned. Knows what he's about.' The chin jutted. 'Bit of a parks-and-gardens man.'

'What does that mean?' Alison, pseudo-naive.

'Bedding plants. In, and out when you've done with them.'

'Isn't that good, then?'

'No.' George rubbed his chin. He might have been taking a turn across the front of his classroom, keeping his class in suspense, letting the bright ones work it out for themselves, before he demonstrated the final stage on the blackboard, solved the problem, completed the theory. 'The best gardens, and Polly will tell you this, teeter,' he paused, daring them to criticise the choice of word, 'on the edge of the wilderness. Their beauty lies in profusion.' Again he stopped. The younger women were delighted, mouths slightly agape for wisdom. 'The real gardener imposes order, or a semblance of it, on this rush of plants upwards and sideways.'

'I see what you mean.' Vernon.

'Not things set out in rows and tidied up. I'm not complaining about that. That's a sensible way with a biggish area and a shortage of labour. But the real garden is ordered by colour and shape and size and allowed to let rip so that an extra branch here and spray there isn't an eyesore but a touch of genius. You've made it possible for nature to fulfil itself.'

'You're always pruning and chopping.' Polly, objecting. 'And weeding.'

'Of course I am, woman. I didn't say a garden was a wilderness, but had some sort of the characteristics of one.' George put out a hand to Polly's shoulder. 'She's no idea of the theory. But you should see her in practice.' He coughed. 'She's been a good wife to me.'

'That's what my father said to the nurse about my mother just before he died.' Polly, with solemn face. 'In the General Hospital.'

'I didn't know that,' George answered, affronted.

They talked without inhibition, watching the London pair.

'I hope you don't mind but we're taking you out for lunch.'

'Oh, hell.'

'George,' Polly expostulated.

'I thought you'd want to see a bit of Karen. You wouldn't, if she was tied up in the kitchen.'

256

'Make other people work on Sundays,' George muttered.

'That's what money's for. To free your wife on holy days. Though God knows we both have to work all day Sunday often enough. Liberty Hall today. No cooking, no serving.'

Vernon took all six in a Rolls he had hired. Only David and his father ate with any gusto, though the meal was deliciously light.

'They do as you tell them,' George said in approval. He had already laid it down as unalterable law that all restaurants soaked everything in oil, wine and cooking fat. Vernon then embarrassed him by retailing the dictum to the Italian chef who walked across to the table. The old man reddened. His grey eyebrows met. David easily saw how his father and grandfather angered each other.

After the leisurely meal they drove back home giving the visitors a tour of the district.

'That wasn't too painful, now, was it?' Vernon chaffed his father.

'No. Not so long as you've some bicarbonate of soda in the cupboard.'

'Ask Karen.'

David and the women took an hour's stroll on Hampstead Heath. Alison and Karen walked ahead of Polly and her step-grandson.

'Your grandfather complains out of habit,' she told him.

'Does it embarrass you?'

'Yes. Sometimes. It's unnecessary. When we are back at home he'll talk for days about going out for lunch in a Rolls-Royce. It's almost as if he can't allow himself to enjoy anything until it's over.'

'Why is that, d'you think?'

'I've no idea. He's always been like it.'

'Still, as long as he realises that there is enjoyment to come.'

'I doubt if he does. Dressing up, going out, putting on a show goes against his grain. From what he says his parents had little social life. They'd go to chapel, for services, or prayer meetings, or concerts, but there weren't birthday parties, or anything like that. Somebody extra, a relative or two, at Christmas was about it. You kept yourself to yourself.'

Ahead of them the younger women seemed to be talking as vigorously as they walked.

'How do you think Karen and Vernon are shaping?' Polly asked.

'They seemed quite normal,' David answered. 'Affectionate.'

'George will put a question or two to Vernon, if I'm any judge.' Polly made a comical, bitter mouth.

'My father won't mind, I guess.'

'Do you think Karen's pouring it all out to Alison?'

'Shouldn't be surprised. But Ally won't probe unless she's encouraged to. She's a devil, when she does. I wouldn't be keen on her examining a literary thesis of mine. But in the ordinary way, she's very quiet. The sympathetic face, the listening ear. She doesn't throw her weight about.'

'Why?'

'I guess she understands the extent of her ignorance more than most. Just because she's so learned.'

Polly eyed the family walkers they passed with approbation.

'George would love to see these children chasing about. He's fond of youngsters shouting and running, as long as they're far enough away. He surprised me. He can, you know. He went to see that Mrs White whose husband died.'

'Did you go with him?'

'Oh, yes. I drove him there. And to the funeral. He puts a suit on, you know, and a black tie for these occasions. And a dark topcoat in winter. He wrote a note of condolence to Mrs White, Betty or whatever her name is. He does it very well. "Praise where you can," he says, "and shut up about the rest." And then a bit after he said, "Poll, we ought to go and see Ma White," that's what he calls her. He made me ring her up. I don't think he likes the 'phone much. A lot of older people don't. And we went. He was really nice. Very considerate. And that's a word I wouldn't usually apply to him. She was a little bit upset, as you'd expect. She talked about moving to a smaller place. She asked him his advice. "You just sit about for a week or two," he said. "At our age we're in no hurry." We didn't stay beyond an hour. She wanted us to, but he was adamant. "No, Bet," he said. "We're not going to wear you out. We'll come again." '

'And have you?'

'It was only last week. But he'll go. Or I expect so. He was bored and uncomfortable, but he didn't show it. I could tell, but I know him. The way he sits, or rolls, in his chair. But he said, "Poll, when I go, and it can't be too long, I want somebody to walk in and say a word of comfort to you." '

'And you said?'

' "You'll live to be a hundred, don't fret yourself." '

'Will he, do you think?'

'I hope so.'

Back in Vernon's house they spent a pleasant couple of hours, setting off for home soon after seven.

'We've stayed just long enough,' George said. 'We'd not worn our welcome out.'

Polly extracted a promise from the London Randalls to visit Beechnall, tied them down exactly to a date.

'And don't work yourself to death,' George warned his son on the pavement.

'Not too likely. And you're not the one to talk.'

'You're like your mother. Terrier with a rat. Obsessive.'

'And you? On the other hand?'

'One of the world's idlers.'

'You're one of the most energetic men I've ever seen.'

'Was. I was. Not now.'

The two men shook hands heartily, watching each other, extending the minute, friends.

In the car David asked his grandfather about Vernon's marriage.

'He never said a word to me,' the old man growled.

'Does that mean you didn't ask him, then?' Alison, lightly.

'It does. I'm not for stirring the waters.' His wife guffawed. 'I leave that to you women. Polly had a good go at him. I could see that.'

'What did you think, Grandpa?' David asked.

'They looked fine. As far as I could tell. She'd gone back. They talked like an old married couple. But they're strangers to me. Both of 'em.'

'He seemed affectionate,' Alison answered. 'He kissed her, and put his arm round her.'

'Not so often as you and Davy,' Polly laughed. 'And do you know what he said to me?'

She made them wait until George blew out his lips in exasperation.

'He said, Vernon said . . .'

'Get on with it. We know who said.'

'He said it did him a world of good to see David and Alison together. They're immersed, no, drowned, in one another.'

'If you're drowned, you're dead,' David objected. 'Not much of a compliment.'

' "Then am I dead to all the globe," ' George quoted with fervour, ' "And all the globe is dead to me." It means paying no attention to, because the whole of the interest is directed elsewhere.'

'Literary criticism now. Watch your step, Ally,' David warned, from the wheel.

'And I said to him,' Polly continued, 'that I expected he and Karen were like that at one time. He answered me, and it seemed sad, that he'd been married once before. But that this young couple, in their new home, happy as children, set the standard.'

'What did you say to that, Poll?' George asked.

'You won't believe it, but I just cried. The tears burst out of my eyes and splashed on my cheeks.'

Alison leaned over to kiss Polly.

'Thank you,' she said.

Polly continued.

'And he took hold of my arm, quite hard. "Their marriage is like a summer's day, with little tufts of cloud. Enough to cast short shadows. But the sun's high and hot and the air crystal clear." It was quite a poem.'

'His marriage, though?' David, delighted.

'He said he'd a good mind to consult you, but he didn't quite dare.' They all laughed in the motorway howl of cars. 'I told him he could do worse.'

Nearly a month later, in September, when hot, long summer had paled the leaves, Vernon and his wife spent three days in Beechnall. On one of the evenings Alison and David took them out to dinner, to a trattoria near the university, where Vernon was recognised. Vernon worked a new schedule, rapidly redrawn, which meant he now kept regular hours, though he started very early in the morning. It had proved a godsend, he claimed, a rest, and he was now used to rising before dawn.

'And we have two or three hours of each other every working day before I slope off to bed.'

'We sleep in separate rooms,' Karen interjected, confident of the relationship. 'He creeps out like a ghost.' They smiled at each other.

After Vernon and Karen had returned to London, David enquired of his grandfather over Sunday lunch how George had found the pair. David himself was on his own as Alison, again in a hurry, spent ten days and four lectures in Boston on the invitation of Rupert Melluish. She had rung that day to say how much she was enjoying herself.

'And what's it like to be a bachelor?' George asked.

'I'm busy. But somewhere in the corner of my mind I'm glad Ally can go and do her stuff.'

'She'll impress?'

'I'm sure. I've never known anyone work as hard as she does. And remember so much. Or put it so well. And I keep the house dusted and ready for her.'

'What about that murder case? Is that over?'

'Yes. We lost. Life. It's what we expected. The judge told our barrister we'd put up a decent showing, and I think that's about right. I couldn't understand the man at all.'

'Young, wasn't he?'

'In his twenties. Mild as milk. Till that day when he went raving mad.'

'Are you disappointed if you lose?'

'Only slightly in this case. More so if we thought we'd win. We did and said everything that could be done and said for him.'

'Matrimonial, wasn't it?'

'Yes. Like many murders. But his wife seemed decent, from all the evidence. Why he exploded in this way I could not fathom.'

The three had reached the highest point of the garden where a stone hut stood squat, perhaps, George suggested, the oldest structure on the property. They sat outside in the sunshine, on a patio built to Edna's specification by her husband in the earliest years of her marriage. Round them the fruit bushes were still green, though the large trees suffered.

'Is it warm enough?' Polly demanded.

'Stop wittling, woman.'

'You'll be complaining about your aches and pains. "I wish I hadn't sat out there in the evening." '

'I bet Alison doesn't nag at Davy like this.'

'There's no need. He's sensible.'

George laughed, clapping and capping his knees with his hands. He spoke, not quickly, in a voice of gravel about Vernon's marriage. He broached a theory that Karen was exactly the right partner at this period of his life, as, surprisingly to the others, raising Polly's eyes comically, Louise had been.

'Louise,' he admonished, 'kept him on his mettle when he was starting. He had to impress her, convince her of his worth. She thought she was more intelligent than he was. The examiners at Oxford University had said so. And he managed it to such an extent that he knocked her off her perch. She realised that she'd married a prodigy. Now he needs somebody to look after him, to hold his hand. And that's Karen.'

'What about you and Edna?' Polly asked, brusquely.

'That was marriage made to last. Till death. We were capable of responding to changes. We live longer these days, and it was a bit unusual in that Edna died first. She was only sixty-seven. Of course she was three years older than I was. But she put up with me and the stress when I was in the RAF, and the calm here. She loved this place. Altered it, knocked it about, made it her life. We suited each other because she would put up with me. We quarrelled. Often enough. I've always been one to throw my weight about, but she didn't mind. She saw her work as a housewife and mother as sufficient occupation. She made jam and bottled fruit, and embroidered, and knitted, and did wood-carvings and decorated and re-designed. She wasn't idle. Nor ambitious for herself. She could be awkward. And when she dug her heels in there was no changing her. Nothing could persuade her, for instance, that Vernon did right in divorcing Louise. "That woman has helped make him what he is, and now he throws her over." She could be sharp.'

'Did she tell Vernon?'

'She did. Plain, blunt John Bull.'

'And did he pay any attention?' Polly asked.

'He took notice. But just said that their life could go no further. I was there. He spoke in a sober voice, one there was no arguing with. She didn't stop, though. "Have you thought of the effect on the child?" You'd be about eight, then. And he answered, "David will suffer more if I stay, believe you me." He could speak solemnly, weigh down his words like an actor. When he married Karen, that would be seven years later, Edna went to London with me to the wedding. It was at a register office, and she wasn't very well, but we appeared. She felt ill, we knew it was cancer, but she was determined to be there. She feared for her son. A great woman. Held me steady. I couldn't live on my own. I was lost.'

'Nobody to shout at,' Polly interrupted.

'I'd still plenty of pupils if that's all I wanted. No. My life was only half there. The better half had gone. I was a shadow. Old Watson-Williams, up at the school, used to quote some Greek poet about man being a dream of a shadow, and that was me. Staggering about, with no idea what I was up to. Oh, I could still do my job and cook, at home, a bit of bacon, or boil an egg, but I was nobody going nowhere. It frightened me, because I'd always judged myself as self-sufficient. I was afraid as I never was on aircrew duty.'

'So he married me.'

'The best thing I ever did. I was retiring from school. Her children, whom I'd taught, were nearly through their education, but gave us a shared interest, and she was lively, could pull my leg.'

'I was terrified of him.'

'You didn't show it. She set me going again. I'd have disappeared, dissipated myself if I'd been left on my own. It's over seven years now. And better than ever. You know, David, we haven't much grip on life, in one sense.' Here the old schoolmaster spoke, waving his hands neatly. 'I see your father day after day on television, reading the news or interviewing or reporting. And yet, more often than not I don't connect that famous, authoritative presence with my son. I know the face, the voice as well as my own, and yet I don't relate to him as the schoolboy who chased about these gardens. Or at least, not without an effort. One's an important, a national figurehead, one was my boy. It was made worse by the fact that we didn't see much of him during his first marriage. He'd call in when you spent your summer holidays here. But he was too busy. Never came this way. His mother felt it. She was proud of him. But she compared herself with her friend, the then rector's wife, who had a son living not three miles off and called in every week without fail.'

George Randall shook his head.

'He's better now,' Polly said. 'A bit.'

'But I've no grasp. For instance when I think back to the war, I know what happened to me, but it seems as if it was some other man. It's getting on for fifty years ago, I realise, but . . . It's not me. It's frightening. Just as that Vernon Randall pinning the Prime Minister back is not the boy who did handstands against this very wall here. I know it was, but I can't believe it. I am certain that I flew over Germany, but the real connection to me, this me, is cut.'

George stood, stumped across the patio, paused like a bent statue, wheeled and lowered himself again to the seat. The other two sat silent.

'Does all this matter?' Polly asked, before he'd time to win his breath back.

'It does and it doesn't.'

'Thank you, thank you.'

'That's why she's so good for me. No bump of reverence.' George waved his arms in the air. 'I sit here waiting for the end.'

'Oh, rubbish George. You're pruning or swatting greenfly or having a bonfire you shouldn't.'

'I'm not telling you I'm thinking about dying from morning to night. I'm not. Especially on days like this when I feel well and the weather's bright. But sometimes when I lie in bed before I get up I look out of the window at that acacia and a silver birch and I think, "That's what I shall see when I'm lying here dying." '

'And you might not.'

'No, I might be otherwise occupied than looking out of the window, or I might die in hospital, or drop dead up here. I admit it. But whenever I do something of note, I think, "That may be the last time." '

'It's all very morbid, George.'

'All right, all right. But if the grim reaper nobbles me up here, I know Poll will come and find me. And that moreover Edna wouldn't have chosen anyone better than Poll to look after the house with me in it or without. They're quite different in every way. But she carries Edna's work on.'

'Your Betty White didn't carry anything on long.' Polly's voice had changed.

'How's that?' David enquired.

'She died last week. We went to the funeral. Say that poem to David. He suddenly came right out with it, on the orchard path. Surprised me.'

'That doesn't take much doing. It was another of old Watty's, Watson-Williams's bits.

"He first deceased – she for a little tried
To live without him, lik'd it not and died."'

'Who wrote that?' David asked.

'Don't know.'

'I'll ask Alison.'

'You do. When's she coming back?'

'Next Tuesday.'

'Are you going down to meet her?'

'I am. I start at the crack of dawn.'

Polly, rising, sang out magnificently loud in a Dame Clara Butt contralto, one hand on heart,

' "O, Love that wilt not let me go." '

'You daft whore.'

She laughed, then tailed off, lacking their approval. The men stood up. George put his arm round his wife's shoulder, drew her into him. Arm in arm they made towards the house, David two steps behind.

George half turned his head.

'I was walking along the street the other day, and I saw an old couple in front of me, arm in arm, waddling along. They both had shopping bags, and they were making hard work of it. Her feet stuck out at a quarter to three and he was bent right over and he wore the most ridiculous panama, a straw hat as shapeless as cow-plop. They tottered and staggered. And do you know what I thought?'

'God knows,' Polly answered.

George made them wait, bringing the party to an unsteady halt.

'I thought, "They were Alison and David once." '

'But they weren't, George.'

'They were, I tell you. The beautiful people.'

He signalled the start of the slow march home.